Tighe Hopkins

The Dungeons of Old Paris

Being the Story and Romance of the most Celebrated Prisons of the Monarchy and

the Revolution

Tighe Hopkins

The Dungeons of Old Paris

Being the Story and Romance of the most Celebrated Prisons of the Monarchy and the Revolution

ISBN/EAN: 9783744622127

Printed in Europe, USA, Canada, Australia, Japan

Cover: Foto ©Andreas Hilbeck / pixelio.de

More available books at **www.hansebooks.com**

IN THE GRIP OF THE BASTILLE.

The Dungeons of Old Paris

Being the Story and Romance
of the most Celebrated Prisons
of the Monarchy and
the Revolution

By

Tighe Hopkins

Author of " Lady Bonnie's Experiment," " Nell Haffenden," " The
Nugents of Carriconna," " The Incomplete Adventurer "
" Kilmainham Memories," etc.

Illustrated

G. P. PUTNAM'S SONS
NEW YORK AND LONDON
The Knickerbocker Press
1897

The Knickerbocker Press, New York

CONTENTS.

ILLUSTRATIONS.

THE DUNGEONS OF OLD PARIS.

CHAPTER I.

INTRODUCTORY.

TRISTE comme les portes d'une prison—Sad as the gates of Prison, is an old French proverb which must once have had an aching significance. To the citizen of Paris it must have been familiar above most other popular sayings, since he had the menace of a prison door at almost every turn! For the "Dungeons of Old Paris" were well-nigh as thick as its churches or its taverns. Up to the period, or very close upon the period, of the Revolution of 1789, everyone who exercised what was called with quite unconscious irony the "right of justice" *(droit de justice)*, possessed his prison. The King was the great gaoler-in-chief of the State, but there were countless other gaolers. The terrible prisons of State—two of the most renowned of which, the Dungeon of Vincennes and the Bastille, have been partially restored in these pages—are almost hustled out of sight by the towers and ramparts of the host of lesser prisons. To every town in France there was its dungeon, to every puissant noble his dungeon, to every lord of the manor

his dungeon, to every bishop and abbé his dungeon.
The dreaded cry of "*Laissez passer la justice du Roi!*"
"Way for the King's justice!" was not oftener heard,
nor more unwillingly, than "Way for the Duke's justice!" or "Way for the justice of my lord Bishop!" For
indeed the mouldy records of those hidden dungeons
and torture rooms of château and monastery, the *car-
ceres duri* and the *vade in pace*, into which the hooded
victim was lowered by torchlight, and out of which
his bones were never raked, might shew us scenes yet
more forbidding than the darkest which these chapters
unfold. But they have crumbled and passed, and
history itself no longer cares to trouble their infected
dust.

Scenes harsh enough, though not wholly unrelieved
(for romance is of the essence of their story), are at
hand within the walls of certain prisons whose names
and memories have survived. I have undone the bolts
of nearly all the more celebrated prisons of historic
Paris, few of which are standing at this day. One or
two have been passed by, or but very briefly surveyed,
for the reason that to include them would have been
to commit myself to a certain amount of not very necessary repetition. I fear that even as the book stands I
must have repeated myself more than once, but this has
been for the most part in the attempt to enforce points
which seemed not to have been brought out or em-
phasised with sufficient clearness elsewhere. Dealing
with prisons which were in existence for centuries,
and some of which were associated with almost every
great and stirring epoch of French history, selection
of periods and events was a paramount necessity.

The endeavour has been to give back to each of these cruel old dungeons, Prison d'État, Conciergerie, or Maison de Justice, its special and distinctive character; to shew just what each was like at the most interesting or important dates in its career; and, as far as might be, to find the reason of that dreary proverb, "Sad as the gates of Prison." Light chequers the shades in some of these dim vaults, and the echoes of the dour days they witnessed are not all tears and lamentations. Something is shewn, it is hoped, of every kind of "justice" that was recognised in Paris until the days of '89, when everything that had been, fell with the terrific fall of the monarchy:—feudal justice, the justice of absolute kings and of ministers who were but less absolute, provosts' and bishops' justice, and the justice of prison governors and lieutenants of police. Often it is no more than a glimpse that is afforded; but the picture as a whole is, perhaps, not altogether lacking in completeness. Once inside a prison, the prisoner is the first study; and there are no more moving or pitiful objects in the annals of France than the victims of its criminal justice in every age. Slit the curtain of cobweb that has formed over the narrow *grille* of the dungeon, put back on their shrill hinges the double and triple doors of the cell, peer into the hole that ventilates the conical *oubliette*, and one may see once more under what conditions life was possible, and amid what surroundings death was a blessing, in the days when Paris was studded with prisons, when every abbot was free to wall-up his monks alive, and every seigneur to erect his gallows in his own courtyard.

For during all these days, dragging slowly into ages, justice has seldom more than one face to shew us: a face of cruelty and vengeance. The thing which we call the "theory of punishment" had really no existence. Punishment was not to chasten and reform; it was scarcely even to deter; it was mainly and almost solely to revenge. What the notion of prison was, I have tried briefly to explain in the chapters on "The Conciergerie," "The Dungeon of Vincennes," and, I think, elsewhere. We are strictly to remember, however, that the vindictive idea of punishment, and the idea of prison as a place in which (1) to hold and (2) to torment anyone who might be unfortunate enough to get in there, were not at all peculiar to France. The history of punishment in our own country leaves no room for boasting; and France has not more to reproach herself with in the memory of the Bastille, than we have in the actual and visible existence of Newgate. France has her *Archives de la Bastille;* we have Howard's *State of Prisons* and Griffiths's *Chronicles of Newgate.* We are not to forget that, in the "age of chivalry" in England, it was unsafe for visitors in London to stroll a hundred yards from their inn after sunset; and that, in the reign of Elizabeth, Shakespeare might have penned his lines on "the quality of mercy" within earshot of the rabble on their way to gloat over the disembowelling of a "traitor," or flocking to surround the stake at which a woman was to die by fire. In a word, the sense of vengeance, and the thirst for vengeance, which underlay the old criminal law of France, and of all Europe, were not less the basis of our own criminal law until well on into the second quarter of this century. But the French, it would seem, have paid the cost of their quick dramatic sense. They have handed down to us, in history, drama, and romance, the picture of Louis XI. arm in arm with his torturer and hangman, Tristan; the spectacle of the noble whose sword was convertible into a headsman's axe; and of the abbot whose girdle was ever ready for use as a halter. Histories akin to these (and, at the root, there is more of history than of legend in all of them) are to be delved out of our own records; but the French have been more candid in the matter, and a good deal more skilled with the pen in chronicles of the sort.

On the other hand, England never had quite such bitter memories of her prisons as France had of hers. The struggle for freedom in England was never a struggle against the prisons; and it was not consciously a struggle against the prisons in France. But the destruction of a prison was the beginning of the French Revolution; and when the Revolution was over, its first historians took the prisons of France as the type and example of the immemorial tyranny of their kings. In one important respect, therefore, the dungeons of old Paris stand apart from the prisons of the rest of Europe.

I had proposed to myself, in beginning this introductory chapter, to attempt a comparison, more or less detailed, between these ruined and obliterated prisons of historic Paris and the French or English prisons of to-day. But a final glance at the chapters as they were going to press counselled me to abstain.

There is no point to start from.   The old and the new prisons have a space between them wider than divides the poles.   The key that turned a lock of the Châtelet, Bicêtre, or the Bastille will open no cell of any modern prison, French or English.   Punishment is systematised, and has its basis in two ideas,—the safety of peoples living in communities, and the cure of certain moral obliquities ; or, it is quite without system, and means only the vengeance of the strong upon the weak.   Between the prison which was intended either as a living tomb, or as a starting-place for the pillory, the whipping-post, or the scaffold ; and the prison which proposes to punish, to deter, or to reform the bad, the diseased, the weak, or the luckless members of society, there is not a point at which comparison is possible.

CHAPTER II.

THE CONCIERGERIE.

I F walls had tongues, those of the Conciergerie
might rehearse a wretched story. This is, I
believe, the oldest prison in Europe; it would speak
with the twofold authority of age and black experi-
ence. Give these walls a voice, and they might say:

"Look at the buildings we enclose. There is a
little of every style in our architecture, reflecting the
many ages we have witnessed. Paris and France, in
all the reigns of all the Kings, have been locked in
here, starved here, tortured here, and sent from here
to die by hanging, by beheading, by dismembering by
horses, by fire, and by the guillotine. We have found
chains and a bitter portion for the victims of all the
tyrannies of France,—those of the Feudal Ages, those
of the Absolute Monarchy, those of the Revolution,
and those of the Restoration. There is no discord,
trouble, passion, or revolution in France which is not
recorded in our annals. Politics, religion, feuds of
parties and of houses, private rancours and the enmi-
ties of queens, the vengeance of kings and the jeal-
ousies of their ministers, have filled in turn the vaults
of this little city of the dead-in-life. We have seen
the killing of the innocent; the torment of a Queen;

the tears of a Dubarry and the stoicism of a hideous Cartouche; the collapse of a Marquise de Brinvilliers under torture and the silent heroism of a Charlotte Corday on her way to the guillotine; the bold immodesty of a La Voisin on the rack and the solemn abandon of the 'last supper' of the Girondins. We have seen the worst that France could shew of wickedness and the best that it could shew of patriotism; we have seen the beginning and the end of everything that makes the history of a prison."

Most French writers who have touched upon the Conciergerie seem to have felt the oppression of the place; their recollections or impressions are recorded in a spirit of melancholy or indignation.

"Ah, that Conciergerie!" exclaims Philarète Chasles; "there is a sense of suffocation in its buildings; one thinks of the prisoner, innocent or guilty, crushed beneath the weight of society. Here are the oldest dungeons of France; Paris has scarcely begun to be when those dungeons are opened."

The strain of Dulaure, the historian of Paris, is not less depressing:

"The Conciergerie, the most ancient and the most formidable of all our prisons, which forms a part of the buildings of the Palais de Justice, one time palace of the kings, has preserved to this day the hideous character of the feudal ages. Its towers, its courtyard, and the dim passage by which the prisoners are admitted, have tears in their very aspect. Pity on the wight who, condemned to sojourn there, has not the wherewithal to pay for the hire of a bed! For him a lodging on the straw in some dark and mouldy chamber, cheek by jowl with wretches penniless like himself." *

In the days when Paris had not so much as a gate

* *Histoire de Paris.*

MADAME DUBARRY.

to shut in the face of the invader, the citizen raftsmen of the Seine thought it well to have a prison, and "dug a hole in the middle of their isle." This, it seems, was the sorry beginning of the Conciergerie ; but the details of that vanished epoch are scant. Palace and prison are thought to have been constructed at about the same date : the palace, which was principally a fortress, was the residence of the kings ; the Conciergerie was their dungeon. Rebuilt by Saint Louis, the Conciergerie became in part—as its name implies—the dwelling of the Concierge of the palace. According to Larousse, the Concierge "was in some sort the governor of the royal house, and had the keeping of the King's prisoners, with the right of *low* and *middle* justice" *(basse et moyenne justice)*. In 1348, the Concierge took the official title of *bailli ;* the functions and privileges of the office were enlarged, and it was held by many persons of distinction, amongst whom was Jacques Coictier, the famous doctor of Louis XI. As the practice was, in an age when every gaoler " exploited " his prisoners, the concierge-bailli taxed the victuals he supplied them with, and charged what he pleased for the hire of beds and other cell-equipments ; while it happened more than once, says Larousse, " that prisoners who were entitled to be released on a judge's order, were detained until they had paid all prison fees." On such a system were the old French gaols administered. The office of concierge-bailli, with its voluminous powers, and its manifold abuses, was in existence until the era of the Revolution.

Justice under the old régime counted sex as nothing.

The physical weakness and finer nervous organisation of woman were allowed no claim upon its mercy. Primary or capital punishment, as to burning and beheading, was the same for women as for men, and the shocking apparatus of the torture chamber served for both sexes. The elaborate rules for the application of the Question published in Louis XIV.'s reign (and abolished only in the reign of Louis XVI.) specified the costume which women *and girls* should wear in the hands of the torturer.*

The black walls of the torture chamber in the Conciergerie, with their ring-bolts and benches of stone, gave back the groans of many thousands of mutilated sufferers. There were the " Question ordinary " and the " Question extraordinary " ; and if the first failed to extract a confession, the second seems almost always to have been applied. The extravagant cruelty of the age frequently added sentence of torture to the death sentence ; and this was probably done in every case in which the condemned was thought to be withholding the name of an accomplice. Far on into the history of France these sentences were dealt out to, and executed upon, women as well as men ; and with as artistic a disregard of human pain or shame in the one sex as in the other.

We are in the presence of a high civilisation, or at least a highly boasted one, in the days of Louis XIV. ; but public sentiment is not offended by the knowledge that a woman is being tortured by the *questionnaire* and his assistants in the Conciergerie ; nor are many

* " Si c'est une femme ou fille, lui sera laissé une jupe avec sa chemise et sera sa jupe liée aux genoux."

persons shocked by seeing a woman on the scaffold semi-nude in the coarse hands of the headsman, or struggling amid blazing faggots in a Paris square. Nowadays, whether in France or in England, the *mauvais quart d'heure* (which, at the guillotine or on the gallows, is usually a half-minute at the utmost) pays the score of the worst of criminals; but in the advanced and cultured France of the seventeenth and eighteenth centuries a Marquise de Brinvilliers must pass through the torture chamber on her way to the block, and a Ravaillac and a Damiens (after a like ordeal) are put to death in a manner which sends a thrill of horror through Europe, and which is not afterwards outdone in any camp of American Red Indians.

The extraordinary criminal drama of the Marquise de Brinvilliers has been vulgarised not a little by legend, by romance, and by the stage; but is there cause for wonder that a series of crimes which made Paris quake from its royal boudoirs to the extremities of its darkest alleys should have inspired writers to the fourth and fifth generations?

In the hands of De Brinvilliers and her lover and accomplice, the Gascon officer Sainte-Croix, poison became a polite art; and the accident of marriage associated the Marchioness with an industrial art which was of great renown in Paris,—I mean, the Gobelin Manufacture, or Royal Manufacture of Crown Tapestries. From the fourteenth century, in the Faubourg Saint-Marcel and on the Bièvre River—the water of which was considered specially good for dyeing purposes,—there were established certain drapers and wool-dyers; and amongst them, in 1450, was a wealthy dyer named Jean Gobelin, who had acquired large possessions on the banks of the river. His business, after his death, was continued by his son Philibert, who made it more than ever profitable, and who on his death-bed bequeathed handsome portions to his sons. The family divided between them, in 1510, ten mansions, gardens, orchards, and lands. Not less fruitful were the labours of their successors, and when the name of Gobelin had grown into celebrity, the popular voice bestowed it, says Dulaure, upon the district in which their establishment was situated.

Immensely enriched, the Gobelins ceased to occupy themselves with business, and took over various employments in the magistracy, army, and finance. Some of them succeeded in obtaining the rank and title of Marquis. From the middle of the sixteenth to the middle of the seventeenth century, the Gobelins held high offices, or married into office; and were notable amongst the merchant princes whose illustrious coffers and power to assert themselves won places for them amid the hereditary aristocracy of France. Into this family entered by marriage, in 1651, Marie Marguerite d'Aubrai, daughter of the *Lieutenant Civil*, or Civil Magistrate of Paris. Her husband, Antoine Gobelin, was the Marquis de Brinvilliers; a title which she was to cover with an infamy as great and enduring as the fame of the Gobelin Tapestries.

The Marquise's gallantries (a term which in the seventeenth century embraced a greater variety of moral eccentricities than the Decalogue has provided for) were quite eclipsed by her celebrity as a poisoner. With her performances in this art—in which she seems to have been trained by Sainte-Croix—began that incredible series of murders, and attempted murders, known as *L'Affaire des Poisons*, which both characterised and lent a *special* character to the morals of the age of the Grand Monarque.

It was the accidental death of her lover, in 1675, which exposed and brought the vengeance of the law on La Brinvilliers. Sainte-Croix was conducting some experiment with poisons in his laboratory, when the glass mask with which he had covered his face suddenly broke, and he fell dead on the spot. Letters of Mme. de Brinvilliers were amongst the suspicious objects found in the laboratory by the police, and she fled to London. One of Sainte-Croix' servants was put to the Question, and his confession did not improve the situation of the Marquise. Leaving London, she hid by turns in Brussels and Liège; and in a convent in the latter town she was discovered by the detective Desgrais, who got her out by a ruse, and brought her back to Paris. Her appearance in the torture chamber of the Conciergerie was not long delayed. All her fascinations failed her with those bloodless cross-examiners, and as she persisted in denying one charge after another, she saw the executioner and his attendants make ready the apparatus for the torture by water. She summoned a little shew of raillery : " Surely, gentlemen, you don't think that with a figure like mine I can swallow those three buckets of water ! Do you mean to drown me ? I

simply cannot drink it." "Madame," replied the ex-
aminer-in-chief, "we shall see"; and the Marchioness
was bound upon the trestle.

For a time her courage sustained her, but, as the
torture grew sharper, avowals came slowly, which
must have amazed the hardened ears that received
them.

"Who was your first victim?"

"M. d'Aubrai—my father."

"You were very devout at this time, attending
church and visiting hospitals?"

"I was testing the powers of our science on the
patients. I gave poisoned biscuits to the sick."

"You had two brothers?"

"Yes . . . we were two too many in my family.
Lachaussée, Sainte-Croix' valet, had instructions to
poison my brothers; they died in the country, with
some of their friends, after eating a pigeon-pie which
Lachaussée used to make to perfection."

"You poisoned one of your children?"

"Sainte-Croix hated it!"

"You wanted to poison your husband?"

"Sainte-Croix for some reason prevented it. After
I had administered the poison, he would give my
husband an antidote."

Before she was released from the trestle, Madame's
confession was complete. Sainte-Croix, imprisoned
in the Bastille, on a *lettre-de-cachet* obtained by M. de
Brinvilliers, had there made the acquaintance of an
Italian chemist, named Exili, who had taught him
the whole art and mystery of poison. Exili's cell in
the Bastille was the first laboratory of Sainte-Croix,

who proved afterwards so apt a pupil that, as his mistress and accomplice avowed, he could conceal a deadly poison in a flower, an orange, a letter, a glove, " or in nothing at all."

After sentence of death had been passed on this most miserable woman, she was denied the consolations of the Church, but a priest found courage to give her absolution as she was carried to the scaffold. The Marchioness was followed to her death by the husband whom she had tried in vain to send to *his* death, and who, it is said, wept beside her the whole way from the Conciergerie to the Place de Grève. Conspicuous in the enormous crowd assembled in the square were women of fashion and rank, whom the noble murderess rallied on the spectacle she had provided for them. One of the ladies was that distinguished gossip, Madame de Sévigné, who wrote the whole scene down for her daughter on the following day. De Brinvilliers was beheaded, and her body burnt to ashes.

This signal example—the torture, beheading, and burning of a peeress of France—was signally void of effect.

The secrets of Sainte-Croix and La Brinvilliers had not been buried with the one, nor scattered with the ashes of the other. Four years later, Paris talked of nothing but poison and the revival of the " black art " which was associated with it ; and, in 1680, the King established at the Arsenal a court specially charged to try cases of poisoning and magic. The notoriety of the widow Montvoisin, more commonly known as La Voisin, who dealt extensively in both arts, was inferior only to that of the Brinvilliers. Duchesses, marchionesses, countesses, and other high dames of the Court were concerned in this scandal, and Louis himself was active in seeking to bring the culprits of title to justice,—or to get them out of the way. He sent a private message to the Comtesse de Soissons, advising her that if she were innocent she should go to the Bastille for a time, in which case he would stand by her, and that if she were guilty, it would be well for her to quit Paris without delay. The Comtesse, who was "famous at the Court of Louis XIV. for her dissolute habits," fled and was exiled to Brussels; the Marquise d'Alluye or d'Allaye was banished to Amboise, Mme. de Bouillon to Nevers, and M. de Luxembourg was imprisoned for two years in the Bastille. A far more terrible expiation was prepared for La Voisin.

Outwardly, this was a woman of a grosser type than the Marchioness Brinvilliers. The Marchioness is described as "*gracieuse, élégante, spirituelle et polie.*" La Voisin was a repellent fat creature, as coarse in speech as in appearance. Yet she lived as a woman of society *(en femme de qualité)* ; and composed and sold to the beauties and gallants of the Court, poisons, charms, philters, and secrets to procure lovers or to outwit rivals; she called up spirits for a fee, and would shew the Devil if one paid the tariff for a glimpse of that celebrity.*

Her attitude in the Salle de la Question of the Conciergerie became her well. She cursed, flouted the examiners, and "swore that she would keep on

* Dulaure.

swearing" if they racked her to pieces. "Here's
your health!" she cried, when the first vessel of
water was forced down her throat; and, as they
fastened her on the rack,—"That's right! One
should always be growing. I have complained all
my life of being too short." It is said that, having
been made to drink fourteen pots of water during the
water torture, she drank fourteen bottles of wine with
the turnkeys in her cell at night. Her sentence was
death at the stake, and on her way to the place of
execution she jeered at the priest who accompanied
her, refused to make the *amende honorable* at Notre-
Dame, and fought like a tigress with the executioners
on descending from the cart. Tied and fettered on
the pile, she threw off five or six times the straw
which was heaped on her. Sévigné, who looked on,
detailed the scene with animation, and without a
touch of feeling, in a letter to her daughter.

Confounding the real crimes with chimerical ones,
the new court continued to prosecute poisoners and
"sorcerers" together; and even at that credulous and
superstitious date, when judges listened gravely to the
most baseless and fantastic accusations, there were
persons interrogated on charges of sorcery who had
the spirit to laugh both judges and accusers in the
face. Mme. de Bouillon said aloud, on the conclusion
of her examination, that she had never in her life
heard so much nonsense so solemnly spoken *(n'avait
jamais tant ouïdire de sottises d'un ton si grave);*
whereat, it is chronicled, his Majesty "was very
angry." It was not until the bench itself began to
treat as mere charlatans the wizards of both sexes

who appeared before it, that trials for sorcery and "black magic" fell away and gradually ceased.

It was the Conciergerie which presided over the examination, torture, and atrocious punishment of Ravaillac, the assassin of Henri IV., and Damiens, who attempted the life of Louis XV. Ravaillac, the first to occupy it, left his name to a tower of the prison.

"You shiver even now in the Tower of Ravaillac," say MM. Alhoy and Lurine in *Les Prisons de Paris*,—"that cold and dreadful place. Thought conjures up a multitude of fearful images, and is aghast at all the tragedies and all the dramas which have culminated in the old Conciergerie, between the judge, the victim, and the executioner. What tears and lamentations, what cries and maledictions, what blasphemies and vain threats has it not heard, that pitiless *doyenne* of the prisons of Paris!"

Ravaillac, most fearless of fanatics and devotees, said, when interrogated before Parliament as to his estate and calling, "I teach children to read, write, and pray to God." At his third examination, he wrote beneath the signature which he had affixed to his testimony the following distich:

> "Que toujours, dans mon cœur,
>   Jésus soit le vainqueur!"

and a member of Parliament exclaimed on reading it, "Where the devil will religion lodge next!"

He was condemned by Parliament on the 2d of May, 1610, to a death so appalling that one wonders how the mere words of the sentence can have been pronounced. Our own ancient penalty for high treason was a mild infliction in comparison with this.

Before being led to execution, Ravaillac did penance in the streets of Paris, wearing a shirt only and carrying a lighted torch or candle, two pounds in weight. Taken next to the Place de Grève, he was stripped for execution, and the dagger with which he had twice struck the King was placed in his right hand. He was then put to death in the following manner. His flesh was torn in eight places with red-hot pincers, and molten lead, pitch, brimstone, wax, and boiling oil were poured upon the wounds. This done, his body was torn asunder by four horses; the trunk and limbs were burned to ashes, and the ashes were scattered to the winds.

Eight assassins had preceded Ravaillac in attempts on the life of Henri IV., and six of them had paid this outrageous forfeit. The torments of the Conciergerie and the Place de Grève were bequeathed by these to the regicide of 1610, and Ravaillac left them a legacy to Robert François Damiens.

The *Tower of Ravaillac* was equally the *Tower of Damiens*. François Damiens, a bilious and pious creature of the Jesuits, not unfamiliar with crime, pricked Louis, as his Majesty was starting for a drive, with a weapon scarcely more formidable than a pen-knife. He was seized on the spot, and there were found on him another and a larger knife, thirty-seven louis d'or, some silver, and a book of devotions,—the assassins of the Kings of France were always pious men. " Horribly tortured," he confessed nothing at first, and it is by no means certain what was the nature or importance of his subsequent avowals. But, although there is little question that Damiens was merely the instrument of a conspiracy more or less redoubtable, no effort was made to arraign, arrest, or discover his supposed accomplices. The examination and trial, conducted with none of the publicity which such a crime demanded, were in the hands of persons chosen by the court, " persons sus- pected of partiality," says Dulaure, " and bidden to condemn the assassin without concerning themselves about those who had set him on—which gives colour to the belief, that they were too high to be touched" *(que ces derniers étaient puissans)*.

One hundred and forty-seven years had passed since the Paris Parliament's inhuman sentence on Ravaillac, but not a detail of it was spared to Damiens on the 28th of March, 1757. Enough of such atrocities.

In the days of the Regency there was in one of the suburbs of Paris a tea-garden which was at once popular and fashionable under the name of La Cour- tille. In the groves of La Courtille, on summer even- ings, amid lights and music, russet-coated burghers might almost touch elbows with "high-rouged dames of the palace"; and here one night Mesdames de Parabère and de Prie brought a party of elegant revellers. As one of the guests strolled apart, hum- ming an air, he was approached softly from behind, and a hand was laid upon his shoulder.

" My gallant mask, I know you ! So you have left Normandy, eh? Well, you have made us suffer much, but I fancy it will be our turn now. One of our cells has long been ready for you, and you shall sleep at the Conciergerie to-night, Cartouche !"

Yes, it was indeed the great Cartouche whom a deft detective had trapped on the sward of La Courtille. The capture was a notable one, and the next day and for many days to come Paris could not make enough of it,—Paris which had suffered beatings, plunderings, and assassinations at the hands of Cartouche and his band for ten years past. He lay three months at the Conciergerie, and every day his fame increased. The Regent's finances and the "ministerial rigours" of Dubois were disregarded ; Cartouche was a godsend to rhymesters, journalists, wits, and diners-out ; pretty lips repeated the dubious history of his amours, and a theatrical gentleman announced a "comedy" named after the distinguished cut-throat. Cartouche awaited stoically enough death by breaking on the wheel. It required a severe application of the Question to bring him to a betrayal of his band, but "his tongue once loosed, he passed an entire night in naming the companions of his crimes." The villain even denounced "three pretty women who had been his mistresses."

He consented one day to the visit of a person whose indiscreet candour was passing cruel. This was the dramatist Legrand who, with his *Cartouche* comedy in preparation, sought the "local colour" of the condemned cell. Cartouche had the vanity which characterises the great criminal, and willingly allowed himself to be "interviewed"; he answered all Legrand's questions, and then asked one himself : "When is your piece to be represented?" "On the day of your execution, my dear Monsieur Cartouche." "Ah, indeed ! Then you had better interview the executioner also; he will come in at the climax, you see."

Having entertained the playwright with his wit, the murderer next essayed the part of patriot, and said to his Jesuit confessor, Guignard, in speaking of the assassination of Henri IV. :

"All the crimes that I have ever committed were the merest peccadilloes *(de légères peccadilles)* in comparison with those which your Order is stained with. Is there any crime more enormous than to take the life of your King, and such a King as that was? The noblest prince in the universe, the glory of France, the father of his country! I tell you that if a man whom I were pursuing had taken refuge at the foot of the statue of Henri IV., I should not have dared to kill him."

The condition of the Conciergerie at this date was at all events better than it had been two or three centuries earlier. No mediæval prisons were fit to live in. Sanitation was a science as yet undreamed of in Europe, and even had there been such a science, it is improbable that the inmates of prisons would have tasted its advantages. In the Middle Ages, nothing was more remote from the official mind, from the minds of all judges, magistrates, governors, gaolers, and concierges, than the notion that prisoners should live in wholesome and decent surroundings. Two very definite ideas the Middle Ages had about prisons, and only two : the first was, that they should be impregnable, and the second was, that they should be "gey ill" to live in ; and their one idea regarding the lot of all prisoners and captives was, that it should be beyond every other lot wretched and unendurable.

In the age we live in, civilised governments setting

about the building of a new prison do not say to their architects, " You must build a fortress which prisoners cannot break, and you must put into it a certain quantity of conical cells below the level of the ground, in which prisoners may be suffocated within a given number of days," but, "You must build a prison of sufficient strength ; and in planning your cells you must secure for every prisoner an ample provision of space, air, and light." Those are the supreme differences between ancient and modern gaols. Prison in the old days was of all places the least healthy to live in ; nowadays, it is often the most healthy. Good control and strict surveillance confer security upon prisons which are not built as fortresses ; but nothing gives such immense distinction to the new system, by contrast with all the earlier ones, as the elaborate and minute regard of everything which may make for the physical well-being of the prisoners.

Then comes the moral question ; and from the standpoint of morals the situation tells even more in favour of the modern system. Imprisonment should never be cruel ; but, when the prisoner is fairly tried and justly sentenced, it should always be both irksome and disgraceful. The disgrace of prison, however, depends upon the absolute impartiality of the tribunal and the soundness of public sentiment. Nobody is disgraced by being sent into prison in a society in which arrest is arbitrary, and in which arraignment at the bar is not followed by an honest examination of the facts. Princes of the blood, nobles, ministers, and judges and magistrates themselves were equally liable with the commonest offend-

ers against the common law to be spirited into prison,
and left there, without accusation and without trial,
during many centuries of French history.   Most
tribunals were corrupt, and during many ages all
were at the mercy of the Crown.   A Daniel on the
bench was rare, and in great danger of being hanged ;
and public sentiment was not yet articulate.

In such insecurity of justice, imprisonment could
carry with it no social stigma, as it carries inevitably
in these days.   But, where there is no shame in imprisonment, there is no question of the reform of the
prisoner, and this—one of the main endeavours of
modern penal systems—was not only quite ignored
by the old régime, but was an aspect of the matter to
which it was entirely indifferent, and which had evidently no place whatever in its conceptions.   In the
progress of civilisation, no institution has been so
completely transformed as the prison.   It was an instrument of vengeance ; it is seeking, not at present
too successfully, to be an instrument of grace.

Prisons neglected or encumbered with filth are
natural hotbeds of disease, and epidemic sicknesses
were frequent.   In 1548, the plague broke out in the
Conciergerie, and then for the first time an infirmary
was established in the prison, though I cannot find
that it made greatly for the comfort of the sick.
Doctor's work was grudgingly and carelessly done in
the prisons of those days, and there was no great dis-
position to hinder the sick from yielding up the
ghost ; the bed or the share of a bed allotted to the
patient was always wanted.   The Conciergerie was
devastated by fire in 1776, and this visitation resulted

in a royal command to rehabilitate the whole interior
of the prison. In this attempt to realise the generous
thought of his minister Turgot, Louis XVI. did not
imagine, we may be sure, that he was preparing a last
lodging for Marie Antoinette !

Here then we stand on the threshold of the Conciergerie of the Revolution—the ante-chamber of the
scaffold, in the fit words of Fouquier-Tinville.

It was at four o'clock on the morning of the 14th
of October, 1793, at the close of the sitting of the
revolutionary tribunal, that the dethroned and wid-
owed Queen was brought to the Conciergerie. Poor,
abandoned, outraged Queen, they thrust her into one
of their common cells, and gave her for attendant a
galley-slave named Barasin. This must have been a
brave, good fellow, with a loyal heart under his galley-slave's vest, for at the risk of his life he waited
devoutly and devotedly on the queenly woman, a
queen no longer, who could in nothing reward his
devotion. One should name also the concierge Richard, who shewed himself not less a man in his care
of the "beautiful high-born," and who for his humanity to her was stripped of all his goods.

The gendarmes guarded her last hours, sat there in
the cell with her, though republican modesty allowed
the intervention of a screen.

It is known what a sublime dignity sustained her to
the end ; and indeed almost the worst was over when
she had quitted Fouquier-Tinville's bar, after the
"hideous indictment" and the condemnation. She
withdrew to die, and she could die as became a
Queen. Louis had gone before her, and all the

mother's dying thoughts and prayers must have been for the children who were to live after her—how long, she knew not. She sat in the dingy cell, clasping her crucifix, waiting her call to the tumbril; "dim, dim, as if in disastrous eclipse; like the pale kingdoms of Dis!"

From this time on to the end of the Reign of Terror, the Conciergerie offered such a spectacle as was never seen before within the walls of any prison. The guillotine

"smoked with bloody execution."

The Revolution was eating not her enemies only but her children, and those victims and prospective victims, men and women, old and young, filled the cells of the Conciergerie, the chambers, the corridors, and the yards. They swarmed there in disorder, dirt, and disease, guarded and bullied by drunken turnkeys, who had a pack of savage dogs to assist them. They went out by batches in the tumbrils, to leave their heads in Samson's basket, and ever fresh parties of proscribed ones took the places of the dead. "I remained six months in the Conciergerie," says Nougaret, one of the historians of the period, "and saw there nobles, priests, merchants, bankers, men of letters, artisans, agriculturists, and honest sansculottes." Often as this population was decimated, Fouquier-Tinville filled up the gap; and throughout the whole of the Terror the condemned and the untried proscribed ones, herded together, seldom had space enough for the common decencies of life.

Then some sort of classification was attempted, and

three orders were established in the prison. The *Pistoliers* were those who could afford to pay for the privilege of sleeping two in a bed. The *Pailleux* lay huddled in parties, in dens or lairs, on piles of stale straw, "at the risk of being devoured by rats and vermin." Nougaret remarks that in some cells the prisoners on the floor at night had to protect their faces with their hands, and leave the rest of their persons to the rats. The *Secrets* were the third class of prisoners, who made what shift they could in black and reeking cells beneath the level of the Seine.

And the sick in the infirmary? Listen once more to Nougaret in his *Histoire des Prisons de Paris et des Départemens* :

" There were frightful fevers there, and you took your chance of catching them. The patients, lying in pairs in filthy beds, were in as wretched a plight as ever mortals found themselves in. The doctors hardly condescended to examine them. They had one or two potions which, as they said, were ' saddles for all horses,' and which they administered quite indiscriminately. It was curious to see with what an air of contempt they made their rounds. One day, the head doctor approached a bed and felt the patient's pulse. ' Ah,' said he to the hospital warder, ' the man 's better than he was yesterday.' ' Yes, doctor, he 's a good deal better,—but it 's not the same man. Yesterday's patient is dead ; this one has taken his place.' ' Really ? ' said the doctor, ' that makes the difference ! Well, mix this fellow his draught. ' "

When the prisoners were to be locked in for the night, there was always a great to-do in getting the roll called. Three or four tipsy turnkeys, with half-a-dozen dogs at their heels, passed from hand to hand an incorrect list, which none of them could read. A wrong name was spelled out, which no one answered

to ; the turnkeys swore in chorus, and spelled out another name.   In the end, the prisoners had to come
to the assistance of the guards and call their own roll.
Then the numbers had to be told over and over again,
and the prisoners to be marched in and marched out
three or four times, before their muddled keepers
could satisfy themselves that the count was correct.

One seeks to know what the feeding was like in the
"ante-chamber of the guillotine."   When, in the midst
of the Terror, Paris was pinched with hunger, the pinch
was felt severely in the Conciergerie.   Rations ran desperately short, and a common table was instituted.
The aristocrats had to pay scot for the penniless, and
came in these strange circumstances to "estimate
their fortunes by the number of *sans-culottes* whom
they fed, as formerly they had done by the numbers
of their horses, mistresses, dogs, and lackeys."

All histories, memoirs, chronicles, and legends are
agreed that the Conciergerie of the Revolution was a
frightful place.   The political prisoners endured all
the horrors, physical and mental, of an unparalleled
régime.   Sick and unattended, hungry and barely
fed, cold and left to shiver in dark and naked cells—
these were amongst the ills of the body.   But greater
by far than these must have been the pangs of the
mind.

Nearly all of these prisoners, men and women both,
regarded death as a certainty ; before ever they were
tried, from the moment that the outer door of the
prison had closed behind them, the guillotine was as
good as promised to them.   They had no help to
count on from without, they had not even the animat-

ing hope of a fair hearing by an upright judge. The judgment bar of Fouquier-Tinville did not pretend to be impartial.

Nevertheless, though the blade of the guillotine was suspended over all heads, and fell daily upon many, an air of mingled serenity and exaltation reigned throughout the gaol. There were few tears, and there was no weak repining. Morning and evening, the political prisoners chanted in chorus the hymns of the Revolution, and these were varied by witty verses on the guillotine, composed in some instances by prisoners on the eve of passing beneath the knife. Some had brought in with them their favourite books, and reading led to long discussions, of which literature, science, religion, and politics were alternately the themes. Devoted priests like the Abbé Emory went about making converts, and opposing their efforts to those of the militant atheist, Anacharsis Clootz, who styled himself the "personal enemy of Jesus Christ." For recreation, old games were played and new ones invented. Imagine a crowd of prisoners of both sexes, living in daily expectation of the scaffold, who played for hours together at the *guillotine!* A hall of the prison was transformed into Tinville's tribunal, a Tinville was placed on the bench who could parody the voice and manner of the terrible original, the prisoner was arraigned, there were eloquent counsel on both sides, and witnesses; and when the trial was finished, and the inevitable sentence had been pronounced, the guillotine of chairs and laths was set up, and amid a tumult of applause the wooden blade was loosed and the victim rolled into the basket. Sometimes the game was interrupted, and there was a general rush to the window to catch the voice of the crier in the street,—" Here's the list of the brigands who have won to-day at the lottery of the blessed guillotine!"

Famous figures, and a few sublime ones, detach themselves from the groups : a Duc d'Orléans, a Duc de Lauzun, a General Beauharnais (who writes to his wife Josephine that letter of farewell which she shewed to Bonaparte at her first interview with him), Charlotte Corday, the great chemist Lavoisier (on whose death Lagrange exclaimed, " It took but a moment to sever that head, and a hundred years will not produce one like it"), Danton the Titan of the Revolution, Camille Desmoulins, and Robespierre himself.

One evening, a few days after the death of Marie Antoinette, the twenty-two Girondins, condemned to die in twenty-four hours, passed into the keeping of Concierge Richard. These were some of the most heroic men of the Revolution, "the once flower of French patriotism," Carlyle calls them ; tribunes, pre-lates, men of war, men of ancient and noble stock, poets, lawyers. One of their number had killed him-self in court on receiving sentence, and the dead body was carried to the prison, and lay in a corner of the room in which the twenty-two spent their last night. They gathered at a long deal table for a fare-well supper, at which, says Thiers, they were by turns, "gay, serious, and eloquent." They drank to the glory of France, and the happiness of all friends. They sang solemnly the great songs of the Revolution, and at five in the morning, when the turnkey came to call the last roll, one of them arose and declaimed the *Marseillaise*.   A few hours later, the twenty-two went chanting to their death ; and the chant was sustained until the last head had fallen.

These are amongst the loftier memories of those bloody days.   It is impossible within the limits of a chapter to give a tithe even of the names that were written in the registers of the *maison de justice* of the Revolution.   Well, indeed, might Fouquier-Tinville have named it the ante-chamber of the guillotine, for two thousand prisoners, drawn from all the other gaols of Paris, went to the scaffold from the Conciergerie. And they died, most of them, as children of a Revolution should die ; virgin girls were no longer timid, women were weak no longer, when their turn came to mount the steps of the scaffold.   A sense of patriotism so high and pure and penetrating as to resemble the spiritual exaltation and abandonment of the Christian martyrs seemed to extinguish in the frailest breasts the natural fear of death.   "*On meurt en riant, on meurt en chantant, on meurt en criant : Vive la France !*"

The fierce political interests of the revolutionary period absorb all others ; those who are not Fouquier-Tinville's victims languish obscurely in their cells, or travel towards the guillotine almost unnoticed.   But who is this in a condemned cell of the Conciergerie in the year '94, not sent there by sentence of Tinville ? It is honest, unfortunate Joseph Lesurques, unjustly convicted of the murder of a courier of Lyons,—one of the saddest miscarriages of justice.   English playgoers are familiar with the dramatic version of the story, which gave Sir Henry Irving the material of one of his most remarkable creations. In the drama, playwright's justice snatches Lesurques from the tumbril within sight of the guillotine, but the Lesurques of real life fared otherwise. He died, innocent and ignorant of the crime, but the shade of the murdered courier had a double vengeance, for the actual assassin, Dubosc, was taken later, and duly stretched on the *bascule*.

In the Napoleonic era, the Conciergerie lost two-thirds of its lugubrious importance. It continued to receive prisoners of note, but their sojourn was brief ; the prison of the Terror passed them on to Sainte-Pélagie, Bicêtre, the Temple, or the Bastille. With the return to France of the dynasty of Louis XVI., the old gaol went suddenly into mourning, as one may say, for Marie Antoinette. When Louis XVIII. commanded the erection of an " expiatory monument " in the Rue d'Anjou, the authorities of the Conciergerie made haste to blot out within its walls all traces of the Queen's captivity. They broke up the mean and meagre furniture of her cell, the wooden table, the two straw chairs, the shabby stump bedstead, the screen behind which her gaolers had gossiped in whispers ; and the cell itself ceased its existence in that form, and was converted into a little chapel or sacristy. Some poor prisoner with a thought above his own distresses may be praying there to-day for the soul of Marie Antoinette.

A ghostly souvenir of 1815 may give us pause for a moment. There is no need to rehearse the story of

CELL OF MARIE ANTOINETTE IN THE CONCIERGERIE.

AII

Marshal Ney, bravest of the sons of France, Napoleon's *le brave des braves*, whose surpassing services in the field might have spared him a traitor's end. A few days after he had "gathered into his bosom" the bullets of a file of soldiers in the Avenue de l'Observatoire, behind the Luxembourg, the public prosecutor, M. Bellart, was entertaining at dinner the great men of the bar, the army, and society. At midnight, the door of the inner salon was suddenly thrown open, and a footman announced: *Le Maréchal Ney!*

M. Bellart and his guests, smitten to stone, looked dumbly towards the door. The talk stopped in every corner, the music stopped, the play at the card-tables stopped. In a moment, the tension passed. It was not the great Marshal, nor his astral. It was a blunder of the footman, who had confounded the name with that of a friend of the family, M. Maréchal Aîné.

CHAPTER III.

THE DUNGEON OF VINCENNES.

I.

LOUIS XI. strolled one day in the precincts of
Vincennes, wrapped in his threadbare surtout
edged with rusty fur, and plucking at the queer little
peaked cap with the leaden image of the Virgin stuck
in the band. There was a smile on the sallow and
saturnine face.

At his Majesty's right walked a thick-set, squab
man of scurvy countenance, wearing a close-fitting
doublet, and armed like a hangman. On the King's
left went a showy person, vulgar and mean of face,
whose gait was a ridiculous strut.

Louis stopped against the dungeon and tapped the
great wall with his finger.

"What's just the thickness of this?" he asked.

"Six feet in places, sire, eight in others," answered
the squab man, Tristan, the executioner.

"Good!" said Louis. "But the place looks to me
as if it were tumbling."

"It might, no doubt, be in better repair, sire," observed the showy person, Oliver, the barber; "but as
it is no longer used——"

"Ah! but suppose I thought of using it, gossip?"

34

"Then, sire, your Majesty would have it repaired."

"To be sure!" chuckled the King—"If I were to shut you up in there, Oliver, you could get out, eh?"

"I think so, sire."

"But you, gossip," to his hangman, "you 'd catch him and have him back to me, *hein?*"

"Trust me, sire!" said Tristan.

"Then I 'll have my dungeon mended," said Louis. "I 'm going to have company here, gossips."

"Sire!" exclaimed Oliver. "Prisoners so close to your Majesty's own apartments! But you might hear their groans."

"Ha! They groan, Oliver? The prisoners groan, do they? But there 's no need why I should live in the château here. Hark you both, gossips, I 'd like my guests to groan and cry at their pleasure, without the fear of inconveniencing their King."

And the King, and his hangman, and his barber fell a-laughing.

From that day, in a word, Louis ceased to inhabit the château of Vincennes, and the dungeon which appertained to it was made a terrible fastness for his Majesty's prisoners of State. It was already a place of some antiquity. The date of the original buildings is quite obscure. The immense foundations of the dungeon itself were laid by Philippe de Valois; his son, Jean le Bon, carried the fortress to its third story; and Charles V. finished the work which his fathers had begun.

All prisons are not alike in their origin. In the beginnings of states, force counts for more than legal prescripts, and ideas of vengeance go above the

worthier idea of the repression of crime. Such-and-
such a prison, renowned in history, is the expression
in stone and mortar of the power or the hatred of its
builders. Thus and thus did they plan and construct
against their enemies. There was no mistaking, for
example, the purpose of the architect of the Bastille,—
it must be a fortress stout enough to resist the enemy
outside, and a place fit and suitable to hold and to
torture him when he had been carried a prisoner
within its walls.

But Vincennes, in its origin, at all events, may be
viewed under other and softer aspects. Those prodigious towers, for all the frightful menace of their
frown, were not first reared to be a place of torment.
The name of Vincennes came indeed, in the end, to
be not less dreadful and only less abhorrent than that
of the Bastille. A few revolutions of the vicious
wheel of despotism, and the King's château was
transformed into the King's prison, for the pain of
the King's enemies, or of the King's too valiant subjects. But the infancy and youth of Vincennes were
innocent enough, a reason, perhaps, why it was always
less hated of the people than the Bastille. Vincennes
lived and passed scathless through the terrors and
hurtlings of the Revolution; and presently, from its
cincture of flowers and verdant forest, looked down
upon that high column of Liberty, which occupied
the blood-stained site of the vanquished and obliterated Bastille.

King Louis lived no more in the château, and his
masons made good the breaches in the dungeon which
neglect, rather than age, had occasioned. When it
stood again a solid mass of stone,—

THE KEEP OR DUNGEON OF VINCENNES.

" Gossip," said Louis to his executioner and torturer-in-chief, "if there were some little executions to be done here quietly and secretly—as you like to do them, Tristan—what place would you choose, *hein?*"

" I 've chosen one, sire; a beautiful chamber on the first floor. The walls are thick enough to stifle the cries of an army; and if you lift the stones of the floor here and there, you find underneath the most exquisite *oubliettes!* Ah! sire, they understood high politics before your Majesty's time."

King Louis caressed his pointed chin, and laughed:

" I think it was Charles *the Wise* who built that chamber."

" No, sire; it was John *the Good!*"

" Ah, so! Go on, gossip. My dungeon is quite ready, eh?"

" Quite ready, sire."

" To-morrow, then, good Tristan, you will go to Montlhéry. In the château there you will find four guests of mine, masked, and very snug in one of our cosy iron cages. You will bring them here."

" Very good, sire."

" You will take care that no one sees you—or them."

" Yes, sire."

" And you will be tender of them, gossip. You are not to kill them on the way. When we have them here—we shall see. Start early to-morrow, Tristan. As for friend Oliver here, he shall be my governor of the dungeon of Vincennes, and devote himself to my prisoners. If a man of them escapes, my Oliver, Tristan will hang you; because you are not a noble-man, you know."

" Sire," murmured the barber, " you overwhelm me."

" Your Majesty owed that place to me, I think,"
said Tristan.

" Are you not my matchless hangman, gossip ? No,
no ! Besides, I 'm keeping you to hang Oliver. Go
to Montlhéry."

Thus was Vincennes advanced to be a State prison,
in 1473, when Louis XI. held the destinies of France.
From that date to the beginning of the century we
live in, those black jaws had neither sleep nor rest.
As fast as they closed on one victim, they opened to
receive another. At a certain stage of all despotic
governments, the small few in power live mainly for
two reasons—to amuse themselves and to revenge
themselves. One amuses oneself at Court, and a
State prison—controlled from the Court—is an ideal
means of revenging oneself. The tedious machinery
of the law is dispensed with. There is no trouble of
prosecuting, beating up witnesses, or waiting in suspense for a verdict which may be given for the other
side. The *lettre de cachet*, which a Court historian
described as an ideal means of government, and which
Mirabeau (in an essay penned in Vincennes itself)
tore once for all into shreds, saved a world of tire-
some procedure to the King, the King's favourites, and
the King's ministers. For generations and for centuries, absolutism, persecution, party spirit, public and
private hate used the *lettre de cachet* to fill and keep
full the cells and dungeons of the Bastille and Vincennes. It was, to be sure, a two-edged weapon,
cutting either way. He who used it one day might

find it turned against him on another day. But, by whomsoever employed, it was the great weapon of its time; the most effective weapon ever forged by irresponsible authority, and the most unscrupulously availed of. It was this instrument which, during hundreds of years, consigned to captivity without a limit, in the *oubliettes* of all the State prisons of France, that "*immense et déplorable contingent de prisonniers célèbres, de misères illustres.*"

Vincennes and the Bastille have been contrasted. They were worthy the one of the other; and at several points their histories touch. In both prisons the discipline (which was much an affair of the governor's whim) followed pretty nearly the same lines, and owed nothing in either place to any central, preconceived and ordered scheme of management. Prisoners might be transferred from Vincennes to the Bastille, and from the Bastille again to Vincennes. For the governor, Vincennes was generally the stepping-stone to the Bastille. At Vincennes he served his apprenticeship in the three branches of his calling —turnkey, torturer, and hangman. Like the callow barber-surgeon of the age, he bled at random, and used the knife at will; and his savage novitiate counted as so much zealous service to the State.

But Vincennes wears a greater colour than the Bastille. It stood to the larger and more famous fortress as the *noblesse* to the *bourgeoisie*. Vincennes was the great prison, and the prison of the great. Talent or genius might lodge itself in the Bastille, and often so did, very easily; nobility, with courage enough to face its sovereign on a grievance, or with power enough to be reckoned a thought too near the throne, tasted the honours of Vincennes. To be a wit, and polish an epigram against a minister or a madam of the Court ; to be a rhymester, and turn a couplet against the Government ; to be a philosopher, and hazard a new social theory, was to knock for admission at the wicket of the Bastille. But to be a stalwart noble, and look royalty in the eye, sword in hand ; to be brother to the King, and chafe under the royal behest ; to be a cardinal of the Church, and dare to jingle your breviary in the ranks of the Fronde ; to be leader of a sect or party, or the head of some school of enterprise, this was to give with your own hand the signal to lower the drawbridge of Vincennes.

At seasons prisoners of all degrees jostled one another in both prisons ; but in general the unwritten rule obtained that philosophy and unguarded wit went to the Bastille ; whilst for strength of will that might prove troublesome to the Crown .   .   .   *voilà le donjon de Vincennes !*

Yes, Vincennes was the *State* prison, the prison for audacity in high places, for genius that could lead the general mind into paths of danger to the throne. The fetters fashioned there were for a Prince de Condé to wear, a Henri de Navarre, a Maréchal de Montmorency, a Bassompierre or a Cardinal de Retz, a Duc de Longueville or a Prince Charles Edward, a La Môle and a Coconas, a Rantzau or a Prince Casimir, a Fouquet or a Duc de Lauzun, a Louis-Joseph de Vendôme, a Diderot or a Mirabeau, a d'Enghien.

History, says a French historian, shews itself never at the Bastille but with manacles in one hand and headsman's axe in the other. At Vincennes, ever and anon, it appears in the rustling silks of a king's favourite, who finds within the circle of those cruel walls soft bosky nooks and bowers, for feasting and for love. Sometimes from the bosom of those perfumed solitudes, a death-cry escapes, and the flowers are spotted with blood : Messalina has dispensed with a *lettre de cachet*. At one epoch it is Isabeau de Bavière, it is Catherine de Médicis at another ; what need to exhaust or to extend the list? Catherine made no sparing use of the towers of Vincennes. It was a spectacle of royal splendours on this side and of royal tyrannies on that ; banquets and executions ; the songs of her troubadours mingling with the sighs of her captives. Often some enemy of Catherine, quitting the dance at her pavilion of Vincennes, fell straightway into a cell of the dungeon, to die that night by stiletto, or twenty years later as nature willed. Yes, indeed, Vincennes and the Bastille were worthy of each other.

Two mysterious echoes of history still reach the ear from what were once the vaulted dungeons of Vincennes. The note of the first is gay and mocking, a cry with more of victory in it than of defeat, and one remembers the captivity of the Prince de Condé. The other is like the sudden detonation of musketry, and one recalls the bloody death of the young Duc d'Enghien, the last notable representative of the house of Condé.

The Prince de Condé's affair is of the seventeenth

century. It was Anne of Austria, inspired by Mazarin,
who had him arrested, along with his brother the
Prince de Conti and their brother-in-law the Duc de
Longueville. A lighter-hearted gallant than Condé
never set foot on the drawbridge of Vincennes. On
the night of his arrival with De Conti and the duke,
no room had been prepared for his reception. He
called for new-laid eggs for supper, and slept on a
bundle of straw. De Conti cried, and De Longueville
asked for a work on theology. The next day, and
every day, Condé played tennis and shuttle-cock with
his keepers ; sang and began to learn music. He
quizzed the governor perpetually, and laid out a garden in the grounds of the prison which became the
talk of Paris. " He fasted three times a week and
planted pinks," says a chronicler. " He studied
strategy and sang the psalms," says another. When
the governor threatened him for breaches of the rules,
the Prince offered to strangle him. But not even
Vincennes could hold a Condé for long, and he was
liberated.

Briefer still was the sojourn of the Duc d'Enghien
—one of the strangest, darkest, and most tragical
events of history. In 1790, at the age of nineteen,
he had quitted France with the chiefs of the royalist
party. Twelve years later, in 1802, he was living
quietly at the little town of Ettenheim, not far from
Strasbourg ; in touch with the forces of Condé, but
not, as it seems, taking active part in the movement
which was preparing against Napoleon. A mere
police report lost him with the First Consul. He
was denounced as having an understanding with the

officers of Condé's army, and as holding himself in readiness to unite with them on the receipt of instructions from England. Napoleon issued orders for his arrest, and he was seized in his little German retreat on March 15, 1804. Five days later he was lodged in the dungeon of Vincennes.

Here the prison drama, one of the saddest enacted on the stage of history, commences. "*Tout est mystérieux dans cette tragédie, dont le prologue même commence par un secret.*" (Everything is mysterious in this tragedy, the very prologue of which begins with a secret.)

The Duke had married secretly the Princess Charlotte de Rohan, who, by her husband's wish, continued to occupy her own house. The daily visits of the constant husband were a cause of suspicion to the agents of Napoleon. They said that he was framing plots ; he was simply enjoying the society of his wife. He was engaged, they said, in a conspiracy with Georges and others against the life of Napoleon ; he was but turning love phrases in the boudoir of the Princess.

The mystery accompanied the unfortunate prisoner from Ettenheim to Strasbourg, from Strasbourg to Paris, and went before him to Vincennes. Governor Harel was instructed to receive "an individual whose name is on no account to be disclosed. The orders of the Government are that the strictest secrecy is to be preserved respecting him. He is not to be questioned either as to his name or as to the cause of his detention. You yourself will remain ignorant of his identity."

As he was driven into Paris at five o'clock on the evening of March 20th, the Duke said with a fine assurance :

" If I may be permitted to see the First Consul, it will be settled in a moment."

That request never reached Napoleon, and the prisoner was hurried to Vincennes. His only thought on reaching the château was to ask that he might have leave to hunt next day in the forest. But the next day was not yet come.

The mystery does not cease. The military commission sent hot-foot from Paris to try the case were " *dans l'ignorance la plus complète* " both as to the name and the quality of the accused. An aide-de-camp of Murat gave the Duke's name to them as they gathered at the table in an ante-chamber of the prison to inquire what cause had summoned them. D'Enghien was abed and asleep.

" Bring in the prisoner," and Governor Harel fetched d'Enghien from his bed. He stood before his judges with a grave composure, and not a question shook him.

" Interrogated as to plots against the Emperor's life, taxed with projects of assassination, he answered quietly that insinuations such as these were insults to his birth, his character, and his rank." *

The inquiry finished, the Duke demanded with insistence to see the First Consul. Savary, Napoleon's aide-de-camp, whispered the council that the Emperor wished no delay in the affair,† and the prisoner was withdrawn.

---

* *Histoire du Donjon de Vincennes.*

† It is moderately certain at this day that everyone representing Napoleon in this miserable affair of d'Enghien *mis*-represented him from first to last.

Some twenty minutes later a gardener of the château, Bontemps by name, was turned out of bed in a
hurry to dig a grave in the trenches against the Pavil-
lon de la Reine ; and the officer commanding the guard
had orders to furnish a file of soldiers.

D'Enghien sat composedly in his room against the
council-chamber, writing up his diary for his wife, and
wondering whether leave would be given him to hunt
on the morrow. Enters, once more, Governor Harel,
a lantern in his hand. It was on the stroke of midnight.

"Would monsieur le duc have the kindness to
follow?" It is still on record that the governor
was pale, looked troubled, and spoke with much
concern.

He led the way that conducted to the Devil's
Tower. The stairs from that tower descended
straight into the trenches. At the head of the staircase, looking into the blackness beyond, the Duke
turned and said to his conductor : "Are you taking
me to an *oubliette?* I should prefer, *mon ami,* to be
shot."

"Monsieur," said Harel, "you must follow me,—
and God grant you courage !"

"It is a prayer I never yet needed to put up,"
responded d'Enghien calmly, and he followed to the
foot of the stairs.

"Shoulder arms !"

A lantern glimmering at either end of the file of
soldiers shewed d'Enghien his fate. As the sentence
of death was read, he wrote in pencil a message to
his wife, folded and gave it to the officer in com-

mand of the file, and asked for a priest.   There was
no priest in residence at the château, he was told.

"And time presses!" said the Duke.   He prayed a
moment, covering his face with his hands.   As he
raised his head, the officer gave the word to fire.

Volumes have been written upon this tragedy, but
to this day no one knows by whose precise word the
blood of the last Condé was spilled in the trenches of
Vincennes.   That d'Enghien was assassinated seems
beyond question—but by whom?   Years after the
event, General Hullin, president of the commission,
asserted in writing that no order of death was ever
signed; and that the members of the commission, still
sitting at the council-table, heard with amazement the
volley that made an end of the debate.   Napoleon
bore and still bears the opprobrium, but the proof
lacks.   Yet who, under the Consulate, dared shoot
a d'Enghien, failing the Consul's word?   The stones
of Vincennes, wherein the mystery is locked, have
kept their counsel.

Let the curtain be drawn for a moment on the
last scene in the tragedy of La Môle and Coconas.
It is a lurid picture of the manners of the time—the
last quarter of the sixteenth century, Charles IX. on
the throne.   The tale, which space forbids to tell at
length, is one of love and jealousy, with the wiles of
a *soi-disant* magician in the background.   The prime
plotter in the affair was the Queen-Mother, Catherine
de Médicis.   La Môle was the lover of Marguerite
de Navarre; Coconas, the lover of the Queen's friend,
the Duchesse de Nevers.   Arrested on a dull and

senseless charge of conspiring by witchcraft against the life of the King, the two courtiers were thrown into Vincennes. The first stage of the trial yielding nothing, the accused were carried to the torture chamber, and there underwent all the torments of the Question. After that, being innocent of the charge, they were declared guilty, and sentenced to the axe.

"Justice" was done upon them in the presence of all Paris, wondering dumbly at the iniquity of the punishment.

Night had fallen, and the executioner was at supper with his family in his house in the tower of the pillory. All good citizens shunned that accursed dwelling, and those who had to pass the headsman's door after dark crossed themselves as they did so. All at once there was a knocking at the door.

On his dreadful days of office the "Red Man" sometimes received the stealthy visit of a friend, brother, wife, or sister, come to beg or purchase a lock of hair, a garment, or a jewel.

"There's money coming to us," said the headsman to his wife. He opened the door, and on the threshold stood a man, armed, and two women.

"These ladies would speak with you," said the man ; and as the headsman stood aside, the two ladies, enveloped in enormous hoods, entered the house, their companion remaining without.

"You are the executioner?" said an imperious voice from behind an impenetrable veil.

"Yes, madame."

"You have here . . . the bodies of two gentlemen."

The headsman hesitated. The lady drew out a purse, which she laid upon the table. "It is full of gold," she said.

"Madame," exclaimed the "Red Man," "what do you wish? I am at your service."

"Shew me the bodies," said the lady.

"Ah! madame, but consider. It is terrible!" said the headsman, not altogether unmoved. "You would scarcely support the sight."

"Shew them to me," said the lady.

Taking a lighted torch, the headsman pointed to a door in a corner of the room, dark and humid.

"In there!" he said.

The lady who had not yet spoken broke into an hysterical sob. "I dare not! I dare not! I am terrified!" she cried.

"Who loves should love unto death . . . and in death," said she of the imperious voice.

The headsman pushed open the door of a cellar-like apartment, held the torch above his head, and from the black doorway the two ladies gazed in silent horror upon the mutilated spoils of the scaffold. In the red ooze upon the bare stone floor the bodies of La Môle and Coconas lay side by side. The severed heads were almost in their places, a circular black line dividing them from the white shoulders. The first of the two ladies, with heaving bosom, stooped over La Môle, and raised the pale right hand to her lips.

"Poor La Môle! Poor La Môle! I will avenge you!" she murmured.

Then to the executioner: "Give me the head! Here is the double of your gold."

"Ah! madame, I cannot. I dare not! Suppose the Provost——"

"If the Provost demands this head of you, tell him to whom you gave it!" and the lady swept the veil from her face.

The headsman bent to the earth: "Madame the Queen of Navarre!"

"And the head of Coconas to me, maître," said the Duchesse de Nevers.*

Amongst Louis XV.'s State prisoners, a long and picturesque array, may be singled out for the present Prince Charles Edward, son of the Pretender. Under the wind of adversity, after Culloden, Prince Charles was blown at length upon French soil. Louis was gracious in his offer of an asylum, and courtly France was enthusiastic over the exploits and fantastic wanderings of the young hero. All went gaily with him in Paris until the signatures had been placed to the Treaty of Aix-la-Chapelle. Then the wind began to blow from the east again.

One morning the visit was announced of MM. de Maurepas and the Duc de Gèvres.

"Gentlemen," said Prince Charles to his friends, "I know what this visit bodes. His Majesty proposes to withdraw his hospitality. We are to be driven out of France."

His handful of followers were stupefied, but the Prince was right. M. de Maurepas announced himself as commanded by the King to request Prince Charles Edward's immediate departure from France.

---

*In effect, Margaret of Navarre bore away the head of La Môle, and the Duchesse de Nevers that of Coconas. It is said that La Môle on the scaffold bequeathed his head to the Queen.

4

"Sir," returned the Prince, "your King has given me shelter, and the title of brother."

"Monseigneur," said M. de Maurepas, "circumstances have changed——"

"To my advantage, sir! For over and above the rights which Louis XV. has acknowledged in me, I have those more sacred ones of misfortune and persecution."

"His Majesty, monseigneur, is beyond doubt deeply touched by your misfortunes, but the treaty he has just signed for the welfare of his people compels him now to deny you his succour."

"Does your King indeed break his word and oath so lightly?" said Prince Charles. "Is the blood of a proscribed and exiled prince, to whom he has but just given his hand, so trifling a matter to him?"

"Monseigneur," said de Maurepas, "I am not here to sustain an argument with you. I am only the bearer of his Majesty's commands."

"Then tell the King from me that I shall yield only to his force."

This was on December 10, 1748.

When Louis's emissaries had retired, Prince Charles announced his intention of going to the Opera in the evening. His followers feared some public scandal, and did their utmost to dissuade him.

"The more public the better!" cried the Prince in a passion.

In effect, he drove to the Opera after dinner. De Maurepas had surrounded the building with twelve hundred soldiers, and as the Prince's carriage drew up at the steps, a troop of horse encircled it, and

he himself was met with a brusque request for his
sword.

"Come and take it!" said young Hotspur, flourish-
ing the weapon.

In a moment he was seized from behind, his hands
and arms bound, and the soldiers lifted him into
another carriage, which was forthwith driven off at a
gallop.

"Where are you taking me?" asked the Prince.

"Monseigneur, to the dungeon of Vincennes."

"Ah, indeed! Pray thank your King for having
chosen for me the prison which was honoured by the
great Condé. You may add that, whilst Condé was
the subject of Louis XIV., I am only the guest of
Louis XV."

M. du Châtelet, governor of Vincennes at that
epoch, had received orders to make the Prince's imprisonment a rigorous one, and fifty men were specially appointed to watch him. But du Châtelet, a
friend and admirer of the young hero, took his part,
and counselled him to abandon a resistance which
must be worse than futile. "You have had triumph
enough," said the prudent du Châtelet, "in exposing
the feebleness and cowardice of the King."

Prince Charlie's detention lasted but six days. He
was liberated on December 16th, and left Paris in the
·keeping of an officer of musketeers to join his father
in Rome.

Absolutism, *l'arbitraire*, all through this period was
making hay while the sun shone, and playing rare
tricks with the liberties of the subject. Vincennes

was a witness of strange things done in the name of the King's justice. Take the curious case of the Abbé Prieur. The Abbé had invented a kind of short-hand, which he thought should be of some use to the ministry. But the ministry would none of it, and the Abbé made known his little invention to the King of Prussia, a patron of such profitable things. But one of his letters was opened at the post-office by the *Cabinet Noir*, and the next morning Monsieur l'Abbé Prieur awoke in the dungeon of Vincennes. He inquired the reason, and in the course of months his letter to the King of Prussia was shewn to him.

"But I can explain that in a moment," said the Abbé. "Look, here is the translation."

The hieroglyphs, in short, were as innocent as a verse of the Psalms, but the Abbé Prieur never quitted his dungeon.

A venerable and worthy nobleman, M. Pompignan de Mirabelle, was imprudent enough to repeat at a supper party some satirical verses he had heard touching Madame de Pompadour and De Sartines, the chief of police. Warned that De Sartines had filled in his name on a *lettre de cachet*, M. de Mirabelle called at the police office, and asked to what prison he should betake himself. "To Vincennes," said De Sartines.

"To Vincennes," repeated M. de Mirabelle to his coachman, and he arrived at the dungeon before the order for his detention.

Once a year, De Sartines made a formal visit to Vincennes, and once a year punctually he demanded of M. de Mirabelle the name of the author of the verses. " If I knew it I should not tell you," was the invariable reply ; " but as a matter of fact I never heard it in my life." M. de Mirabelle died in Vincennes, a very old man.

A Swiss, by name Thoring, in the service of Madame de Foncemargue, told a dream in which his mistress had appeared to him with this message : " You must assassinate the King, and I will save you. You will be deaf and dumb until the deed is accomplished."

The man was clearly of unsound mind, but weak intellects were not allowed to murder kings in their sleep, and he was cast into Vincennes. Twenty years later he was seen chained by the middle to the wall of his cell, half naked and wholly mad.

But we may leave the prisoners for a while, and throw a glance upon the great castellany itself. It is best viewed, perhaps, as it stood at the commencement of the eighteenth century. Nine gigantic towers composed the fortress. A tenth out-topped them—the tower of the dungeon, distinguished as the royal manor. Two drawbridges gave access to the prison proper, the one small and very narrow, the other of an imposing size, to admit vehicles. Once beneath the wicket, the prisoner saw himself surrounded on every side by walls of prodigious elevation and thickness. He stood now immediately at the foot of the dungeon, which reared its vast height above him. Before beginning the ascent, three heavy doors must be opened for him, and that which communicated directly with the dungeon could be unfastened only by the joint action of the turnkey from within and the sergeant of the guard from without. Straight from this inner door rose the steep staircase which led to the dungeon towers. There were four of these towers, one at each angle, and communication between them was by means of immense halls or chambers, each defended by its own iron-ribbed doors.

To each of the four towers, four stories; and at each story a hall thirty feet long, and from fifteen to eighteen feet wide. At the four corners of the hall, four dismal chambers—the prisoners' cells. These cells were like miniature fortresses. A solid outer door being opened, a second one presented itself. Beyond the second was a third; and the third, iron-plated on both sides, and armed with two locks and three bolts, was the door of the cell. The three doors acted upon one another in such a manner that, unless their secret were known, the second barred the first, and the third barred the second. Light entered the cells through four loopholes, of which the inner orifices were a foot and a half in width, and the outer only six inches.

In the great halls on which the cells opened, prisoners were exercised for a limited time (never more than an hour) on rainy days, or when the orders of the governor forbade them to descend to the walled garden of the dungeon.

The hall of the first floor, celebrated in the annals of barbarism, was called the *Salle de la Question*, or torture chamber. It had its stone benches, on which the miserable creatures were placed to wait and watch the preparations for their torment; and great iron hoops or rings attached to the walls, to compress their limbs when the Question was to be put. Hard by this frightful chamber—which was fitted with every contrivance for the infliction of bodily suffering—were certain diminutive cells, deprived of light and air, and furnished with plank beds, on which prisoners were chained for a moment of repose between the first and second applications of the torture.*

On the ground floor of the dungeon were the dark cells. These were in no way connected with the *Salle de la Question*, but served as the abodes for months, or even for years, of those unhappy prisoners against whom absolutism had a special grudge, or whom the governor took a pleasure in reducing to the last extremity of misery. Here was a bed hollowed in the stone wall, and littered with mouldy straw; and rings in the wall and floor for waist-chains and leg-irons. Such a dwelling as this might receive the unfortunate whose *lettre de cachet* bore the appalling legend: *Pour être oublié!—(To be forgotten!)*.

But there were darker profundities yet in this Tartarus of the Kings of France. Almost as far as its towers rose above the ground, the dungeon plunged downwards in subterranean abysses, deep below deep. How many victims sank in those secure abysses, and were silently extinguished!

In a place which witnessed so many last earthly moments, a chapel was a necessity. Hasty abso-

---

* Up to the reign of Louis XVI., every prison in Paris and the principal courts of justice had a torture-chamber, and precise rules existed as to the various kinds of torture that might be resorted to, the mode in which each was to be applied, the persons who were to be present during the Question, the preliminary examination of the prisoner by a surgeon, the manner of binding, stretching, etc., together with the minutest details respecting the several forms of the Question, and the means to be employed to restore the sufferer for a second application.

lution was often given for the crimes real or imaginary which were so rudely expiated within the royal
manor; and sometimes prisoners were carried in a
dying state from the *Salle de la Question* to receive
the last rites of the Church in one of the three small
chapel cells with double doors.   Here, on the very
threshold of death, one lay in semi-darkness to hear
the mass which was pronounced on the other side of
the wall.   Over the chaplain's apartment was the
singular inscription, *Carcer sacerdotis (Prison of the
Priest)*, which allows the inference that the chaplain,
whilst in the exercise of his functions, was not allowed to communicate with the outer world.

A narrow stone staircase of two hundred and sixty-
five high steps, obstructed at frequent intervals by
sealed doors, conducted to a small and well made
terrace at the very top of the dungeon.   It is probable that this terrace is still in existence.*   It was
little used—perhaps because it was the pleasantest
place in the prison,—but tradition has represented
Mirabeau as taking an occasional airing on that
superb summit.   The little lantern-shaped tower
placed here contained the chapel which was once
the oratory of the Kings of France.   Some nerve
must have been needed for Majesty to pray at ease,
whilst crushing with its knees that mass of human
wretchedness !

The great court below was parcelled into little
close gardens, where, under rigid surveillance, favoured prisoners took their dreary exercise.

* Vincennes is now a fort and artillery barracks, and may neither be sketched
nor photographed.

Few prisons the like of Vincennes have been erected. Those tremendous towers, those almost impenetrable walls, those double and triple doors garnished with iron, the trenches forty feet in depth, those wide outer galleries to give the sentries command at every point—what more could genius and industry invent to combat the prisoner's passion for liberty? There were, indeed, few escapes from Vincennes. The prisoner who broke prison from the Bastille, and won his way into the trenches, nearly always made good his flight; but in the trenches of Vincennes, if he ever reached them, he was more helpless than a rat in a bucket. The architect of Vincennes was up some half-hour earlier than the architect of the Bastille.

Twice every hour of the twenty-four the patrol made a complete tour of the dungeon; and night and morning, before the closing and opening of the doors, the trenches (which were forbidden to the turnkeys except by express order) were surveyed from end to end, that no letters might be thrown there by prisoners upon whom the State had set a seal like that of the *Masque de Fer*.

Over and above all these *précautions barbares*, the sentries had orders to turn the eyes of every passer-by from the dungeon towers. No one might stand or draw bridle in the shadow of Vincennes. It might be a relative or friend seeking to learn in what exact cell the captive was lodged! From light to dusk, the sentry reiterated his changeless formula: *Passez votre chemin!*

We have yet to see what life the prisoners led.

II.

The hour, the manner, and the circumstances of his reception at Vincennes were little adapted to lessen the apprehensions of a prisoner regarding the fate that awaited him. It was generally at night that the arrest was effected, and the dismal ceremony of admission lost nothing amid the general gloom of the scene, streaked here and there by the thin light of the warders' lanterns. It would have been distressing enough to pass into that black keep as the King's prisoner, after a fair trial in open court, and with full knowledge of the term of one's captivity; how much more so to find oneself thrust in there on some vague or fabulous charge, a victim not of offended laws but of some cold caprice of vengeance, to stay the pleasure of an enemy who might forget his prisoner before he forgot his wrath. At Vincennes as in the Bastille, prisoners lived on, hopelessly forgotten, years after the death of their accusers.

On arrival at the dungeon the prisoner was searched from head to foot, and all papers, money, or other valuables were taken from him. This was done under the eyes of the governor, who then, preceded by two turnkeys, led his charge up that steep, narrow and winding staircase which has been described. One vast hall after another was slowly traversed, with frequent halts for the unbarring of doors which creaked on their rusty hinges. The flicker of the lanterns amid that sea of shadows brought into dim evidence huge locks and padlocks, loopholes and casements, garnished with twisted iron bars; and every footfall found an echo in the vaulted ceilings.

At the end of this oppressive journey, the prisoner came to his den, a miserable place containing a wooden stump bedstead, a couple of rush chairs, and a table stained with the dishes of every previous occupant. If it were past the hour at which prisoners were served with supper, he would probably be denied a morsel of food; and the governor left him, after bestowing his first injunction: "I would have you remember, monsieur, that this is the house of silence."

The prisoner had now to keep himself in patience until the governor decided on his lot—that is to say, on the life that he should lead. There was no ordered system such as regulates the existence of an army of convicts undergoing sentence of penal servitude in these days. The power of the governor was all but autocratic, and though he made constant reference to "the rules," he interpreted those shadowy prescriptions entirely as it pleased him. "It is the rule," said the governor, when enforcing some petty tyranny. "It is not the rule," he said, when denying some petty favour. Sometimes the prisoner was forbidden by superior order the use of books and writing materials, but more frequently such an order issued from the lips of the governor himself. If permission to read and write were accorded, new difficulties arose. There was no special library attached to the dungeon, and as the governor's tastes were seldom literary, his store of books was scanty, and the volumes were usually in the keeping of those few prisoners whom he favoured. As for writing materials, little books of note-paper were sparsely doled, each sheet numbered and to be accounted for; and no letter could leave the prison without the governor's scrutiny.

As the prisoner read and wrote, so also did he eat and drink, by favour of the governor. An allowance sufficient for each prisoner's maintenance was authorised and paid by the State, but most of the King's bounty contributed to swell the governor's private fortune. The tariff allowed and paid out of the royal treasury was:

For a prince of the blood, about £2 *per diem.*

For a marshal of France, about £1 10s.

For a lieutenant-general, about £1.

For a member of Parliament, about 15s.

For an ordinary judge, a priest, a captain in the army, or an official of good standing, about 7s. 6d.

For a barrister or a citizen of means, about 2s. 6d.

For a small tradesman, about 1s. 6d.

At such rates as these, all prisoners should have been well cared for in those days; but the truth is that the governors who entered Vincennes with small means left it rich men. Not only the moneys allotted for food, but the allowances of wood, lights, etc., were shamelessly pilfered; and prisoners who were unable or forbidden to supplement the royal bounty from their own purses were often half-starved and half-frozen in their cells. As for the quality of the food, warders and kitchen-assistants sometimes tried to sell in Vincennes meat taken from the prison kitchen, but it had an ill name amongst the peasants: "That comes from the dungeon; it's rotten." On the other hand, wealthy prisoners who enjoyed the governor's favour, or who could bring influence to bear on him from without,

were allowed to beguile the tedium of captivity by
unlimited feasting and drinking. The inmate of one
cell, lying in chains, dirt, and darkness, might be kept
awake at night by the tipsy strains of his neighbour
in the cell adjoining. Governors avaricious above
the common generally had their dark cells full, so as
to be able to feed on bread and water the prisoners
for whom they received the regular daily tariff.
Ordinarily, there were but two meals a day, dinner
at eleven in the morning and supper at five in
the evening; hence, if your second ration were in-
sufficient, you must go hungry for eighteen hours.
A privileged few were allowed a valet at their own
charge, but the majority of the prisoners of both sexes
were served by the turnkeys.

The turnkeys visited the cells three times a day,
rather as spies, it seems, than as ministers to the
needs of the prisoners. " They came like heralds of
misfortune," says one. " A face hard, expressionless,
or insolent; an imperturbable silence; a heart proof
against the sufferings of others. Useless to address
a question to them; a curt negative was the sole response. 'I know nothing about it,' was the turnkey's
eternal formula."

Some prisoners, but by no means all, were allowed
to walk for an hour a day in one of the confined
gardens at the base of the tower; always in company
with a warder, who might neither speak nor be
spoken to. As the hour struck, the exercise ceased.

Such seems to have been the external routine of
life at Vincennes. Beneath the surface was the perpetual tyrannous oppression of the governor and his

subordinates on the one side, and on the other a
weight of suffering, extended to almost every detail
of existence, endured by the great majority of the
prisoners ; silently even unto death in some instances,
but in others not without desperate resistance, long
sustained against overwhelming odds.

The recital of Mirabeau's captivity throws into
curious relief the inner life of the dungeon. The
governor was a certain De Rougemont, of most unrighteous memory, whom Latude describes as having
written his name in blood on the walls of every cell.
Elsewhere the same narrator says that prisoners occasionally strangled themselves to escape the rage of
De Rougemont, who was seventeen years in charge
of Vincennes.

The fiery, impetuous Mirabeau was ceaselessly at
variance with this " despotic ape," who delighted in
trying to repress by the most contemptible annoyances that irrepressible spirit. Complaint was a fault
in the eyes of De Rougemont, impatience a crime.

The future tribune,* whose head was always in the
clouds, complained incessantly and was impatience
incarnate. Night or day he gave his gaoler no peace.
Mirabeau's lodging in the fortress was a small tower-
chamber between the second and third story, rarely
visited by the sun ; it was in existence fifty years ago,
and bore the number 28. De Rougemont began by

---

* He was imprisoned mainly on the order of the Marquis de Mirabeau, his
father, whose lifelong jealousy of that brilliant son is matter of history , a
finished example of the domestic bully, and a matchless humbug and hypocrite,
whose every action gave the lie to his by-name *Friend of Man*. In the course
of his life, the Marquis procured no fewer than fifty *lettres de cachet* against
members of his own family.

MIRABEAU ON THE TERRACE OF VINCENNES.

submitting him to all the rigours of "the rules." Mirabeau demanded leave to write, it was refused; to read, it was refused; to take a daily airing, it was refused. He could not get scissors to cut his hair, nor a barber to dress it for him. He was four months in altercation with De Rougemont before he could obtain the use of a blunt table-knife. He could not get at his trunk to procure himself a change of linen.

"Is it by 'the rules' that my trunk is kept from me?" he demanded of the governor.

"What need have you of your trunk?"

"Need! I want clothes and linen. I am still wearing what I brought into this rat-hole!"

"What does it matter? You see no company here."

"I am to go foul, then, because I see no company! Is that your rule? Once more, let me have my trunk."

"We have not the key of it."

"Send for a locksmith,—an affair of an hour."

"Where am I to find the hour? Have I no one and nothing else to attend to? Are you the only prisoner here?"

"That is no answer. You are here to take care of your prisoners. Give me my trunk, I tell you!"

"*It is against the rules.* We shall see by-and-bye."

"As usual! 'We shall see.' In the meantime perhaps you will have the goodness to send a barber to shave me and cut my hair."

"Ah! I must speak about that to the minister."

"What! The minister's permission to——"

" Yes. *It is the rule.*"

" Indeed !   The doctor said as much, but I refused to credit him."

" You were wrong, you see !"

" Now that I remember, he told me something else, that in the present state of my health a bath, with as little delay as possible, was indispensable. Perhaps he did not mention that to you ?"

" I fancy he did say something about it."

" Oh, he did !   But the King and the Government have not debated it yet, I suppose ? Well, sir, I want a bath and I 'm going to have one."

" You have no right to give orders here, sir."

" Nor have you the right to withhold what the doctor prescribes for me."

" M. de Mirabeau, you are insolent.   Do you forget that I represent the King ?"

" He could not be more grotesquely represented. The distance between you and his Majesty is short, sir."

The governor (to make the joke more apparent) was short and of a full habit.   He went out speechless, and Mirabeau would doubtless have felt the effects of his rage had it not been for the interest of Lenoir, Lieutenant-General of Police, who was always ready to stand between the prisoner and the vengeful gaoler.   Through Lenoir, who won for him the intercession of the Princesse de Lamballe, Mirabeau got the use of books and pen, and some other small indulgences.   He wrote to his father : " Will you not ease me of my chains ? Let me have friends to see me ; let me have leave to walk.   Let me ex-

change the dungeon for the château. There as here I
should be under the King's hand, and close enough to
the prison, if I should abuse that measure of liberty."
The implacable *Friend of Man* vouchsafed no response to this entreaty. The prisoner buried himself
in the books that were given him, but they were for
the most part "*de mauvais auteurs,*" who had nothing
to teach him. He flung them from him one by one, and
as he paced his cell he began those brilliant improvi-
sations which were soon to electrify France, and which
struck absolutism at its root. In this way he worked
out the scheme of the *Lettres de Cachet,* that work of
flaming eloquence in which the genius of liberty approaches, seizes, and strangles the dragon of despotism. Deprived of all but his pen, Mirabeau let fall
from the height of his dungeon on the head of royalty
that thunderbolt of a treatise. Since De Rougemont
would never, for a hundred chiefs of police, have aided
him with materials for this purpose, he tore out of all
the books he could lay hands on the fly-leaves and
blank spaces, and covered them with his fine close
writing. Each completed slip he concealed in the
lining of his coat, and in this manner did the tribune
compose and preserve his work, every page of which
was a prophecy of the coming Revolution. When
inspiration lacked for a time, he prostrated himself
on the flags of his cell and wept for his absent mistress, or he renewed hostilities with De Rougemont.
The battle of the trunk was followed by the battle of
the looking-glass.

He could not go through his toilet without a looking-glass, he insisted ; and in a letter to the governor

which must have filled several manuscript pages he exhausted his logic and his sarcasm in enforcing this modest request.   He got his mirror in the end, and then renewed his fruitless correspondence with his father, and made an eloquent attempt to move the clemency of the King.   " Deign, sire, to save me from my persecutors," he wrote to Louis.   " Look with pity on a man twenty-eight years of age, who, buried in full life, sees and feels the slow approach of brutish inertia, despair, and madness, darkening and para- lysing the noblest of his years."   M. Lenoir himself placed this letter in the King's hands, but nothing came of it for Mirabeau, who continued in the pauses of astonishing literary labours his fight for liberty from behind his prison bars.   By clamours and entreaties he succeeded at length in forcing his way through them.

Amongst the prisoners of renown of the eighteenth century Latude must not pass unnoticed.   His sojourn in and escape from the Bastille have been much more widely bruited than his captivity at Vincennes, where also he did things wonderful and suffered pains and indignities incredible.   Needless to say that he gave his guards the slip, and equally needless to add that he was recovered and brought back.   His second in- carceration was in one of De Rougemont's *cachots* (De Rougemont always had a *cachot* available), from which, on the surgeon's declaration that his life was in danger, he was removed to a more habitable cham- ber.   On his way thither he found and secreted one of those handy tools which fortune seemed always to

leave in the path of Latude, and used it to establish
a most ingenious means of communication with his
fellow prisoners.   No one ever yet performed such
wonders in prison as Masers de Latude.   No one accomplished such unheard-of escapes.   No one, when
retaken, paid with such cruel interest the penalty of
his daring.   Was the man only a splendid fable, as
some latter-day sceptics have suggested?   The question has been put, but no one will ever affirm it with
authority, and the weight of the evidence seems to lie
with Latude the man and not with Latude the legend.

No great distance separated the chamber of Latude
from the *cachot* of the Prévôt de Beaumont.   The
Prévôt was a great criminal : he had had the courage to denounce and expose that gigantic State fraud,
the *pacte de famine*, in which the De Sartines before
named and other persons of consequence were involved.   Those were not the days for Prévôts de
Beaumont to meddle as critics with criminal ventures
of this sort, and the Prévôt had his name written on
the customary form.   He spent twenty-two years in
five of the State prisons of France, and fifteen of
them in the dungeon of Vincennes.

"There is not in the *Saints' Martyrology*," he wrote (in the
record which he gave to the people of the Revolution of his ex-
periences in the dungeon of the Monarchy), "such a tale of
tribulations and torments as were suffered by me on twelve separate occasions in the fifteen years of my captivity at Vincennes.
On one occasion I was confined four months in the *cachot*, nine
months on another occasion, eighteen months on a third ; of my
fifteen years in the dungeon, *seven years and eight months* were
passed in the black hole.   The cruel De Sartines never ceased
to harry me ; the monster De Rougemont surpassed the orders

of De Sartines. Yes, I have lain almost naked and with fettered ankles for eighteen months together. For eighteen months at a time, I have lived on a daily allowance of two ounces of bread and a mug of water. I have more than once been deprived of both for three successive days and nights." *

The dramatic interest of the Prévôt's imprisonment culminates in an assault upon him in his cell, renewed at four several ventures by the whole strength of the prison staff " and the biggest dog that I have ever seen." The Prévôt had devoted five years to the stealthy composition of an essay on the *Art of True Government*, which was actually a history of the *pacte de famine*. His attempts to get it printed were discovered by the police, and the attack on his cell was designed to wrest from him the manuscript. He sets out the affair in detail with the liveliest touches —" First Round," " Second Round," etc.—shews himself levelling De Rougemont with a brick in the stomach, the dog with a blow on the nose, and blinding a brace of warders with the contents of his slop-bucket. At last, faced by an order in the King's writing, he allowed himself to be transferred from Vincennes to Charenton, on the express understanding that his precious manuscript should be transferred with him. The Prévôt himself arrived duly at Charenton, but he never again set eyes on the essay on the *Art of True Government*. De Rougemont had arranged that it should be stolen on the journey, and

* I have summarised here the extracts in the original from the pamphlet of the Prévôt de Beaumont quoted at great length by the authors of the *Histoire du Donjon de Vincennes*. As a curiosity of prison literature, the Prévôt's pamphlet, if correctly cited, goes above the little eighteenth century work on Newgate by " B. L. of Twickenham."

the manuscript was last seen in the archives of the Bastille.

Mirabeau was not the only polemic of genius who helped to sharpen against the gratings of Vincennes the weapons of the dawning Revolution. Was not Diderot of the *Encyclopedia* there also? He paid by a month's rigorous imprisonment in the dungeon, and a longer period of mild captivity in the château, the publication of his *Letter on the Blind for the Use of those who See*. This, at least, was the ostensible reason of his detention; the true reason was never quite apparent. At the château he was allowed the visits of his wife and friends, and amongst the latter Jean Jacques Rousseau was frequently admitted. Literary legend is more responsible than history for the statement that the first idea of the *Social Contract* was the outcome of Rousseau's talks with Diderot and Grimm in the park of Vincennes.

Year after year, reign after reign, the picture rarely changes within the four walls of the dungeon. Vincennes was perhaps fuller under Louis XV. than in the reigns of preceding or succeeding sovereigns, but the difference could not have been great. During the twenty years of Cardinal Fleury's ministry under Louis XV., 40,000 *lettres de cachet* were issued by him, mostly against the Jansenists. Madame de Pompadour made a lavish use of the *lettres* in favour of Vincennes; Madame Dubarry bestowed her patronage chiefly on the Bastille. Richelieu at one epoch, Mazarin at another, found occupants in plenty for the

cells of Vincennes.   It was Richelieu who passed a
dry word one day apropos of certain mysterious deaths
in the dungeon.

"It must be grief," said one.

"Or the purple fever," said the King.

"It is the air of Vincennes," observed Richelieu,
"that marvellous air which seems fatal to all who do
not love his Majesty."

Ministers themselves were apt to fall by the weapon
of their own employment.   A minister of Louis XIV.,
who had chosen for his proud device the motto, *Quò
non ascendam?—What place too high for me?*—and
whom chroniclers have suspected of pretensions to the
gallant crown of Mademoiselle de la Vallière, fell one
day from a too giddy pinnacle plump into the dungeon of Vincennes.   It was Fouquet the magnificent.

Up to a point, Fouquet was the best courtier in
France.   The King's passion was for pomp and glitter; the minister cultivated a taste for the dazzling.
Louis was prodigal to extravagance; Fouquet became
lavish *jusqu'à la folie*.   The King dipped both hands
into the public moneys; the minister plunged elbow-
deep into the coffers of the State.   The King offered
to his servitors fêtes the most sumptuous; the minister regaled his friends with spectacles beyond compare.
Then Louis wearied of this too splendid emulation,
and Fouquet the magnificent was attached.   He all
but sacrificed his head to his lust of rivalry; but Louis
relented, and took from him only his goods and his
freedom.   Despoiled and dishonoured, the ex-minister
fared from prison to prison,—Vincennes, Angers,
Amboise, Moret, the Bastille, and Pignerol.   *Quò non*

ascendam ?—Whither may I not mount ? The unfortunate minister, who had thought to climb to the
sun of Louis XIV., sank to his death in a *cachot.*

The contrasts presented by the diverse fates of
certain prisoners are sufficiently striking. Fouquet
was preceded at Vincennes by Cardinal de Retz, the
last prisoner of distinction whom Anne of Austria
sent to the dungeon. The Cardinal's was a gilt-edged
captivity. He lived *en prince* at Vincennes ; he had
valets, money, and a good table ; great ladies came
to distract him, friends to flatter him, and players to
divert him. Literature, politics, gallantry, and the
theatre—the Cardinal found all of these at Vincennes.
When he chanced to remember his priestly quality,
he obtained leave to say mass in the chapel of the
château, "carefully concealing the end of his chain
under the richest of vestments." But the chain was
there, and the lightest of fetters grows heavy in
prison ;—the Cardinal resolved on flight.

It was a clever and most original plan. On a certain day, a party of the Cardinal's friends, mounted as
for a desperate ride, were to assemble under the walls
of the keep, and at a given signal were to whirl away
in their midst a man attired at all points like the
Cardinal himself. A rope hanging from a severed
bar in the window of the cell was to give his guards
to suppose that the prisoner had escaped that way ;
but all this while the Cardinal was to lie *perdu* in a
hole which he had discovered on the upper terrace of
the prison. When the excitement over the imaginary
flight had subsided, and the vigilance of the sentries
was relaxed, the Cardinal was to issue from his hiding-

place, disguised as a kitchen-man, and walk out of the dungeon. It might have succeeded, but the elements played into the hands of Anne d'Autriche. A storm blew up on the night that the Cardinal was to have quitted his chamber, and the wind closed a heavy door on the staircase that led to the terrace. All the Cardinal's efforts to wrest it open were unavailing, and he was forced to return to his cell. He was removed to the château of Nantes, and the imaginative daring of his flight from that place has ranked it high in the annals of prison-breaking.

One echo more shall reach us from these lugubrious caverns. Towards the beginning of the eighteenth century, a young man, Du Puits by name (victimised by an Italian abbé into forging orders on the King's treasury), received as cell-companion the Marquis de la Baldonnière, a reputed or suspected alchemist. Du Puits, a laughing philosopher now on the verge of tears, recovered his spirits when he learned the new-comer's name.

"I heard all about you, sir, before I came here," he said. "I was secretary to M. Chamillart, the minister, and you were often talked of at the bureau. I told M. Chamillart that if you could turn iron into gold, it was a pity you were not appointed manager of the iron mines. But it is never too late to turn one's talents to account, monsieur le marquis, and as a magician of the first water you shall effect our escape."

The achievements of the noble wizard came short of this end, but they were far from contemptible.

He took surreptitious impressions in wax of the keys dangling from the very belt of the warder who visited them, and manufactured a choice set of false ones, which gave the two prisoners the range of the dungeon. There was no night watch within the tower, and when the warders had withdrawn after the prisoners' supper-hour, Du Puits and the Marquis ran up and down the stairs, and from hall to hall, called on the other prisoners in their cells, and made some agreeable acquaintances, including that of a pretty and charming young sorceress. Trying a new lock one night, they found themselves in the governor's pantry—after this, some rollicking supper parties. The feasts were organised nightly in one cell or another, Du Puits and the Marquis furnishing the table from the ample larder of the governor. Healths were being drunk one night, when the door was rudely opened, and the guests found themselves covered by the muskets of the guard. An unamiable prisoner whose company they had declined had exposed the gay conspiracy, and there were no more supper parties.

The last years of Vincennes as a State prison have little of the interest either of romance or of tragedy. Its fate in this respect was settled by Mirabeau's *Lettres de Cachet.* Vincennes was the only prison of which he had directly exposed the callous and cruel régime, and the ministry thought well to close it, as a small concession to the rising wrath of the populace. In 1784, accordingly, Vincennes was struck off the list of the State prisons of France. A singular and

oddly ludicrous fate came upon it in the following
year, when it was transformed into a sort of charitable
bakery under the patronage of Louis XVI.! The
cachot in which the Prévôt de Beaumont had lain
hungry for eighteen months, and for three days without food, was stored with cheap loaves for the work-
ing people of Paris. A little later, the dungeon was a
manufactory of arms for the King's troops. After
the destruction of the Bastille, Vincennes was attacked
by the mob, but Lafayette and his troops saved it
from their hands. Under the Republic it was used
for a time as a prison for women. The wretched fate
of the Duc d'Enghien, Napoleon's chief captive in
this fortress, has been told ; and there is only to add
that the last prisoners who passed within the walls of
Vincennes were MM. de Peyronnet, de Guernon
Ranville, de Polignac, and Chantelauze, the four
ministers of Charles X. whose part in the " Revolution of July " belongs to the history of our own times.
Brave old General Daumesnil, " Old Wooden-Leg,"
who died August 17, 1832, was the last governor of
the Dungeon of Vincennes.

CHAPTER IV.

THE GREAT AND LITTLE CHÂTELET, AND THE FORT-L'ÉVÊQUE.

LOUIS VI., called le Gros, whose reign was from 1108 to 1137, did much to enlarge and to embellish the mean and narrow Paris of his day. He built churches and schools both in the Cité and beyond the river, and thanks to the lectures of Abelard his schools were famous. He built a wall around the suburbs, and for the further defence of the Cité he set up the two fortresses called Le Grand and Le Petit Châtelet, "at the extremities of the bridge which united the Cité with the opposite bank."

Here was established the court of municipal justice, and here the Provost of Paris had his residence. The prison of the Châtelet became one of the most celebrated in Paris, and prison and fortress were not completely demolished until 1802.

The functions of the Châtelet—*cette justice royale ordinaire à Paris*—were great and various. It was charged in effect, says Desmaze,* with the maintenance of public safety in the capital, with the settlement of divers causes, with the repression of popular agitations, with the ordering of corporations and

* *Le Châtelet de Paris.*

trades, with the verification of weights and measures. It punished commercial frauds, defended "minors and married women," and kept in check the turbulent scholars of the University. Its magistrates were fifty-six in number; it had its four King's Counsel and its King's Procurator; its clerk-in-chief and his host of subordinates; its receivers, bailiffs, and ushers; its gaolers and its sworn tormentor; its "sixty special experts"; its surgeon and his assistants, including a *sage-femme* or mid-wife; and its two hundred and twenty *sergents à cheval*.

All in all, the Châtelet was one of the most formidable powers in Paris. The court of the Châtelet comprised four divisions, administered by councillors who sat in rotation. The four sections were distinguished as the *parc civil*, the *présidial*, the *chambre du conseil*, and the *chambre criminelle*.

But the Prison of the Châtelet is our principal concern. Although, says Desmaze, the prison was instituted for the safe-keeping and not for the maltreatment of the accused, the law's design was too often eluded or ignored. Much the same might be said in respect of any other prison in Europe at that epoch. Antique papers cited by Desmaze show, nevertheless, that Parliaments of Paris sought by successive decrees to modify the rigour of the prisoner's lot, to restrain the cupidity of his gaolers, and to maintain decent order within the prison. There were provisions against gambling with dice, rules for the distribution of alms amongst the prisoners, and penalties for those who absented themselves from chapel. In 1425, a new *ordonnance* fixed the scale of fees *(geôlage)* which prisoners were to pay to the governor or head gaoler on reception. (This ironic jest of compelling persons to pay for the privilege of going to prison obtained for centuries in Newgate.) A count or countess was charged ten livres, a knight banneret *(chevalier banneret)* passed in for ten sols, a Jew or a Jewess for half that sum ; and so on to the end of the scale. There were particular injunctions as to the registering of prisoners, and as to the mode of keeping the prison books. The bread served out was ordered to be *de bonne qualité*, and not less than a pound and a half a day for each prisoner : in 1739, the baker who supplied the Châtelet was condemned to a fine of 2000 livres for adulterating the prisoners' bread. A special ration of bread and meat was distributed at the Châtelet on the day of the annual feast of the confraternity of drapers, and the goldsmiths of Paris gave a dinner on Easter Day to such of the prisoners as would accept their bounty.

The deputies of the *Procureur Général* were instructed to visit the prison once a week, to examine and receive in private the requests and complaints of the prisoners, and to see that the doctors did their duty by the sick. The first Presidents of the Paris Parliament seem to have visited the Châtelet frequently from the end of the fourteenth to the middle of the sixteenth century.

But there was one circumstance which, in mediæval Paris and in the Paris of a much later date, must have gone far to nullify all good intentions and humane precautions of kings and parliaments

alike.   Under an *ordonnance* of July, 1319, Philippe
le Long decreed that the governorships of gaols
should be sold at auction.   The purchasers were, of
course, to be "respectable persons" (*bonnes gens*),
who should pledge their word to deal humanely by
(*de bien traiter*) the prisoners ; but of what use were
such provisos ?   In no circumstances, indeed, could a
saving clause of any description ensure the proper
administration of a prison the governor of which had
bought the right to make private gain out of his
prisoners.   For this was what the selling of gaoler-
ships came to.   Having paid for his office (having
bought it, moreover, over the heads of other bidders),
the governor recouped himself by fleecing his wealthy
prisoners and by stinting or starving his poorer ones.
It was no worse in France than elsewhere ; until Howard demanded reform, prisoners in Newgate were
plundered right and left under a similar system, and
those who could not pay the illegal fees of the governor and his subordinates were lodged in stinking
holds, and fed themselves as they could.

We shall see what the prisons of the Châtelet and
the Fort-l'Évêque were like amid the luxuries and
refinements which surrounded them in the eighteenth
century.   An *ordonnance* of 1670 had enjoined that
the prisons should be kept in a wholesome state, and
so administered that the prisoners should suffer nothing in their health.   Never, says Desmaze, was a
decree so miserably neglected.

What are the facts ?   He quotes from an " anonymous eighteenth-century manuscript " ("by a magistrate") entitled : *Projet concernant l'établissement*

de nouvelles Prisons dans la Capitale. The Fort-l'Évêque and the Châtelet are turned inside out for such an inspection as Howard would have made with a gust.

In the court or principal yard of Fort-l'Évêque, thirty feet long by eighteen wide, from four to five hundred prisoners were confined. The prison walls were so high that no air could circulate in the yard; the prisoners were "choked by their own miasma." The cells "were more like holes than lodgings"; and there were some under the steps of the staircase, six feet square, into which five prisoners were thrust. Other cells, in which it was barely possible to stand upright, received no light but from the general yard. The cells in which certain prisoners were kept at their private charge were scarcely better. Worst of all were the dens below-ground. These were on a level with the river, water filtered in through the arches the whole year round, and even in the height of summer the sole means of ventilation was a slit above the door three inches in width. Passing before one of the subterranean cells, it was as though one were smitten by fire (*on est frappé comme d'un coup de feu*). They gave only on to the dark and narrow galleries which surrounded them. The whole prison was in a state of dilapidation, threatening an immediate ruin.

The Châtelet was "even more horrible and pestilential." The prison buildings, having no external opening, received air only from above; there was thus "no current, but only, as it were, a stationary column of air, which barely allowed the prisoners to breathe." This is far from a realisation of the *ordon-*

nance of 1670! Like the Fort-l'Évêque, the Châtelet had its horrors of the pit. Dulaure * has a curious passage on the subject. It appears, says one of the best of the historians of Paris, that prisoners were let down into a dungeon called *la fosse,* as a bucket is lowered into a well; here they sat with their feet in water, unable to stand or to lie, "and seldom lived beyond fifteen days." Another of these pits, known as *fin d'aise* (a name more bodeful than the Little Ease of old Newgate), was "full of filth and reptiles"; and Dulaure adds that the mere names of most of the Châtelet cells were "frightfully significant."

The Provost of Paris, rendering justice in the King's name, took cognisance of all ordinary causes, of capital crimes, and of petty offences. His officers arrested and imprisoned "all manner of criminals, vagabonds, and disturbers of the public peace." In the reign of Philippe-Auguste, he was charged with the duty of "bringing to justice the Jews" who at that epoch were "accused of seeking to convert Christians to Judaism, of taking usurious interest, and of profaning the sacred vessels which the churches gave them in pledge." After the King, said Pasquier, the Provost of Paris was the most powerful man in the kingdom.

The headsman of Paris depended on the jurisdiction of the Châtelet. There was a small chamber in the prison called the *réduit aux gehennes,* where, when an execution was to take place, Monsieur de Paris

* *Histoire de Paris.*

THE GREAT CHÂTELET.

CALIFORNIA

received the Provost's warrant. In 1418, the headsman Capeluche was himself sentenced to be beheaded, and in the *réduit aux gehennes* he put the
new Monsieur de Paris through his facings with the
axe.

An account of the sentences decreed by the Châtelet would be little less than a history of punishment
in France. The Châtelet gave reasons for its sentences, à practice not followed by the superior courts.
Terrible were the pains and penalties decreed sometimes from beneath the Provost's dais. Torture
wrung some avowal from the frothy lips of the accused, and then he was shrived and carried to the
place of execution. The fierce canonical law lent its
ingenuity in punishment to the judges of the Châtelet ; but many of the penalties, such as hanging,
beheading, burning, whipping, mutilation, and the
pillory, are found on our own criminal registers of
the same period. Coiners and forgers were boiled
alive ; there is an entry of twelve livres for the purchase of a cauldron in which to boil to death a *faux
monnoyeur*. In 1390, a young female servant, convicted of stealing silver spoons from her master, was
exposed in the pillory, suffered the loss of an ear,
and was banished from Paris and its environs, "not
to return under penalty of being buried alive." For
the crime of marrying two wives, one Robert Bon-
neau was sentenced to be "hanged and strangled."
Geoffroy Vallée was burned, in 1573, for the publication of a pamphlet entitled *The Heavenly Felicity of
the Christians, or the Scourge of the Faith ;* and, in

6

1645, a bookseller was sent to the galleys "for having printed a libel against the Government."

Some of the old registers of the Châtelet examined by Desmaze showed entries of charges of pocket-picking and card-sharping at public processions, fairs, and spectacles. Little thieves defended themselves before the magistrates in the style familiar at Bow Street to-day,—a lad of fifteen charged with stealing handkerchiefs from pedestrians said he had "picked up one in the street."

The Châtelet, or rather the Little Châtelet, was the Provost's residence until the end of the sixteenth century. In 1564, the Provost was Hugues de Bourgueil, "distinguished for the possession of a terrific hump and a beautiful wife." One day Parliament consigned to the cells of the Little Châtelet a young Italian, accused of having set up in Paris a "gambling-house and fencing-saloon," where he corrupted the morals of the young nobility, "teaching them a thousand things unworthy of Christians and Frenchmen."

In his quality of Italian, the prisoner, Gonsalvi by name, invoked the protection of Catherine de Médicis. The Queen-Mother, while respecting the decree of Parliament, recommended the young compatriot to the Provost's particular care. De Bourgueil accordingly lodged him in his own house, where Gonsalvi was soon on intimate terms with the family. One night he eloped with the Provost's wife. Madame had contrived to possess herself of the keys of the prison, thinking that if she let loose the whole three hundred prisoners, M. le Prévôt would have a

good night's work on hand, and the course would be
clear for her lover and herself. And so it resulted;
for the Provost, faithful to his duty, despatched horse
and foot after his three hundred fugitives, and let
Madame and Gonsalvi take their way.

The next day, an errant wife was missing from the
Little Châtelet, but at night the keys were turned as
usual on the full contingent of three hundred prisoners. It was the scandal of this affair, say MM. Alhoy
and Lurine, which decided the King to shift the
Provost's residence from the Châtelet to the Hôtel
d'Hercule, wherein was presently installed Nantouillet,
"successeur de ce pauvre diable de Bourgueil."

Nantouillet was not too well off, it would seem, in
the Hôtel d'Hercule. No sooner was he established
there than he was bidden to prepare for the visit of
three Kings,—France, Poland, and Navarre,—who
would do themselves the pleasure of lunching with
him. Nantouillet, who had just declined to marry a
cast-off mistress of the King of Poland, suspected
some scheme of vengeance on their Majesties' part;
he could not, however, refuse to spread his board for
them. He spread it, and the Kings came down and
swept it bare. They swooped upon Nantouillet's
silver plate and sacked his coffers of fifty thousand
francs. There was a fierce fight in the Hôtel, but
the Kings got away with the plunder. On the following day, the First President of Parliament waited
upon Charles IX. and said that all Paris was shocked;
and his Majesty in reply bade him "not trouble himself about that." This *tableau moral* of the period is
presented by several historians.

With such examples in the seats of Royalty, one
can feel little surprise at the charges of venality, and
worse, which were brought from time to time against
the Provosts. In the reign of Philippe le Long, a
certain wealthy citizen lay under sentence of death in
the Châtelet. The Provost Henri Caperel made him
a private proposal of ransom, a bargain was struck,
Dives was set free, and the Provost hanged some
obscure prisoner in his stead. Provost Hugues de
Cruzy is said to have trafficked openly at the Châtelet
in much the same way, Royalty itself sharing the
booty with him. Now and again, justice took her
revenge; and both Henri Caperel and Hugues de
Cruzy finished on the gallows. The noble brigand,
highwayman, and cut-throat, Jourdain de Lisle, who
led a numerous band in the fourteenth century, bought
the interest of the Provost of Paris; and the Châtelet
" refused to take cognisance of his eighteen crimes,
the least of which would have brought to an ignominious death any other criminal." A new Provost had
to be appointed before Jourdain de Lisle, tied to the
tail of a horse, could be dragged through the streets
of Paris to the public gallows. He had married a
niece of Pope Jean XXII., and when justice had been
done, the curé of the church of Saint-Merri wrote to
Rome : " Scarcely had your Holiness's nephew been
hanged, when, with much pomp, we fetched him from
the gibbet to our church, and there buried him *honor-
ablement et gratis*."

Ordinarily, the Châtelet relied for its defence upon
the archers of the Provost's guard, a reedy support

when the mob turned out in force. It was seized in 1320 by the *Pastoureaux*, a swarm of peasants who had united themselves under two apostate priests, and who said they were " going across the sea to combat the enemies of the faith and conquer the Holy Land." To rescue some of their number who had been arrested and thrown into the Châtelet, they marched on that place, broke open the gaol, and effected a general delivery of the prisoners, as Madame de Bourgueil was to do some two centuries later.

Between the conflicting powers of the Châtelet, as represented by the Provost of Paris, and the University, which was accountable only to the ecclesiastical tribunals, and intensely jealous of any interference by the secular arm, a long and bitter struggle was sustained. In 1308, Provost Pierre Jumel hanged a young man for theft on the highway. Unfortunately for Jumel, this was a scholar of the University, and the clergy of Paris went in procession to the Châtelet and briefly harangued the Provost : " Come out of that, Satan, accursed one ! Acknowledge thy sin, and seek pardon at the holy altar, or expect the fate of Dathan and Abiram, whom the earth swallowed." While they were thus engaged, a messenger came from the Louvre with the announcement that the King had sacrificed his chief magistrate to the wrathful demands of the clergy and University. For a like encroachment on the sacred privileges of the University, Guillaume de Thignonville was degraded from his office of Provost, led to the gallows, and there compelled to take down and kiss the corpses of two students whom he had hanged for robbery.

In 1330, Hugues Aubriot, in his capacity of Provost, lent the shelter of the Châtelet to a party of
Jews flying for their lives before the mob.   This
service to the causes of humanity and public order
renewed against the Provost an ancient enmity of
the clerics and University, by whom, in the words of
MM. Alhoy and Lurine, "it was determined that
Aubriot should be ruined."   Condemned by the ecclesiastical tribunal "for the crime of impiety and
heresy," he was ordered to be "preached against and
publicly mitred in front of Notre-Dame."   On his
knees, he demanded absolution of the bishop, and
promised an offering of candles for his iniquity in be-
friending the Jews.   " His crimes were read aloud by
the Inquisitor of the Faith, and the bishop consigned
him to perpetual imprisonment, with the bread of sor-
row and the water of affliction, as an abettor of the
Jewish infidelity, and a contemner of the Christian
faith."   From that, the Provost descended to an
oubliette of the Fort-l'Évêque.

The Fort-l'Évêque, in the Rue Saint-Germain-
l'Auxerrois, was one of the two prisons of the Bishop
of Paris.   Its *oubliettes* were subterranean dungeons,
separated from one another by stout timbers.   The
prisoners, attached to a common chain, were fastened
to the wall by iron rings, in such a manner that they
could not approach one another.   They never saw
their gaolers, and their meagre rations were handed
in through a narrow wicket in the door.   Hugues
Aubriot occupied his *oubliette* for many years.   In the
insurrection of the *Maillotins* he was discovered by the

rioters and set free. In 1674, the Bishop's jurisdiction was reunited with that of the Châtelet, but the prison of the Fort-l' Évêque was in existence until 1780.

Dulaure says that the penalties imposed by the episcopal court were inflicted in various places, according to the gravity of the offence. Sentences of hanging or burning were carried out beyond the precincts of Paris; but if it were "a mere bagatelle of cutting off the culprit's ears," justice was done at the Place du Trahoir.

In the middle of the seventeenth century, the Fort-l'Évêque was the prison for "debtors and refractory comedians"; and about a hundred years later, in 1765, it received the entire company of the Comédie-Française. The episode is one of the oddest in the history of the House of Molière. A second-rate member of the famous troupe, named Dubois, who had been under medical treatment for some malady, refused to pay the doctor's bill. Mademoiselle Clairon, the tragic actress, delicate on the point of honour, summoned the rest of the company, and it was resolved to appeal to M. de Richelieu, *gentilhomme de la chambre*. This functionary treated it as "an affair of vagabonds," and told the company to settle it amongst themselves. Dubois, accordingly, was put out of the troupe. His daughter carried her father's grievance and her own charms (*elle met en œuvre tous ses charmes*) to the Duc de Fronsac, through whose intervention she succeeded in forcing for Dubois the doors of the Comédie-Française. But the company were resolved not to act with him again, and put a sudden stop to

the performances of that very successful piece, the
Siége de Calais.   De Sartines, of the police, now came
forward in the pretended interests of the public, and
ordered the arrest of Dauberval, Lekain, Molé, Bri-
sard, Mademoiselle Clairon, and others of the company.   The public, however, were on the side of the
players, and Mademoiselle Clairon and her fellows
had a semi-royal progress to the Fort-l' Évêque ;
roses and rhetoric were showered on them, and *les
plus nobles dames de Paris* disputed the honour of
attending the tragédienne to the threshold of the
prison.   Their captivity lasted, nevertheless, for five-
and twenty days ; but the final victory was with the
players, for Dubois was dismissed with a pension,
and appeared no more on the stage of the Théâtre
Français.

Fêted every day in her chamber in the ecclesiastical
prison—for there was scarcely question of an *oubliette*
in her case,—receiving the visits of noblemen and
dames of fashion, artists, wits, and poets, Mademoiselle
Clairon had small leisure to bethink her that, under
the litter of flowers pressed by her dainty feet, lay the
bones of whole generations of victims of the church's
tyranny ; victims of those too familiar charges of
magic, heresy, and sacrilege.

Yet (I quote again from MM. Alhoy and Lurine)
had she in the still night lent a listening ear to those
grey walls, the wailing murmurs of the phantoms of
Fort-l'Évêque might have chilled her heart :—

"We expiated in the *oubliettes* of the Fort-l'Évêque, under the
reign of Francis I, the wrong of believing in God without believ-

ing also in the infallibility of the Pope. Look . . . there is blood on our shrouds!"

"We are two poor Augustine monks. They accused us, in Charles VI.'s time, of being idolaters, invokers of evil spirits, utterers of profane words. They accused us of making a pact with the powers below ; our only crime was believing that our science might heal the madness of the King. Look . . . there is blood on our shrouds!"

"I am the sorcerer of the château of Landon. I promised an abbé of Citeaux to find, by magic, a sum of money that had been stolen from him. Alas! it was a dear jest for me ; torture, and death on the Place de Grève. Look . . . there is blood upon my shroud!"

"I am a poor madman. I thought that heaven had given me the glorious mission of sustaining on earth the servants of Jesus Christ. I went humbly to the bishop and said : The envoy of God salutes you! They brought me here to an *oubliette*, and I left it only with the headsman. Look . . . there is blood on my shroud!"

The factions of the Armagnacs and the Bourguignons cost Paris a river of blood in the early years of the fifteenth century, and the massacre of the Armagnacs in May–August, 1418, was a terrible affair. On the first day, five hundred and twenty-two were put to the sword by the Bourguignons in the streets of the capital. Every Armagnac, or suspected Armagnac, was laid hold of, and the prisons overflowed with the captives. The Bourguignons assailed the Châtelet, "and the threshold of the prison became the scaffold of fifteen hundred unfortunates." The attack upon the Châtelet was renewed by the Bourguignons in August ; and the Provost of Paris, powerless to check or even to stem their fury, bade them at length "Do what they would": *Mes amis, faites*

ce qu'il vous plaira. This time the prisoners organised
a defence, and a regular siege began. On the north
side of the fortress was a lofty terrace, crowning the
wall, so to say, and running the length of the prison.
Here the imprisoned Armagnacs threw up barricades,
but the Bourguignons reared scaling-ladders, and made
light of climbing the walls, sixty feet in height. The
attack on the one side and the defence on the other
were long, bloody, and desperate; but the advantage
was with the assailants. Foiled at this point and that,
they fired the prison; and where the flames did not
penetrate, they hacked their way in, and drove their
game to take refuge on the heights. As the fire
soared upwards, the Armagnacs flung themselves over
the walls, and were caught upon the pikes of the
Burgundians, "who finished them with axe and
sword."

The name of Louis XI., which is writ large in the
histories of the Bastille and the Dungeon of Vincennes, attaches to one curious episode in the history
of the Châtelet. In 1477, on the day of the festival
of Saint Denis, Louis "took the singular fancy of
giving their liberty" to the prisoners of the Great and
Little Châtelet. A chronicler of this fact, evidently
puzzled, "hastens to add" that at that epoch the two
Châtelets "held merely robbers, assassins, and vagabonds. Not even to honour the memory of Saint
Denis could Louis bring himself to liberate his political prisoners in Vincennes and the Bastille." It was
in Louis XI.'s reign that one Charlot Tonnelier, a
hosier turned brigand, lying in the Châtelet on a score

of charges, and dreading lest the Question should weaken him into betrayal of his companions, snatched a knife from a guard at the door of the torture chamber, and deliberately cut his tongue out.

The Fort-l'Évêque and the Little Châtelet were suppressed in 1780, in virtue of an *ordonnance* of Louis XVI., countersigned by Necker ; and the prisoners were transferred to La Force. The buildings, which were even then in a state of ruin, were thrown down two years later. The Great Châtelet existed as a prison for another decade, and the fortress itself was not demolished until 1802–4. A triumphal column replaced the ancient dungeon of the Provosts of Paris.

CHAPTER V.

THE TEMPLE.

WHEN they came to Paris in the twelfth century, the Templars obtained leave to settle
in the Marshes, whose baleful exhalations cost the
town a plague or two every year. In no long time
they had completely transformed that dismal and pestilential swamp. Herculean labours witnessed as their
outcome oaks, elms, and beeches growing where the
rotten ooze had bred but reeds and osiers. Vast buildings, too, arose as if by magic, with towers and turrets protecting them, drawbridges, battlemented walls,
and trenches. The principal tower of the pile enclosed the treasure and arsenal of the Order, and
four smaller towers or turrets served as a prison
for those who had trangressed the stark monastic
rules. On the broad terrace of the Temple three
hundred men had space for exercise at cross-bow
and halberd.

Philip III. bestowed a royal recompense on the
laborious monks who had reclaimed those miasmatic
marshes and given new means of defence to the capital ; and towards the close of the thirteenth century
the Templars had become an extraordinary power
in France. In Paris they exercised large justiciary

rights, and had their gallows standing without the Temple walls. They were concerned in all enterprises, civil, political, and military; their sovereignty was such that princes had to reckon with them, on pain of contact with the monkish steel. They had great monopolies of grain, and owned some of the richest lands in the kingdom; they touched the revenues of from eight to ten thousand manors. The Templars guarded at need the towns, treasures, and archives of royalty; and kings, popes, and nobles were their visitors and guests.

The fortress dwelling of the Temple which had sprung fairy-like from the foul marshes of Paris shone with a splendour above that of the royal residence. Twenty-four columns of silver, carved and chased, sustained the audience-chamber of the grand master; and the chapter-hall, paved in mosaic, and enriched with woodwork in cedar of Lebanon, contained sixty huge vases of solid gold and a veritable armoury of Arabian, Moorish, and Turkish weapons, chiselled, damascened, and crusted with precious stones. The private chamber of every knight of the Order was distinguished by some particular object of beauty; whilst the chambers of the officers and commanders were stored with riches " so that they were a wonder to behold."

How great a gulf separated the wealthy and powerful Templars of Paris from those " poor brothers of the Temple who rode two on one horse, lived frugally, without wives or children, had no goods of their own, and who, when they were not taking the field against the infidels, were employed in mending their

weapons and the harness of their horses, or in pious
exercises prescribed for them by their chief."

The first institution of the Order of the Temple
dates from the year 1118, when "certain brave and
devout gentlemen" obtained from King Baudouin
III. "the noble favour of guarding the approaches
to Jerusalem." The Council of Troyes, in 1128,
confirmed the religious and military Order of the
Templars. The knights clothed themselves in long
white robes adorned with a red cross; and the
standard of the Order, called the *Beaucéant*, was white
and black, for an emblem of life and death,—death
for the infidels and life for the Christians of the
Holy Land. Bravery in battle was almost an article of their faith; no Templar would fly from three
opponents.

In the day of their military and political power, the
Templars of France acknowledged none but the
authority of the grand master of the Order, and
treated with royalty as between power and power.
Up to the reign of Philippe le Bel, the Kings of
France were little more than courtiers of the Temple,
Royalty knocked humbly at those august, defiant
portals, for leave to deposit within them its treasures
and its charters, or to solicit a loan from the golden
coffers of the knights. Not so, however, Philippe
le Bel.

This was the sovereign who, in 1307, broke the
power of the Knights Templars of France. The
act of accusation which he flung at the Order proscribed its members as "ravening wolves," "a per-
fidious and idolatrous society, whose works, nay,

whose very words soil the earth and infect the air."
The last grand master, Jacques de Molay, seized by
the King's Inquisitor, passed through the torments of
the torture chamber, and thence to the torments of
the stake. The Knights of the Temple in their turn,
loaded with chains, were led before the Inquisitor,
Guillaume de Paris, to answer his charges of heresy
and idolatry. The Templars were pursued through
all the States of Europe, the Pope encouraging the
hue and cry. Jacques de Molay, and his companion
in misfortunes, Gui, Dauphin of Auvergne, were
burned alive in Paris; and the persecution of the
Templars lasted for six years. Their Order was
abolished, and most of their wealth was bestowed by
Philippe upon the Knights of St. John of Jerusalem.

The prison of the Temple became a prison of the
State; and the Temple and the Louvre were the
forerunners of the Bastille. The Dukes of Aquitaine
and Brabant were confined in the Temple under
Philippe V. and Philippe de Valois, the Counts of
Dammartin and Flanders under King John. Four
sovereigns, indeed, Charles VII., Louis XI., Charles
VIII., and Louis XII., seemed to have forgotten the
dungeon which the Templars had bequeathed them
(they might well have done so, since mediæval Paris
had its prisons at every turn); and the cells and
chambers in the great tower of the Temple remained
closed,—to be opened no more until after the 10th of
August, 1792.

But there were social passages of interest in the
history of this famous fastness, and it was not unfitting
that Francis I., the magnificent monarch of the

Renaissance, should repair the palace of the Templars, restore those historic ruins, re-establish the spreading gardens, gild afresh those illustrious halls,—re-create, in a word, the once brilliant dwelling of the Chevaliers of the Cross: in 1540, the Temple became the sumptuous abode of the Grand Priors of France.

In the last years of the seventeenth century, Philippe de Vendôme, prince of the blood and knight of Malta, was named Grand Prior of the Temple. He would have his priory worthy of the gallant and graceful Court of the Palais Royal; and the handsomest and most amiable of ladies, and the finest and gayest of wits were bidden to his historic suppers. The oaks that had shadowed the cross of Jacques de Molay lent their shelter now to " all the gods of Olympus," summoned within the green enclosure of the Temple by the lively invocations of La Fare and de Chaulieu.

In the eighteenth century, this same enclosure had a population of four thousand souls, divided into three distinct classes. There was first the house of the Grand Prior, the dignitaries of the Order, and certain nobles; then, a numerous body of workers of all grades; and lastly, a rather heterogeneous collection of debtors who were able to elude their creditors within these precincts, in virtue of a mediæval prescript—which justice ceased to respect in 1779.

At this epoch, the Government of Louis XVI.— as if with a presentiment of what the Temple was shortly to become for the King of France—ordered the demolition of the old fortress of the Templars. But the destroyers of 1779 overthrew only a portion

THE TEMPLE PRISON.

of the tower; the dungeon itself remained, to be witness of a royal agony.

See, then, at length, after the revolution of the 10th of August, Louis XVI. and Marie Antoinette prisoners in the prison of the Temple! Marie Antoinette, most imprudent and most amiable, most unfortunate and most calumniated of women; Louis XVI., poor honest gentleman, whose passive intelligence drew from Turgot this prophetic word: "Sire, a weak prince can make choice only between the musket of Charles IX. and the scaffold of Charles I." The King was without force and without prestige; the Queen was incapable either of giving or of receiving a lesson in royalty.

Taciturn, and subject to sudden fits of temper; as much embarrassed by his wife as by his crown, Louis divided his time between hunting and those little harmless hobbies which showed that, had the fates desired, he might have made an excellent artisan. As for Marie Antoinette, what rôle was there for her, the victim of perpetual suspicion, in the midst of a tremendous political reaction? It was reproached against her, not without reason, that she could never fashion for herself the conscience of a queen. She felt herself a woman, young and beautiful; she forgot that she was also the partner of a throne. Full of personal charm, liking to toy with elegant pleasures, wedded to a man so little made for her, surrounded by gallant courtiers whom her beauty and graces intoxicated, Marie Antoinette had her share of ardent emotions, and more than once she was at last forgetful of her pride, *cette pudeur des reines;* but her posi-

7

tion at the Court of France was so false and so
complicated that, let her have done what she would,
she might not have escaped the abyss towards which
her own feet impelled her.

To the Temple, then, they were hurried, Louis and
his family, on the 14th of August, 1792. The tower of
the fortress was allotted to them, and a portion of the
palace and all the adjacent buildings were levelled, so
that the dungeon proper was completely isolated. The
space of garden reserved for their daily exercise was
enclosed between lofty walls. Louis occupied the first
floor of the prison and his family the second. Every
casement was protected by thick iron bars, and the
outer windows were masked in such a manner that
the prisoners obtained scarcely a glimpse of the world
beyond their cage. Six wickets defended the staircase which led to the King's apartment ; so low and
narrow that it was necessary to squeeze through them
in a stooping posture. Each door was of iron, heavily
barred, and was kept locked at all hours. After Louis'
imprisonment, a seventh wicket with a door of iron was
constructed at the top of the stairs, which no one could
open unassisted. The first door of Louis' chamber was
also of iron ; so here were eight solid barriers betwixt
the King and his friends in freedom,—not counting
the dungeon walls. A guard of some three hundred
men watched night and day around the Temple.

These costly preparations on his Majesty's account
(great sums, it is said, were spent on them) were not
completed in a day, and in the meantime the Royal
family inhabited that portion of the palace of the
Temple which had been left standing. In his daily

walks in the garden, King Louis looked on at the building of his last earthly mansion, and must have noticed the desperate haste with which the builders worked! In the middle of September, he passed into the shades of the dungeon.

Once locked in there, he was forbidden the use of pens, ink, and paper; no writing materials were allowed him until the national convention had commanded his appearance at the bar.

The large chamber assigned to the King was partitioned into four compartments; the first served as a dining-room, the second was Louis' bed-chamber, and his valet slept in the third; the fourth was a little cabinet contrived in a turret, to which the royal prisoner was fond of retiring. His bed-chamber was hung in yellow and decently furnished. A little clock on the chimney-piece bore on its pedestal the words "Lepante, Clockmaker for the King." When the convention had decreed France a republic, Louis' gaolers scratched out the last three words of the inscription. They hung in his dining-room the declaration of the rights of the Constitution of 1792, at the foot of which ran the legend: "First year of the Republic." This was their announcement to Louis that he had fallen from his king's estate.

Like a murderer of these days in the condemned hold, Louis had two guards with him night and day. They passed the day in his bed-chamber, following him to the dining-room when he took his meals; and in the dining-room they slept at night, after locking the doors of the apartments.

Their captivity was full of indignity for the illustri-

ous unfortunates, whose guards were incessantly suspicious. If Louis addressed a question during the
night to the valet who slept close to him, the answer
must be spoken loudly. The members of the family
were not allowed to whisper in their conversations,
and if at dinner Louis, or his wife, or his sister chanced
to speak low in asking anything of the servant who
waited on them, one of the guards at the door cried,
"*Parlez plus haut !*"

Apart from suspense as to the future, a terrible
dreariness must have marked those days in the Temple. The early morning was given by the King to
his private devotions, after which he read the office
which the Chevaliers of the Order of the Saint-Esprit
were accustomed to recite daily. His piety was not
without its inconveniences to himself. The table was
furnished with meat on Fridays, but Louis dipped a
slice of bread in his wine glass with the remark:
"*Voilà mon diner !*" To the gentle suggestion that
such extreme abstinence might be dispensed with, he
replied: "I do not trouble your conscience; why
trouble mine? You have your practices, and I have
my own; let each hold to those which he believes the
best."

His devotions engaged the King until nine o'clock,
at which hour his family joined him in the dining-
room,—that is to say, during the period in which it
was still permitted him to communicate with them.
He sat with them at breakfast, eating nothing himself; he had made it a rule in prison to fast until the
dinner-hour. After breakfast the King took his son
for lessons in Latin and geography, and whilst Marie

Antoinette taught their daughter, sister Elizabeth plied her needle. The children had an hour's play at mid-day, and at one o'clock the family assembled for dinner. The table was always well supplied, but Louis ate little and drank less, and the Queen took nothing but water with her food.

After dinner the parents amused their children again as best they could, round games at the table being the favourite recreation. To these poor little pleasures succeeded reading and conversation, and at nine the prisoners supped. After supper, Louis took the boy to his bed-chamber, where a little bed was placed for him beside his own. He heard him recite his prayers, and saw him to bed. Then he returned to reading, and fell to his own prayers at eleven. When the doomed King, husband, and father was denied the solace of his family, the time that he had devoted to them was given almost wholly to his books. The Latins were his favourite authors, and a day seldom passed on which he had not conned afresh some pages of Tacitus, Livy, Seneca, Horace, Virgil, or Terence. In French he was especially fond of books of travel. He read the news of the day as long as he was supplied with it, but his not unnatural interest in the affairs of revolutionary France seemed to trouble his gaolers, and the newspapers were withdrawn from him. Thrown back upon his books, he studied more than ever, and on the eve of his death he summed up the volumes he had read through during the five months and seven days of his captivity in the Temple : the number was two hundred and fifty-seven.

Towards the end he suffered some brusque inter-
ruptions of his ignominious solitude. Three times
he awoke to find a new valet in his bedroom. Chamilly's place in this capacity was taken by Hue, and
Hue was succeeded by Cléry, who was all but a
stranger to the King. Chamilly and Hue barely
came off with their lives in the prisons to which they
were removed from the Temple. The abandoned
King took shock upon shock with not a little fortitude. He was skimming his Tacitus one day when
the cannibals of September stopped under his window to brandish on a pike the bleeding and disfigured
head of the Princess Lamballe.

Severely as they had guarded him, his gaolers
began to double their precautions. The concierge
of the dungeon, the chief warder,—all, in a word,
who were specially charged with the keeping of the
King, were themselves constituted prisoners of the
Temple. Did you wait on Louis, or were you suffered to approach him, your person was searched
minutely at the governor's discretion. Not the commonest instrument of steel or iron was allowed to be
carried by anyone who went near the King: Cléry
was deprived of his penknife. Every article of food
passed into the prison for Louis' table was rigor-
ously examined; and the prison cook had to taste
every dish, under the eyes of the guard, before it
was permitted to leave the kitchen. Never was
suicide more strenuously denied to a man who had
no thought of it.

The prisoners themselves were not spared the indignity of the search. Louis, his wife, and his sister

had their cupboards, drawers, and closets ransacked;
they were spoiled of knives, scissors, and curling-
irons. Louis' pains were prolonged to the end. The
courage he had mustered for death, and it was a very
commendable portion, failed him a moment at the
last. In his confessor's hands, on the morning of his
death, whilst the carriage was waiting for him in the
courtyard, he halted in his prayers. He had, as he
thought, caught a note of tears on the other side of
the partition, and he dreaded a second last embrace.
His ear strained at the wall, whilst the priest's hand
was on his head. But there was no weeping there,
for Marie Antoinette was on her knees under her
crucifix; and Louis went down to his carriage. There
is no need to tell again the last scene of all. . . .

Marie Antoinette was removed to the Conciergerie, which she quitted only for the scaffold. After
the parents had passed under the knife, the young
dauphin and his sister Marie Thérèse continued in
the prison of the Temple "the sorrowful Odyssey of
the Royalty of France." The daughter of Marie
Antoinette must quit the Temple to go into exile,
the son of Louis XVI. must die wretchedly in the
prison of his father. The "education" of the poor
little dauphin was entrusted to Simon the shoemaker,
whose wife, it is said, used to teach him ribald songs.
He had a charming face and a crooked back, "as if
life were already too heavy for him." In the hands
of those singular preceptors he came to lose nearly
all his moral faculties, and the sole sentiment which
he cherished was that of gratitude, "not so much for
the good that was done him—which was small—as

for the ills that were spared him. Without uttering
a word, he would precipitate himself before his guards,
press their hands, and kiss the hems of their coats." *
After the retreat of Simon, who had not used his
gentle captive over-tenderly, the dauphin's imprisonment was somewhat kinder, though he continued to
be watched as closely as before. His gaoler one day
asked him : "What would you do to Simon, little
master, if you were to become king?" "I would
have him punished as an example," answered the
young Capet. He had had no news of Simon for
two years, and did not know that the ungentle shoemaker had perished on the scaffold.†

The little dauphin's own untimely death, while still
a prisoner in the Temple, induced more than one
audacious adventurer to seek to assume the mask of
Louis XVI.'s son. Hervagaut, Mathurin Bruneau,
and more recently the Duc de Normandie essayed in
turn the rôle of pretender, "draped in the shroud of
Louis XVII." The first-named, condemned in 1802
to four years' imprisonment, died ten years later in
Bicêtre. The second, tried at Rouen in 1818, received a sentence of seven years ; and the Duc de
Normandie ended his days in Holland.

The Convention seems to have given no political
prisoners to the tower of the Temple, which was
again a prison of State under the Directory, the
Consulate, and the Empire.

It was the Directory which consigned to the
Temple the celebrated English Admiral, Sir Sidney
Smith, M.P. for Rochester, who had defended Acre

---

* Nougaret.   † Idem.

against Napoleon, and who was arrested at Havre "on the point of setting fire to the port." He was transferred to the Temple from the Abbey, the order of transfer bearing the signature of Barras.

On the 10th of May, 1798, certain friends of the Admiral, disguised in French uniform, presented to the concierge of the Temple a document purporting to be an order of the Minister of War for the removal of Sir Sidney to another prison. The concierge fell into the trap, and bade adieu to his prisoner, who, a few days later, found himself safe in London.

The mysterious conspiracy of the Camp de Grenelle furnished the Temple with a batch of one hundred and thirty-five prisoners; and the *coup d'État* which swept them in proscribed also the editors of twenty-two French journals. During the next eight years the most distinguished of the "enemies of the Republic" whose names were entered on the Temple register were Lavalette; Caraccioli, the Ambassador of the King of Naples to the Court of Louis XVI.; Hottinguer, the banker of the Rue de Provence; Hyde de Neuville; the journalist Bertin; Toussaint-Louverture, the hero of Saint-Domingue, who had written to Buonaparte: "*Le premier homme des noirs au premier homme des blancs*"; the two Polignacs, the Duc de Rivière, George Cadoudal, Moreau, and Pichegru.

General Pichegru, arrested on the 28th of February, 1804, "for having forgotten in the interests of the English and the Royalists what he owed to the French Republic," was found dead in his cell on the 6th of April following, having strangled himself with a black silk cravat. Moreau, liberated by the First

Consul, took service in the ranks of the enemy, and was slain by a French bullet before Dresden, in 1813.

Toussaint-Louverture's detention in the Temple is an episode which reflects little credit upon the military and political history of the Consulate. Certainly the expedition of Saint-Domingue, under the command of General Leclerc, Napoleon's brother-in-law, makes a poor page in the annals of that period. After having received Toussaint-Louverture's submission, Leclerc, afraid of the great negro's influence, made him a prisoner by the merest trick, and despatched him to France. Confined at first in the Temple, he was afterwards removed to the fort of Joux, where he died in April, 1803.

Five years after this, in June, 1808, the prisoners of the Temple were transferred by Fouché's order to the Dungeon of Vincennes. Amongst them was General Malet, that bold conspirator who, in 1812, "*devait porter la main sur la couronne de l'Empereur.*"

The tower of the Temple was demolished in 1811, and, four years later, Louis XVIII. instituted, on the ruins of the ancient dwelling of the Templars and the prison of Louis XVI., a congregation of nuns, who had for their Superior a daughter of Prince de Condé.

CHAPTER VI.

BICÊTRE.

"WHERE there are monks," exclaimed brusque-
ly the authors of *Les Prisons de Paris*,
"there are prisoners." The folds of the priestly
garb concealed a place of torment which monastic
justice, with a grisly humour, named a *Vade in Pace ;*
the last bead of the rosary grazed the first rings of a
chain which bore the bloody impress of the sworn
tormentor. At Bicêtre, as at the Luxembourg, ages
ago, big-bellied cenobites sang and tippled in the cosy
cells piled above the dungeons of the church.

Bicêtre—more anciently Bissestre—is a corrupt
form of Vincestre, or Winchester, after John, Bishop
of Winchester, who is thought to have built the
original château, and who certainly held it in the
first years of the thirteenth century. It was famous
amongst the pleasure-houses of the Duc de Berri,
who embellished it with windows of glass, which at
that epoch were only beginning to be an ornament of
architecture—"objects of luxury," says Villaret, "reserved exclusively for the mansions of the wealthiest
seigneurs." In one of the rather frequent "popular
demonstrations" in the Paris of the early fifteenth
century, these "objects of luxury" were smashed, and

little of the château remained except the bare walls.
It was rebuilt by the Duc de Berri, a noted amateur
of books, and was by him presented to an order of
monks in 1416.

A colony of Carthusians under St. Louis; John of
Winchester under Philippe-Auguste; Amédée le
Rouge, Count of Savoy, under Charles VI.; the
Bourguignons and the Armagnacs in the fifteenth
century; the canons of Notre-Dame de Paris under
Louis XI.; the robbers and *bohémiens* in the sixteenth
century; the Invalides under Cardinal Richelieu, and
the foundlings of St. Vincent de Paul,—all these preceded at Bicêtre the vagabonds, the *bons-pauvres*, the
epileptics and other diseased, the lunatics, and "all
prisoners and captives." In becoming an asylum and
hospital, in a word, Bicêtre became also one of the
most horrible of the countless prisons of Paris; it
grew into dreadful fame as "the Bastille of the canaille and the bourgeoisie."

The enormous numbers of the poor, the hordes of
sturdy mendicants who "demanded alms sword in
hand," and the soldiers who took the road when they
could get no pay, became one of the chief scourges
of Paris. Early in the seventeenth century it was
sought to confine them in the various hospitals or
houses of detention in the Faubourg Saint-Victor,
but under the disorders and weaknesses of the Government these establishments soon collapsed. Parliament issued decree after decree; all strollers and
beggars were to be locked up in a prison or asylum
specially appropriated to them; the buildings were
commenced and large sums of money were spent on

them, but they were never carried to completion. In course of time the magistrates took the matter in hand, dived into old records, but drew no counsel thence, for the evil, albeit not new, was of extraordinary proportions; went to the King for a special edict, and procured one "which ordered the setting-up of a general hospital and prescribed the rules for its governance." The Château of Bicêtre and the Maison de la Salpêtrière were ceded for the purpose.

Children and women went to the Salpêtrière; at Bicêtre were placed men with no visible means of subsistence, "widowers," beggars, feeble or sturdy, and "young men worn out by debauchery." Before taking these last in hand, the doctors "were accustomed to order them a whipping."

This destiny of Bicêtre is pretty clear, and as hospital and asylum combined it should, under decent conduct, have played a useful part in the social economy of Paris. But the absolutism of that age had its own notions as to the proper functions of "hospitals," and the too-familiar *ordres du roi*, and the not less familiar *lettres de cachet* (which Mirabeau had not yet come forward to denounce), were presently in hot competition with the charitable *ordonnances* of the doctors. Madness was a capital new excuse for vengeance in high places, and the cells set apart for cases of mental disease were quickly tenanted by "luckless prisoners whose wrong most usually consisted in being strictly right." Bicêtre, it must be admitted, did the thing conscientiously, and with the best grace in the world. Rational individuals were despatched there whom, according to the authors of

Les Prisons de Paris, Bicêtre promptly transformed into imbeciles and raging maniacs.

Indeed the "philanthropists" and the criminologists of the early part of this century need not have taxed their imaginations for any scheme of cellular imprisonment. The system existed in diabolical perfection at Bicêtre. That much-abused "depôt" of indigent males, "widowers," and young rakes had an assortment of dark cells which realised *à merveille* the conditions of the vaunted programme of the penitentiary—isolation and the silence of the tomb. Buried in a *cabanon* or black hole of Bicêtre, the prisoner endured a fate of life in death ; he was as one dead, who lived long, *tête-à-tête with God and his conscience.* If a human sound penetrated to him, it was the sobbing moan of some companion in woe.

There was a subterranean Bicêtre, of which at this day only the dark memory survives. For a dim idea of this, one has to stoop and peer in fancy into a far-reaching abyss or pit, partitioned into little tunnels : in each little tunnel a chain riven to the wall ; at the end of the chain a man. Now there were men in these hellish tunnels who had been guilty of crimes, but far oftener they stifled slowly the lives or the intelligences, or both, of men who had done no crimes at all. Innocent or guilty, Bicêtre in the long run had one way with all its guests ; and when the prisoners and their wits had definitely parted company, the governor of the prison effected a transfer with his colleague the administrator of the asylum. It was expeditious and simple, and no one asked questions or called for a report.

It is on record, nevertheless, that existence in underground Bicêtre was a degree less insupportable than a sojourn in the *cabanons*. Hear the strenuous greet of Latude, with its wonted vividness of detail :

" When the wet weather began, or when it thawed in the winter, water streamed from all parts of my cell. I was crippled with rheumatism, and the pains I had from it were such that I was sometimes whole weeks without getting up. . . . In cold weather it was even worse. The ' window ' of the cell, protected by an iron grating, gave on the corridor, the wall of which was pierced exactly opposite at the height of ten feet. Through this aperture (garnished, like my own window, with iron bars), I received a little air and a glimmer of light, but the same aperture let in both snow and rain. I had neither fire nor artificial light, and the rags of the prison were my only clothing. I had to break with my wooden shoe the ice in my pail, and then to suck morsels of ice to quench my thirst. I stopped up the window, but the stench from the sewers and the tunnels came nigh to choke me ; I was stung in the eyes, and had a loathsome savour in the mouth, and was horribly oppressed in the lungs. The eight-and-thirty months they kept me in that noisome cell, I endured the miseries of hunger, cold, and damp. . . . The scurvy that had attacked me showed itself in a lassitude which spread through all my members ; I was presently unable either to sit or to rise. In ten days my legs and thighs were twice their proper size ; my body was black ; my teeth, loosened in their sockets, were no longer able to masticate. Three full days I fasted ; they saw me dying, and cared not a jot. Neighbours in the prison did this and that to have me speak to them ; I could not utter a word. At length they thought me dead, and called out that I should be removed. I was in sooth at death's gate when the surgeon looked in on me and had me fetched to the infirmary." *

* *Mémoires.*

Whether Masers de Latude existed, or was but a creature projected on paper by some able enemy of La Pompadour, those famous and titillating *Mémoires* are excellent documents—all but unique of their kind —of the prisons of bygone France. If the question be of the Bastille, of the Dungeon of Vincennes, of Charenton, or of Bicêtre, these pungent pages, with a luxuriance and colour of realistic detail not so well nor so plausibly sustained by any other pen, are always pat and complete to the purpose. To compare great things with small, it is as unimportant to inquire who wrote *Shakespeare* as to seek to know who was the author of the *Mémoires* of Latude. It is necessary only to feel certain that the writer of this extraordinary volume was as intimately acquainted with the prisons he describes as Mirabeau was with the Dungeon of Vincennes, or Cardinal de Retz with the Château de Nantes. His book (an epitome of what men might and could and did endure under the absolute monarchy, when his rights as an individual were the least secure of a citizen's possessions) is the main thing, and the sole thing ; the name and identity of the author are not now, if they ever were, of the most infinitesimal consequence.

A fine sample of the work of Bicêtre, considered as a machine for the manufacture of lunatics, is offered in the person of that interesting, unhappy genius, Salomon de Caus. A Protestant Frenchman, he lived much in England and Germany, and at the age of twenty he was already a skilled architect, a painter of distinction, and an engineer with ideas in advance of his time. He was in the service of the Prince of Wales in 1612, and of the Elector Palatine, at Heidelberg, 1614–20. In 1623 he returned to live and work in France, *dans sa patrie et pour sa patrie.* He became engineer and architect to the King.

Eight years before his return to France, De Caus had published at Frankfort his *Raison des Forces Mouvantes*, a treatise in which he described "an apparatus for forcing up water by a steam fountain," which differs only in one particular from that of Della Porta. The apparatus seems never to have been constructed, but Arago, relying on the description, has named De Caus the inventor of the steam engine.

It is not, however, with the inventive genius that we are concerned, but with the ill-starred lover of Marion Delorme. The minister Particelli took De Caus one day to the *petit lever* of the brilliant and beautiful Aspasia of the Place Royale. Particelli, one of the most prodigal of her adorers, wanted De Caus to surpass, in the palace of Mademoiselle Delorme, the splendours he had achieved in the palace of the Prince of Wales. " At my charge, look you, Monsieur Salomon, and spare nothing ! Scatter with both hands gold, silver, colours, marble, bronze, and precious stuffs—what you please. Imagine, seek, invent,—and count on me ! "

But Monsieur Salomon had no sooner seen the goddess of Particelli than he too was lifted from the earth and borne straight into the empyrean. At the moment of leaving her, when she suffered him to kiss her hand, and let him feel the darts of desire which shot from those not too prudish eyes, Salomon de

Caus "*devint amoureux à en perdre la tête.*"   Thence-
forth, in brief,

> " His chief good and market of his time "

was to obey and anticipate every wild and frivolous
fantasy of Marion Delorme.   Michel Particelli's hy-
perbolical commission should be fulfilled for him beyond his own imaginings !   He threw down the palace
of Marion and built another in its place.   The new
palace was to cede in nothing to the Louvre or Saint-
Germain.   With his own hands Salomon de Caus
decorated it ; and then, at the bidding of his pro-
tector, Particelli, he consented, *bon gré*, *mal gré*, to
paint the picture of the divinity herself.

" Alone one morning with his delicious model," the
distracted artist flung brushes and palette from him,
and cast himself at her feet.   " *Mon cœur se déchire,
ma tête se perd. . . . Je deviens fou, je vous aime,
et je me meurs !*"   It was a declaration of much in
little, and Marion, a *connaisseuse* of such speeches,
absolved and accepted him with a kiss.

Installed by right of conquest in that Circean
boudoir, which drew as a magnet the wit and gallantry of Paris, Salomon stood sentinel at the door
" like a eunuch or a Cerberus."   Brissac and Saint-
Evremont received the most Lenten entertainment,
and the proposals of Cinq-Mars were rejected.
Marion was even persuaded to be not at home to
Richelieu himself.   But the happy Salomon grew unhappy, and more unhappy.   Every moment he came
with a sigh upon some souvenir, delicately equivocal,

of the *vie galante* of his mistress ; and when love began to feed upon the venom of jealousy, his com-
placent goddess grew capricious, vexed, irritated,
and at length incensed. After that, she resolved
coldly on Salomon's betrayal. It was the fashion of
the age to be cruel in one's vengeance. Marion
penned a note to Richelieu :

> " I want so much to see you again. I send with this the little
> key which opens the little door. . . . You must forgive every-
> thing, and you are not to be angry at finding here a most learned
> young man whom the love of science and the science of love have
> combined to reduce to a condition of midsummer madness. Does
> your friendship for me, to say nothing of your respect for your-
> self, suggest any means of ridding me instantly of this embarrass-
> ing lunatic? The poor devil loves me to distraction. He is
> astonishingly clever, and has discovered wonders—mountains
> that nobody else has seen, and worlds that nobody else has im-
> agined. He has all the talents of the Bible, and another, the
> talent of making me the most miserable of women. This genius
> from the moon, whom I commend to your Eminence's most par-
> ticular attention, is called Salomon de Caus."

A missive of that colour, from a Marion Delorme
to a Richelieu, was the request polite for a *lettre de
cachet*. Salomon de Caus was invited to call upon
the Cardinal. Behind his jealous passion for his mistress, Salomon still cherished his passion for science,
and he went hot-foot to Richelieu with his hundred
schemes for changing the face of the world, with steam
as the motive power. It must have been a curious
interview. At the end, Richelieu summoned the captain of his guard.

" Take this man away."

" Where, your Eminence ?"

"To what place are we sending our lunatics just
now?"

"To Bicêtre, your Eminence."

"Just so! Ask admission for Monsieur at Bicêtre."

So, from the meridian of his glory, Salomon de Caus
hastened to his setting, and at this point he vanishes
from history. Legend, not altogether legendary,
shows him once again.

Some eighteen months or two years after he had
been carried, "gagged and handcuffed," to Bicêtre, it
fell to Marion Delorme (in the absence of her new
lover Cinq-Mars) to do the honours of Paris for the
Marquis of Worcester. The marquis took a fancy to
visit Bicêtre, which had even then an unrighteous
celebrity from one end of Europe to the other. As
they strolled through the *quartier des fous* a creature
made a spring at the bars of his cell.

"Marion—look, Marion! It is I! It is Salomon!
I love you!   Listen : I have made a discovery which
will bring millions and millions to France! Let me
out for God's sake! I will give you the moon and all
the stars to set me free, Marion!"

"Do you know this man?" said Lord Worcester.

"I am not at home in bedlam," said Marion, who
on principle allowed no corner to her conscience.

"What is the discovery he talks of?" asked Lord
Worcester of a warder.

"He calls it steam, milord. They 've all discovered
something, milord."

Lord Worcester went back to Bicêtre the next
morning and was closeted for an hour with the madman. At Marion Delorme's in the afternoon he said :

"In England we should not have put that man into a madhouse. Your Bicêtre is not the most useful place. Who invented those cells? They have wasted to madness as fine a genius as the age has known."

Salamon de Caus died in Bicêtre in 1626.

Earlier than this, Bicêtre the asylum shared the evil renown of Bicêtre the prison. To prisoners and patients alike popular rumour assigned an equal fate. The first, it was said, were assassinated, the second were "disposed of." Now and again the warders and attendants amused themselves by organising a pitched battle between the "mad side" and the "prison side"; the wounded were easily transferred to the infirmary, the dead were as easily packed into the trench beneath the walls.

The very name of Bicêtre—dungeon, mad-house, and *cloaca* of obscene infamies—became of dreadful import; not the Conciergerie, the Châtelet, Fort-l'Évêque, Vincennes, nor the Bastille itself inspired the common people and the bourgeoisie with such detestation and panic fear. The general imagination, out-vieing rumour, peopled it with imps, evil genii, sorcerers, and shapeless monsters compounded of men and beasts. Mediæval Paris, at a loss for the origins of things, ascribed them to the Fairies, the Devil, or Julius Cæsar. It was said that the Devil alighted in Paris one night, and brought in chains to the "plateau de Bicêtre" a pauper, a madman, and a prisoner, with which three unfortunates he set agoing the prison on the one side and the asylum on the other, to minister to the *menus plaisirs* of the deni-

zens of hell. Such grim renown as this was not easily
surpassed; but at the end of Louis XIV.'s reign the
common legend went a step farther, and said that the
Devil had now disowned Bicêtre! Rhymes sincere
or satirical gave utterance to the terror and abhor-
rence of the vulgar mind.

Throughout the whole of the eighteenth century, up
to the time of the Revolution, say MM. Alhoy and Lurine,[1] Bicêtre continued a treatment which in all respects is not easily paralleled : the helot's lot and
labour for pauperism ; the rod and worse for sickness
of body and of mind ; the dagger or the ditch, upon
occasion, for mere human misfortune. Till the first
grey glimmer of the dawn of prison reform, in the
days of Louis XVI., Bicêtre offered to "mere prisoners" the "sanctuary of a lion's den," and lent boldly
to king, minister, nobles, clergy, police, and all the
powers that were, the cells set apart for the mad as
convenient places for stifling the wits and consciences
of the sane.

In 1789, Paris had thirty-two State prisons. Four
years later, the Terror itself was content with twenty-
eight. One of the earliest acts of that vexed body,
the National Assembly, was to appoint a commission
of four of its members to the decent duty of visiting
the prisons. The commissioners chosen were Fré-
teau, Barrière, De Castellane, and Mirabeau. Count
Mirabeau at least—whose hot vagaries and the undy-
ing spite of his father had passed him through the

---

[1] *Les Prisons de Paris.*

hands of nearly every gaoler in France—had qualifications enough for the task!

The commissioners found within the black walls of *ce hideux Bicêtre* a population of close upon three thousand creatures, including "paupers, children, paralytics, imbeciles and lunatics." The administrative staff of all degrees numbered just three hundred. The governor, knowing his inferno, was not too willing to accord a free pass to the explorers, and Mirabeau and his colleagues had to give him a taste of their authority before he could be induced to slip the bolts of subterranean cells, whose inmates "had been expiating twenty years the double crime of poverty and courage," against whom no decree had been pronounced but that of a *lettre de cachet*, or who had been involved, like the Prévôt de Beaumont, in the crime of exposing some plot against the people's welfare. Children were found in these cells chained to criminals and idiots.

In April, 1792, Bicêtre gave admission to another set of commissioners. This second was a visit of some mystery, not greatly noised, and under cover of the night. It was not now a question of diving into moist and sunless caverns for living proofs (in fetters and stinking rags) of the hidden abuses of regal justice. The new commissioners came, quietly and almost by stealth, to make the first official trial of the Guillotine.

The invention of Dr. Guillotin (touching which he had first addressed the Constituent Assembly in December, 1789: "With this machine of mine, gentle-

men, I shall shave off your heads in a twinkling, and
you will not feel the slightest pain ") does not date in
France as an instrument of capital punishment until
1792 ; but under other names, and with other accesso-
ries, Scotland, Germany, and Italy had known a similar
contrivance in the sixteenth century.   In Paris, where
sooner or later everything finishes with a couplet, the
newspapers and broadsheets, not long after that midnight *essai* at Bicêtre, began to overflow gaily enough
with topical songs *(couplets de circonstance)* in praise
of the Doctor and his " razor."   Two fragmentary
samples will serve :—

> Air—" Quand la Mer Rouge apparut."

> " C'est un coup que l'on reçoit
>   Avant qu'on s'en doute ;
> A peine on s'en aperçoit,
>   Car on n'y voit goutte.
> Un certain ressort caché,
> Tout à coup étant laché,
>   Fait tomber, ber, ber,
>   Fait sauter, ter, ter,
>   Fait tomber,
>   Fait sauter,
>   Fait voler la tête . . .
>   C'est bien plus honnête."

II.

" Sur l'inimitable machine du Mèdecin Guillotin, propere à
couper les têtes, et dite de son nom Guillotine."

> Air—" Du Menuet d'Exaudet."

> " Guillotin,
>   Médecin
>   Politique,

Imagine un beau matin
Que pendre est inhumain
Et peu patriotique ;
Aussitôt,
Il lui faut
Un supplice
Que, sans corde ni poteau,
Supprime du bourreau
L'office," etc.

It was on the 17th of April, 1792, that proof was made of the first guillotine—not yet famed through France as the nation's razor. Three corpses, it is said (commodities easily procured at Bicêtre), were furnished for the experiment, which Doctors Guillotine and Louis directed. Mirabeau's physician and friend Cabanis was of the party, and—a not unimportant assistant—Samson the headsman, with his two brothers and his son. "The mere weight of the axe," said Cabanis, "sheared the heads with the swiftness of a glance, and the bones were clean severed (*coupés net*)." Dr. Louis recommended that the knife should be given an oblique direction, so that it might cut saw-fashion in its fall. The guillotine was definitely adopted ; and eight days later, the 25th of April, it settled accounts with an assassin named Pelletier, who was the first to "look through the little window," and "sneeze into the sack (*éternuer dans le sac*)."

Four months after the first trial of the "inimitable machine" Bicêtre paid its tribute of blood to the red days of September. In Bicêtre, as elsewhere in Paris, that Sunday, 2d of September, 1792, and the three days that followed were long remembered. "All

France leaps distracted," says Carlyle, "like the winnowed Sahara waltzing in sand colonnades!" In Paris, "huge placards" going up on the walls, "all steeples clangouring, the alarm-gun booming from minute to minute, and lone Marat, the man forbid," seeing salvation in one thing only—in the fall of "two hundred and sixty thousand aristocrat heads." It was the beginning or presage of the Terror.

The hundred hours' massacre in the prisons of Paris, beginning on the Sunday afternoon, may be reckoned with the hours of St. Bartholomew. "The tocsin is pealing its loudest, the clocks inaudibly striking three." The massacre of priests was just over at the Abbaye prison ; and there, and at La Force, and at the Châtelet, and the Conciergerie, in each of these prisons the strangest court—which could not be called of justice but of revenge—was hurriedly got together, and prisoner after prisoner, fetched from his cell and swiftly denounced as a "royalist plotter," was thrust out into a "howling sea" of *sansculottes* and hewn to pieces under an arch of pikes and sabres. "Man after man is cut down," says Carlyle ; "the sabres need sharpening, the killers refresh themselves from wine-jugs." Dr. Moore, author of the *Journal during a Residence in France*, came upon one of the scenes of butchery, grew sick at the sight, and "turned into another street." Not fewer than a thousand and eighty-nine were slaughtered in the prisons.

The carnage at Bicêtre, on the Paris outskirts, was on the Monday, and here it seems to have been of longer duration and more terrible than elsewhere.

Narratives of this butchery are not all in harmony. Prud'homme, author of the *Journal des Révolutions de Paris*, says that the mob started for Bicêtre towards three o'clock, taking with them seven pieces of cannon; that a manufactory of false paper-money *(assignats)* was discovered in full swing in the prison, and that all who were concerned in it were killed without mercy; that Lamotte, husband of the " Necklace Countess," was amongst the prisoners, and that the people " at once took him under their protection"; that the debtors and " the more wretched class of prisoners," were enlarged; and that the rest fell under pike, sabre, and club.

Barthélemi Maurice contradicts Prud'homme wholesale. The attack was at ten in the morning, he says, and not at three; there were no cannon; the paper-notes manufactory existed only in M. Prud'homme's imagination; prisoners for debt were not lodged in Bicêtre; the sick and the lunatics suffered no harm; and the famous Lamotte " never figured in any register of Bicêtre."

Thiers * insists upon the cannon, says the killing was done madly for mere lust of blood, and that the massacre continued until Wednesday, the 5th of September.

Peltier in his turn, royalist pamphleteer, gives his version of the tragedy. This Bicêtre, says Peltier, was " the den of all the vices," the sewer, so to speak, of Paris. " All were slain; impossible to figure up the number of the victims. I have heard it placed at as many as six thousand!" Peltier is not easily

* *Histoire de la Révolution.*

satisfied. " Eight days and eight nights, without one instant's pause, the work of death went forward." Pikes, sabres, and muskets " were not enough for the ferocious assassins, they had to bring cannon into play." It was not until a mere handful of the prisoners remained " that they had recourse again to their small-arms " *(que l'on en revenait aux petites armes)*.

Doubtless the most accurate account of this merciless affair is contained in the statement made to Barthélemi Maurice by Père Richard, *doyen* of the warders of Bicêtre, and an eye-witness. It may be summarised from the pages of MM. Alhoy and Lurine :

" Master Richard traced on paper the three numbers, 166, 55, and 22.—What are those ? I asked him.—166, that is the number of the dead.—And 55 and 22, what are they ?—55 was the number of children in the prison, and only 22 were left us. The scoundrels killed 33 children, besides the 166 adults.—Tell me how it began.—They came bellowing up at ten that Monday morning, all in the prison so still that you might have heard a fly buzzing, though we had three thousand men in that morning.— But you had cannon they say ; you defended yourselves.—Where did you get that tale, sir ? We had no cannon, and we did n't attempt to defend ourselves.—What was the strength of the attacking party ?—A good three thousand, I should say ; but of those not more than about two hundred were active, so to speak. —Did they bring cannon ?—It was said they did, but I saw none, though I looked out of the main gate more than once.—What were their arms, then ?—Well, a few of them had second-hand muskets *(de méchants fusils)*, others had swords, axes, bludgeons *(bûches)*, and bills *(crochets)*, but there were more pikes than anything else.—Were there any well-dressed people amongst them ? —Oh, yes ; the ' judges ' especially ; though the bulk of them were not much to look at.—How many ' judges ' were there ?—

A dozen ; but they relieved one another.—If there were judges, there was some sort of formality, I suppose. What was the procedure? How did they judge, acquit, and execute?—They sat in the clerk's office, a room down below, near the chapel. They made us fetch out the register ; looked down the column of ' cause of imprisonment,' and then sent for the prisoner. If you were too frightened to feel your legs under you, or could n't get a word out quick, it was ' guilty ' on the spot.—And then ?—Then the 'president' said : ' Let the citizen be taken to the Abbaye.' They knew outside what that meant. Two men seized him by the arm and led him out of the room. At the door he was face to face with a double row of cut-throats, a prod in the rear with a pike tossed him amongst them, and then . . . well, there were some that took a good deal of finishing off.—They did not shoot them then ?—No, there was no shooting.—And the acquittals ?—Well, if it was simply, 'take the citizen to the Abbaye,' they killed him. If it was 'take him to the Abbaye,' with *Vive la nation !* he was acquitted. It was n't over at nightfall. We passed the night of the 3d with the butchers inside the prison ; they were just worn out. It began again on the morning of the 4th, but not quite with the same spirit. It was mostly the children who suffered on the Tuesday.—And the lunatics, and the patients, and the old creatures—did they get their throats cut too ?—No, they were all herded in the dormitories, with the doors locked on them, and sentinels inside to keep them from looking out of window. All the killing was done in the prison.—And when did they leave you? At about three on Tuesday afternoon ; and then we called the roll of the survivors.—And the dead ?—We buried them in quicklime in our own cemetery."

The hideous *mise-en-scène* of Père Richard is, at the worst, a degree less reproachful than that of Prud'homme, Peltier, or M. Thiers.

There was one worthy man at Bicêtre, Dr. Pinel, whose devotion to humanitarian science (a form of devotion not over-common in such places at that day)

very nearly cost him his life at the hands of the revolutionary judges.   Dr. Pinel, who had the notion that
disease of the mind was not best cured by whipping,
was accused by the Committee of Public Safety (under
whose rule, it may be observed, no public ever went
in greater terror) of plotting with medical science for
the restoration of the monarchy !   It was a charge
quite worthy of the wisdom and the tenderness for
" public safety" of the *Comité de Salut Public*.   Pinel,
disdaining oratory, vouchsafed the simplest explanation of his treatment at Bicêtre,—and was permitted
to continue it.

Not so charitable were the gods to Théroigne de
Mericourt, a woman singular amongst the women of
the Revolution.   Readers of Carlyle will remember
his almost gallant salutations of her (a handsome
young woman of the streets, who took a passion for
the popular cause, and rode on a gun-carriage in the
famous outing to Versailles) as often as she starts
upon the scene.   When he misses her from the procession, in the fourth book of the first volume, it is :

" But where is the brown-locked, light-behaved, fire-hearted
Demoiselle Théroigne?   Brown eloquent beauty, who, with thy
winged words and glances, shalt thrill rough bosoms—whole steel
battalions—and persuade an Austrian Kaiser, pike and helm lie
provided for thee in due season, and alas ! also strait waistcoat
and long lodging in the Salpêtrière."

Théroigne was some beautiful village girl when the
echo first reached her of the tocsin of the Revolution.
She thought a woman was wanted there, and trudged
hot-foot to Paris, perhaps through the self-same quiet
lanes that saw the pilgrimage of Charlotte Corday.

In Paris she took (for reasons of her own, one must suppose) the calling of "unfortunate female"—the euphemism will be remembered as Carlyle's—and dubbed herself the people's Aspasia—"l'Aspasie du peuple." In "tunic blue," over a "red petticoat," crossed with a tricolour scarf and crowned with the Phrygian cap, she roamed the streets, "*criant, jurant, blasphémant,*" to the tune of the drum of rebellion. One day the women of the town, in a rage of fear or jealousy, fell upon her, stripped her, and beat her through the streets. She went mad, and in the first years of this century she was still an inmate of Bicêtre. When the "women's side" of Bicêtre was closed, in 1803, Théroigne was transferred to the Salpêtrière, where she died.

During the hundred years (1748–1852) of the prisons of the Bagnes—those convict establishments at Toulon, Brest, and Rochefort, which took the place of the galleys, and which in their turn gave way to the modern system of transportation,—it was from Bicêtre that the chained cohorts of the *forçats* were despatched on their weary march through France. The ceremony of the *ferrement*, or putting in irons for the journey, was one of the sights of Paris for those who could gain admission to the great courtyard of the prison. At daybreak of the morning appointed for the start, the long chains and collars of steel were laid out in the yard, and the prison smiths attended with their mallets and portable anvils ; the convicts, for whom these preparations were afoot, keeping up a terrific din behind their grated windows. When all was ready for them, they were tumbled out by batches and placed in rows along the wall. Every man had to strip to the skin, let the weather be what it might, and a sort of smock of coarse calico was tossed to him from a pile in the middle of the yard ; he did not dress until the toilet of the collar was finished. This, at the rough hands of the smith and his aids, was a sufficiently painful process. The convicts were called up in alphabetical order, and to the neck of each man a heavy collar was adjusted, the triangular bolt of which was hammered to by blows of a wooden mallet. To the padlock was attached a chain which, descending to the prisoner's waistbelt, was taken up thence and riveted to the next man's collar, and in this way some two hundred *forçats* were tethered like cattle in what was called the *chaine volante*. The satyr-like humours of the gang, singing and capering on the cobbles, shouting to the echo the name of some criminal hero as he stepped out to receive his collar, and sometimes joining hands in a frenzied dance, which was broken only by the savage use of the warder's bâtons—all this was the sport of the well-dressed crowd of spectators.

As far as the outskirts of Paris, the convicts were carried in *chars-à-bancs,* an armed escort on either side ; and when the prison doors were thrown open to let them out, the whole canaille of the town was waiting to receive them with yells of derision, to which the *forçats* responded with all the oaths they had. This was one of the most popular spectacles of Paris until the middle of the present century.

An essential sordidness is the character most persistent in the history of Bicêtre—a dull squalor, with perpetual crises of unromantic agony. There is no glamour upon Bicêtre; no silken gown with a domino above it rustles softly by lantern-light through those grimy wickets. It is not here that any gallant prisoner of state comes, bribing the governor to keep his table furnished with the best, receiving his love-letters in baskets of fruit, giving his wine-parties of an evening. In the records of Vincennes and the Bastille the novelist will always feel himself at home, but Bicêtre has daunted him. It is poor Jean Valjean, of *Les Misérables*, squatting "in the north corner of the courtyard," choked with tears, "while the bolt of his iron collar was being riveted with heavy hammer-blows." This is the solitary figure of interest which Bicêtre has given to fiction.

If a shadowy figure may be added, it is from the same phantasmagoric gallery of Victor Hugo. Bicêtre was the prison of the nameless faint-heart who weeps and moans through the incredible pages of *Le Dernier Jour d'un Condamné*. Then, and until 1836, Bicêtre was the last stage but one (*l'avant-dernière étape*) on the road to the guillotine. The last was the Conciergerie, close to the Place de Grève. The shadow-murderer of *Le Dernier Jour d'un Condamné*—for there is no real stuff of murder in him, and he is the feeblest and least sympathetic puppet of fiction—is useful only as bringing into relief the old, disused, and forgotten *cachot du condamné*, or condemned cell, of Bicêtre. It was a den eight feet square; rough stone walls, moist and sweating,

9

like the flags which made the flooring; the only
"window" a grating in the iron door; a truss of
straw on a stone couch in a recess; and an arched
and blackened ceiling, wreathed with cobwebs.

Starting out of sleep one night, Hugo's condemned
man lifts his lamp and sees spectral writings, figures
and arabesques in crayons, blood and charcoal dancing
over the walls of the cell—the "visitors' book" of
generations of *condamnés à mort* who have preceded
him. Some had blazoned their names in full, with
grotesque embellishments of the capital letter and a
motto underneath breathing their last defiance to the
world; and in one corner, "traced in white outline, a
frightful image, the figure of the scaffold, which, at
the moment that I write, may be rearing its timbers
for me! The lamp all but fell from my hands."

VII.

SAINTE-PÉLAGIE.

THE prison of Sainte-Pélagie owed its name to a frail beauty whom playgoers in Antioch knew in the fifth century of this era. Embracing Christianity, she forsook the stage, and built herself a cell on the Mount of Olives. The Church bestowed on her the honours of the Calendar.

Twelve centuries later, in the reign of Louis XIV., a Madame de Miramion, inspired by the memory, not of Pélagie the *comédienne*, but of Sainte-Pélagie the recluse, built in Paris a substantial Refuge for young women whose virtue seemed in need of protection. Letters-patent were obtained from the King, and Madame de Miramion sought her recruits here and there in the capital; gathering within the fold, it was said, a considerable number "who had no longer anything to fear for their virtue." But the rule of the house was strait, and one by one Madame's young persons absconded, or were withdrawn from her keeping by their parents. Nothing daunted, and sustained by her fixed idea of making penitents at any price, Madame de Miramion descended boldly upon the haunts of Aspasia herself, and there laid hands on all those votaries of Venus who were either weary of

their calling or whose calling was wearying of them.
The crown of the *joyeuse vie* fits loosely, and the
lightest shock unfixes it. Madame's campaign in
this quarter was successful, and she was soon at the
head of a battalion of more or less repentant graces.
New letters-patent were granted by a Majesty so desirous of the moral well-being of his female subjects,
the establishment of Sainte-Pélagie was confirmed,
and, thanks to the invaluable assistance of the police, the complement of Magdalens was maintained.
Sainte-Pélagie continued its pious destiny until the
days of the Revolution, when the cloister of the Magdalens became a prison.

As a prison, Sainte-Pélagie (which is in existence
to-day as a *maison de correction*, or penitentiary) has
known many and strange guests. From 1792 to 1795,
it held a mixed population of both sexes, political
prisoners and others. Between the years 1797 and
1834, debtors of all degrees were confined there, and
at one period the debtors shared the gaol with a
motley crew of juvenile delinquents. Under the
Restoration and under the two Empires Sainte-Pélagie served the uses of a State prison. The first Napoleon had the cells in constant occupation. The
Restoration sent there, within the space of a few
days, one hundred and thirty-five individuals, arrested
by the police of Louis XVIII. for their connection,
as officers, with the old Imperial Guard. Innumer-
able indeed, from 1790 onwards, were the victims
who found a lodging, not of their choosing, behind
the ample walls which the widow Miramion had con-

secrated a shelter for tottering virtue or gallantry in
mourning for its past. The men of the Revolution
found Sainte-Pélagie excellently suited to their needs;
Madame de Miramion had housed her Magdalens
strongly. In form a vast quadrilateral, the buildings
were easily converted to the uses of a prison; and at
a later date the prison was arranged in three divisions.
On the west side were confined petty offenders under
sentences ranging between six months and one year.
The debtors' was the second division; and here also
were imprisoned young rogues, thieves, and vagabonds, and (up to 1867) "certain men of letters and
journalists." The east side seems to have been reserved principally for political offenders. But the
divisions were never very strictly observed; and a
political prisoner relegated by mischance or for lack
of space to the west side of the prison was treated in
all respects as a common criminal. Ordinary prisoners were kept at work, and received a small percentage on the profits of their industry. Political
prisoners, journalists, and "men of letters" were ex-
empted from labour; and a third class called *pistoliers*, purchased this exemption at a cost of from six
to seven francs a fortnight.

It was by order of the Convention that Sainte-
Pélagie was transformed from a convent-refuge into
a prison, and during the revolutionary period a crowd
of unknown or little-known suspects passed within its
keeping before being summoned to the bar. Not a
few quitted it only for the scaffold.

Madame Roland was cast there on the 25th of
June, 1793. Three years earlier, Carlyle notes her

at Lyons, "that queen-like burgher woman; beautiful, Amazonian-graceful to the eye" with "that strong
Minerva-face." We shall return to Madame Roland,
wife of the "King's Inspector of Manufactures."

In the same month, if not on the same day, were
sent to Sainte-Pélagie the Comte de Laval-Montmo-
rency, and the Marquis de Pons. In August of the
same year went to join them (not now with popular
acclamation, as when, in 1765, Mademoiselle Clairon
and her fellow players were haled to the Châtelet)
nine ladies of the Théâtre-Français. After the 9th
Thermidor (July 27, 1794), which saw the sudden
downfall and death of Robespierre, Sainte-Pélagie
received most of the victims of the reaction,—the
Tail of Robespierre,—including the Duplaix family.

Madame Roland had known the indignities of a
revolutionary prison before her sojourn at Sainte-
Pélagie. Imprisoned first in the Abbaye, it was
from there that she wrote :

"I find a certain pleasure in enforcing privations on myself, in
seeing how far the human will can be employed in reducing the
'necessaries' of existence. I substituted bread and water for
chocolate, at breakfast ; a plate of meat with vegetables was my
dinner ; and I supped on vegetables, without desert."

But having "as much aversion from as contempt
for a merely useless economy" *(autant d'aversion que
de mépris pour une économie inutile)*, Madame Roland
goes on to say that what she saved by the retrench-
ments of her own cuisine she spent in procuring ex-
tra rations for the pauper prisoners of the Abbaye ;
and adds : "If I stay here six months I mean to go

out plump and hearty [*je veux en sortir grasse et
fraîche*], wanting nothing more than soup and bread,
and with the satisfaction of having earned certain
bénédictions incognito."

Transferred to Sainte-Pélagie, this heroic woman
of the people saw herself confounded with women of
the town (the descendants of the widow Miramion's
Magdalens), thieves, forgers, and assassins. She
made the best of the situation, cultivated flowers in
a box in the window of her cell, and wrote incessantly.
When told that her name had been included in the
process against the Girondins, she said : " I am not
afraid to go to the scaffold in such good company ; I
am ashamed only to live among scoundrels." Her
friends had contrived a plan for her escape, but could
not induce her to profit by it : " Spare me !" she cried.
" I love my husband, I love my daughter ; you know it ;
but I will not save myself by flight." When the axe
fell on the heads of the twenty-two Girondins, October 31, 1793 (10th Brumaire of the Republican
calendar), Madame Roland was removed to the
Conciergerie. Knowing well the fate that awaited
her, she lost neither her courage nor her beautiful
tranquillity ; and used to go down to the men's wicket
of the prison, exhorting them to be brave and worthy
of the cause. In the tumbril, on her way to the guillotine, she was robed in white, her superb black hair
floating behind her ; and at the place of execution,
bending her head to the statue of Liberty, she murmured : " O Liberty ! what crimes are done in thy
name !"—*O Liberté ! que de crimes on commet en ton
nom !*

It was not Madame Dubarry's to show this sublime
fortitude in death ; but after all one dies as one must.
Sainte-Pélagie will tell us that poor Dame Dubarry
was the feeblest and most faint-hearted of its recluses
of the Revolution.   She wept, and called on heaven
to save her, and shuffled and cut her cards, and consulted the lines in her hand ; and when her name was
called at the wicket on the fatal morning, she swooned
on the flags of the prison, and was carried scarcely
animate to the tumbril.

The story of governor Bouchotte, who had charge
of Sainte-Pélagie at this terrible epoch, is a noble one.
The September massacres had begun, and the red-
bonnets in detachments were sharing the butchery at
the prisons.   The Abbaye, the Carmes, the Force,
and the Conciergerie had given them prompt entrance ; the turnkeys saluting the self-styled judges,
say MM. Alhoy and Lurine, as the grave-digger salutes the hangman.   Not so governor Bouchotte of
Sainte-Pélagie.   The mob swarmed at the doors, but
to their clattering on the panels no answer was vouchsafed.   Pikes, hammers, and axes resounded on the
solid portals, but silence the most complete reigned
behind them.

" Can citizen Bouchotte have been beforehand
with us ?—*Le citoyen Bouchotte, nous aurait-il de-
vancés ?* " cried one.   " Not an aristocrat voice to be
heard ! Bouchotte has perhaps finished them off
himself."

The neighbouring houses were ransacked for tools
proper to effect an entrance, and the doors were burst

open. The mob poured in ; and there, bound hand and foot on the flags in the court-yard of the prison, they found the governor and his wife.

"Citizens," cried Bouchotte, "you arrive too late ! My prisoners are gone. They got warning of your coming, and after binding my wife and myself as you see us, they made their escape."

Bouchotte was taken at his word, he and his wife were released from their cords, and the red-bonnets went off to wreak a double vengeance at Bicêtre. At the risk of his own and of his wife's life, the admirable Bouchotte had tricked the cut-throats. He had uncaged his birds and given them their liberty through a private postern, and had then ordered his warders to tie up his wife and himself. Honour to the brave memory of Bouchotte ! The history of the French Revolution has few brighter passages than this.

Nougaret gives us a curious picture of the interior of Sainte-Pélagie under the bloody rule of Robespierre.* The prison itself he describes as "damp and unwholesome" (humide et malsaine). There were about three hundred and fifty prisoners, detained they knew not why, for they were not allowed to read the charges entered on the registers.

To each prisoner was allotted a cell six feet square, "with a dirty bed and a mattress as hard as marble." The turnkey's first question to a new-comer was : " Have you any money?" If the answer was, Yes, he was supplied with " a basin and a water-jug and a few cracked plates, for which he paid triple their

* _Histoire des Prisons de Paris et des Départements._

worth." If the prisoner entered with empty pockets, it was: "So much the worse for you; for the rule here is that nothing buys nothing" (*on n'a rien pour rien*). In this plight, says Nougaret, the prisoner was obliged to sell some poor personal effect in order to obtain the strictest necessaries of life. " A citizen who occupied, in the month of Floréal, cell number 10 in the corridor of the second story, sacrificed for twenty-five francs a gold ring worth about £20, to procure for himself those same necessities." The rations at this date consisted of " a pound and a half of bad bread and a plate of flinty beans [*haricots très-durs*], larded with stale grease or tallow." Prisoners who could afford it paid an exorbitant price for a few supplementary dishes. Later, the diet was rather more generous.

Although communication between the prisoners was forbidden, they had invented a sort of club; perhaps the most singular in the annals of clubdom. The "meetings" were at eight in the evening, but no member left his cell. Despite the thickness of the doors, it was found that, by raising his voice, a prisoner could be heard from one end of the corridor to the other; and by this means the members of the club exchanged such news as they had gleaned during the day from the warders on duty. In order that no one might be betrayed or compromised (in the event of the conversation being overheard by the gendarmes posted under the windows), instead of saying " I heard such-and-such a thing to-day," the formula was, " I dreamt last night."

When a candidate presented himself (that is to say,

A TURNKEY.

when a new prisoner arrived), the president inquired, in behalf of the club, his name, quality, residence, and the reason of his imprisonment ; and if the answers were satisfactory he was proclaimed a member of the society in these terms : "Citizen, the patriots imprisoned in this corridor deem you worthy to be their brother and friend. Permit me to send you the *accolade fraternelle !*"

Two circumstances excluded from membership of the club,—to have borne false witness at Fouquier-Tinville's bar, and to have been concerned in the fabrication of false *assignats*. The club held its "meetings" regularly, until the date at which the prisoners were allowed to exercise together in the corridors.

We saw Madame Roland, "brave, fair Roland," at the men's wicket of Sainte-Pélagie, passionately exhorting them ; and Comtesse Dubarry answering her summons to the guillotine by a swoon.

Another woman, not famous yet, but destined to fame, was on the women's side of Sainte-Pélagie in 1793 : Joséphine de Beauharnais, who was to stand one day with Napoleon on the throne. A tradition of the prison affirmed that Joséphine left her initials carved or traced on a wall of her cell.

The Terror seems almost to have emptied Sainte-Pélagie, and it is not until the days of the Empire that we find its cells once more in the occupation of political prisoners. Prisoners of that quality were not lacking there in Buonaparte's despotic era ; but (and this may have been of design) the registers were

not too well kept, and prisoners' names and the
motives of their imprisonment are hard to arrive at.
Had we the lists in full, however, they would ex-
cite small interest at this day. Between 1811 and
March, 1814, when the records were more precise,
two hundred and thirty-four persons were confined
in this prison for causes more or less political. In
April, 1814, we have the Russian Emperor giving
their freedom to some seventy of the prisoners of
Napoleon. The Restoration sends the officers of the
old Imperial Guard to Sainte-Pélagie. The record
of the Hundred Days, so far as this prison is concerned, is a clean one ; but Charles X. continues the
use of Sainte-Pélagie as a prison of State, and Béran-
ger, Cauchois-Lemaire, Colonel Duvergier, Bonnaire,
Dubois, Achille Roche, and Barthélemy are amongst
the names on the gaoler's books. The Constitutional
Monarchy from 1830 to 1848, the Republic succeeding
it, and the reign of Napoleon III. (who swept into it
five hundred citizens in the space of a few days) kept
alive the political tradition of Sainte-Pélagie. M.
Rochefort, who had his turn there from 1869–1870,
was one of the last of Napoleon III.'s prisoners, to
whom the revolution of the 4th of September gave
back their liberty. From that date, the "political
boarders" of Sainte-Pélagie were few, the governments of MM. Thiers and De Broglie preferring
rather to suppress newspapers than to pursue their
editors.

Under the Empire and the Restoration the
organisation and administration of Sainte-Pélagie
evidently left much to be desired. It was not rare,

says one chronicler, for accused persons to remain six
or seven months without being interrogated.

A certain M. Poulain d'Angers lay there a quarter
of a year quite ignorant as to the cause of his arrest.
Another accused, a certain M. Guillon, who had
been attached to the Emperor's Council, weary of the
perpetual shufflings of the police of the succeeding
reign, constituted himself a prisoner *de facto* without
having received judgment ; and remained six months
a captive, although there was no entry against his
name : one morning, they showed him the door,
malgré lui. An adventure which befell this gentleman attests sufficiently the disorder which reigned in
the prison service.

Being to some extent indisposed, the doctor had
given M. Guillon an order for the baths. Not
knowing in what part of the prison the infirmary was
situated, he presented his order to a tipsy turnkey,
who promptly opened the door which gave on the
Rue du Puits-de-l'Ermite. M. Guillon, a free man
without being aware of it, took the narrow street to
be a sentry's walk, and went a few paces without find-
ing any one to direct him. Returning to the sentry
at the door, he inquired where were the baths.
"What baths?" said the sentinel.—"The prison
baths." "The prison baths," said the sentinel, "are
probably in the prison ; but you can't get in there."—
"What? I can't get into the prison ! Am I outside
it, then?"—"Why, yes ; you're in the street ; you
ought to know that, I should think." "I did not
know it, I assure you," said M. Guillon ; "and this
won't suit me at all." He rang the prison bell, and

was readmitted; and the recital of his adventure restored to sobriety the turnkey who had given him his freedom.

It was related that under the Directory a criminal condemned to transportation managed to conceal himself in Sainte-Pélagie, persuaded that there at all events he was safe, nor were his hopes deceived.

It appears to have been after the Revolution of 1830—that brief week of July which "paragons description"—that some kind of method was attained or attempted in the management of Sainte-Pélagie. A new wing had been built, which was reserved for the politicals,—but the builder had reckoned without his guests, and without the King's Attorney. It was considered that thirty-six beds in ten chambers, to say nothing of a small spare dormitory, would be accommodation enough for prisoners of this class. At the same epoch, a droll idea took possession of the administration. It was, that if the *gamins* and 'prentice-thieves raked into the police-courts were mixed pell-mell with the political prisoners, the former might get a polish on their morals, and the latter an agreeable distraction! As a scheme of reform for the artful dodger it was perhaps elementary, but it shewed at least a kindly anxiety on the part of the administration to prepare diversions for political offenders. Alas! it was a dream; for there were presently so many political delinquents to be accommodated, that the question was no longer how to distract their captivity, but how to lodge the newcomers. The artful dodger was exiled.

More buildings were called for, and another court; and the political wing of Sainte-Pélagie became a colony by itself. A colonist of the early thirties bestowed on it the following appreciation :—"Sainte-Pélagie is death by wasting (*le supplice par la langueur*), torture by ennui, homicide by process of decline. It is a sort of pneumatic machine applied to the brain, which saps and exhausts it by inches. It is not an active irritation, and it is nothing resembling repose. It is not Paris, and it is not a desert solitude. It is a *mélange* of everything : air, a modicum ; elbow-room, rather less ; friends, one or two ; bores, any number. It is a prison with a mirage of the world ; a world not made for a prison. It is not severe, and it is infinitely wearisome. It is a kind of civilised police ; it is a prodigious and perpetual paradox. . . . Sainte-Pélagie is insupportable !"

Here is another appreciation of about the same date :—"Sainte-Pélagie is a hurly-burly (*pêle-mêle*) of all imaginable ideas and opinions ; a species of political Pandemonium. The *Caricature* runs foul of the *Quotidienne*, the *Courrier de l'Europe* elbows the *Revolution*, the *Gazette* pirouettes between the *Tribune* and the *Courrier Français*. . . . All colours and all races, all ages and all tongues are confounded. It is a Babel ; it is a common camp in which friends and foes are flung together after a general rout. As a huge anomaly it is curious to see, but it has the depressing effect of a monster !"

Let us turn to the debtors' side. Dulaure quotes in this connection a description given by De la Borde in his *Memoirs*, which is worth translating :

" The debtors' wing of Sainte-Pélagie, which is intended to accommodate a hundred, has one hundred
and twenty and sometimes one hundred and fifty
tenants.   The building is in three stories, each story
consisting of one narrow corridor, the rooms in which
receive no light except from loopholes beneath the
roof.   There are no fire-places in the rooms, some of
which are cruelly cold, whilst in others the heat is
unbearable.   With proper space for three persons
at the most, they are generally made to hold from five
to six ; and the dirt everywhere is revolting.   The
wretched occupants can only take exercise in a corridor four feet wide, and a court-yard thirty feet
square.   For years they have asked in vain for some
contrivance which would give them a proper current
of air ; there is not a decent ventilator in the place.
In winter they are locked in from eight P.M. until
seven A.M.; and, whatever his necessities, not one of
the five or six cell-mates can possibly quit his cell between those hours.   The dirtiest and worst-kept part
of the whole prison is the infirmary.   Two or three
patients are put into one bed,—an excellent means of
spreading the itch, and other maladies."

The reproach of this unseemly state M. de la Borde
laid upon the chiefs of the prison service for their
indifference, and the subordinates for their wholesale
negligence.

To obtain leave to visit a friend on the debtors'
side, you climbed the dingy staircase of the Préfecture
de Police, to the office marked *Bureau des Prisons*,
where orders were issued for the principal gaols ; and

you took your place in the waiting-room amongst a very motley crowd whose relatives or acquaintances had been "put away" for murder, arson, forgery, house-breaking, or a simple difficulty with a creditor.

Furnished with the necessary passport, a literary Frenchman made the pilgrimage to Sainte-Pélagie seventy years ago, and wrote a most interesting account of his visit. The authors of *Les Prisons de Paris* transferred it to their entertaining pages, and I cannot do better than translate from them. It chanced to be pay-day in the prison, that is to say, the day on which the debtors received the stingy pittance which their creditors were compelled to pay them once a month,—an excellent opportunity of observing the stranded victims of the most nonsensical law in the universe. To clap into prison a man who could not satisfy his creditors, and thereby to encourage the indolent debtor in his indolence and to dry up for the industrious debtor all possible sources of industry, was perhaps, in this country as in France, the summit of folly ever attained by legal enactment.

"I found myself in a world of which those who have described it only from the other side of the wall have given us an entirely false notion. Where were all the gaieties which the novelists and the rhymesters have depicted for us? Where were the bevies of fair women who, as we have been assured, flock here by day to scatter the cares of the forlorn imprisoned debtor? I strained my ear in vain for any note of those bacchic concert-parties and mad festivities (*ces bruyants éclats de l'orgie*) which are to be met with in the novels. I threw a glance into the court-yard, and calculated the amount of space which each man could claim in the only spot in the whole prison where there is any circulation of air; I came to the conclusion that, when the

10

prisoners were assembled here of an evening, after their friends had left, each might possess for himself a fraction of a fraction of a square yard of mother earth."

The debtors trooped down to the office to finger their doles.

"I watched a procession of artisans and labourers, whose speech and costume contrasted oddly with the title of 'merchants' (*négociants*), under which their creditors had filched them from the workshops and yards to which they belonged; next, some physiognomies of men of the world, some representatives of the middle classes, and a crowd of young bloods (*étourneaux*).

"One of the first comers was an officer, decorated and seamed with wounds, who had been four times in Sainte-Pélagie to purge the same debt. After five months' captivity he came to an arrangement with his creditor, to whom he owed a couple of thousand francs, agreeing to pay him in ninety days five hundred more. He was let out, failed to redeem the debt, and returned to take up his old quarters in Sainte-Pélagie. At the end of a year, he acknowledged a debt of three thousand francs to the same creditor, and obtained six months' grace. He paid a thousand on account, could not furnish a penny more, and went back to prison for the third time. Thus, after nearly three years in prison, the captain owes one-third more than he did on first coming in, and has paid a thousand francs to boot,—to encourage his creditor.

"The old fellow who followed him was a monument of the speculative spirit of a certain class of creditors. He was half-blind, and had lost his left arm; his whole debt amounted to £20. Eight days before the King's birthday his creditor cast him into Sainte-Pélagie, in the hope that one of the civil-list bonuses would fall to the old man. Unhappily, the hope was not realised, and the creditor is now looking forward to next year's list.

"Amongst the swarm of debtors, I recognised my old water-carrier, who needed little coaxing to tell me the story of his imprisonment.

"Léonard was a native of Auvergne. After hawking water in

buckets for several years, his ambition rose to a water-cart ; and behold him now with his sphere of operations extended from the Rue du Faubourg-Poissonnière to the Marais.   Unluckily for Léonard the water-cart was not yet his own property, and he began to fall into arrears with his monthly payments.   When the arrears had become what the bailiffs call an 'exploitable' sum, Léonard was haled to the bar.   Here he suddenly ceased to be a water-carrier ; they promoted him to the rank of 'merchant,' and under that style and dignity they condemned poor Léonard for debt.   In this strait Léonard thought, " Why not become bankrupt at once ? " but when he went to deposit his balance-sheet they told him he was not a 'merchant' at all, but a mere water-carrier.   Fifteen days later, Léonard had joined the ranks of the impecunious in Sainte-Pélagie.

" His next idea was to lodge an appeal, and his brother was willing to bear the costs ; but Léonard's debt was a bagatelle of £12, and the lawyer whom he consulted said that the blessings of appeal were reserved for persons owing £20 and upwards. The code of the Osages, if they have one, probably does not contain such exquisite burlesque as this.

" I asked Léonard what had become of his wife.   'Oh,' he said, 'poor Jeanne has gone back to Auvergne ; otherwise they 'd have had her too, for they made Jeanne a "merchant" also' (*elle était aussi négociante*).

" I gave Léonard a trifle, and he went off to drink it.   It is the commonest recreation, when it can be indulged ; and the majority of the debtors, when their day of liberation comes, return to their homes with the two incurable habits of idleness and liquor."

Another who came to touch his allowance was a tradesman whose clerk had robbed him of one thousand crowns.   " The tradesman being unable in consequence to meet his engagements is condemned to spend five years in Sainte-Pélagie, and from the grating of his cell he can see in the penal wing the scoundrelly clerk, who gets off with six months' imprisonment ! "

Another comes

"tripping cheerfully through the crowd ; he is receiving his last
payment ; in a few days he will be a free man. An anonymous
letter has loosed his bonds with the happy tidings that his
creditor has been dead a year, and that a speculative bailiff
has been prolonging his captivity on the chance of the debt
being paid into his own pocket."

To this victim of a negligent law succeeded two
who had made the law their dupe. One was an officer who had had himself arrested for debt to escape
joining an expedition to Morea. The other was a
tradesman "who was nobody's prisoner but his own,
and who had arranged with a friend to deposit the
monthly allowance for food. He was speculating on
the article of the code which gave a general exemption from arrest for debt to all who had passed five
consecutive years in the gaol."

A new-comer, "with his face all slashed," was

"recounting the details of the siege he had sustained in his house
against the bailiff's men. He had wanted to give himself up
without fuss, but was told when he presented himself at the office
that a person condemned for debt must be forcibly arrested (*doit
être appréhendé au corps avec brutalité*), and pitched into a cab
under the eyes of all the loungers on the foot-way,—who no
doubt often imagine that they are assisting at the capture of some
eminent criminal. This enterprise on the part of the bailiff and
his men is charged to the unfortunate debtor, and the field of
battle is as often as not some public thoroughfare."

But by far the most interesting and sympathetic
personality on the debtor's side of Sainte-Pélagie at
this date was the American Colonel Swan. The nature and amount of the colonel's debt are not set out,

but the interest seems to have been the main cause
of offence, and he had made it a matter of conscience
to refuse payment.

"The French law had ordered his temporary arrest, and,
twenty years after his incarceration, he was still 'temporarily'
in confinement. Compatriot and friend of Washington, Colonel
Swan had fought in the War of Independence with Lafayette,
and the grand old French republican often bent his white head
beneath the wicket of the gaol, on a visit to his brother-in-arms."

His own private means, the aid of wealthier friends,
or even a successful project of escape, might have restored him to the free world; but so greatly had he
used himself to his captivity, that no thought of liberty seems ever to have crossed his mind.

"It was not altogether without emotion that one saw this
comely veteran—whose features were almost a copy of Benjamin
Franklin's—pacing the narrow and sombre passages of the prison,
drawing a breath of air at the loop-hole above the little garden.
His long robe of swanskin or white dimity announced his coming, and it was both curious and touching to see how the groups
of prisoners made way for him in the corridors, and how some
hastened to carry into their cells the little stoves on which they
did their cooking, lest the fumes of the charcoal should offend
him."

This respect and love of the whole prison the old
colonel had justly won; not a day of his long confinement there but he had marked by some service of
kindness, for the most part mysterious and anonymous. No hungry debtor went in vain to the door
of the colonel's little cell; and often, seeking a supper, the petitioner went away with the full price of
his liberty.

There were two classes in the debtors' wing; those with certain resources of their own to supplement the miserable allowance of their creditors, and those who were dependent for their daily rations on the handful of centimes allowed them by law.

These last used to hire their services to the others for a gratuity, and were among the regular suitors of Colonel Swan's inexhaustible bounty. They were known in the prison as "cotton-caps" (*bonnets de coton*). One of these, hearing that the American had lost his "cotton-cap," went to beg the place. The colonel knew all about the man, a poor devil with a large family, stranded there for a few hundred francs. He asked a salary of six francs a month.

"That will suit me very well," said the colonel; and, opening a little chest, "here is five years' pay in advance." It was the amount precisely of the man's debt,—and a fair instance of the colonel's benefactions.

Towards the year 1829, prisoners taking their airing in the garden saw an old man strolling an hour or two in the day on the high terrace or gallery at the top of the prison. It was Colonel Swan, for whom, in failing health, the doctor had demanded that privilege. He had accepted it gratefully, but—as if admonished from within—he said to the doctor: "My proper air is the air of the prison; this breath of liberty will kill me."

A few months later, the cannon of the 27th of July was belching in the streets of Paris. On the 28th, the doors of the "commercial Bastille" were thrown open, and the prisoners went out.

Colonel Swan, who went out with them, died on the 29th.

There were a few clever escapes, *evasions* as the French call them, from Sainte-Pélagie. What was known as the *procès d'Avril*, 1835, resulted in the condemnation of Guinard, Imbert, Cavaignac, Marrast, and others, who were lodged in the political wing. Forty of them joined in a scheme of evasion, and a subterranean passage was dug from the northeast angle of the prison into the garden of No. 9, Rue Copeau. The tunnel, nearly twenty yards in length, was completed on the 12th of July, and of the forty prisoners twenty-eight made good their escape from Sainte-Pélagie the "insupportable."

The excitement of a well-conducted escape is contagious, and in September of the same year the Comte de Richmond, who gave himself out as the son of Louis XVI., with his two friends in durance, Duclerc and Rossignol, broke prison ingeniously enough. By bribery or some other means, Richmond procured a pass-key which gave admission to the sentry-walk; and, head erect and a file of papers under his arm, he walked boldly out, followed by Rossignol and Duclerc. To the sentinel who challenged them, the Count with perfect *sang-froid* introduced himself as the director of the prison; "and these gentlemen," he added, "whom you ought to know, are my chief clerk, and my architect." The sentry saluted and let them pass, and M. de Richmond and his friends opened the door and walked out.

In 1865, an Englishman named Jackson, condemned to five years' hard labour, managed to get himself transferred to Sainte-Pélagie. On a wet wild night in the last week of January, he squeezed out of his cell, crawled over the roof to a convenient wall, and by the aid of a cord and grappling iron let himself down into the street. The night was pitchy black, rain was falling in torrents, the sentry was in his box, and Jackson footed it leisurely home.

Better than these, however, was the escape of Colonel Duvergier, one of the State prisoners of Charles X. Colonel Duvergier had been condemned to five years' "reclusion" for no apparent reason except that he was one of the most distinguished soldiers of his day. The story of his escape is one of the happiest in the romantic annals of prison-breaking, but the credit of the affair rests principally with a young littérateur, a certain Eugène de P——.

Colonel Duvergier was on the political, and Eugène de P—— on the debtors' side of Sainte-Pélagie, but they had succeeded in establishing a correspondence by letter ; and Eugène, not over-eager for his own liberty, seems to have taken upon himself to procure the colonel's. With Colonel Duvergier was one Captain Laverderie, and the colonel refused to go out unless the captain could share his escape. Eugène de P—— said the captain should go also, and the plot went forward.

The first step was to get the colonel and his friend from the political to the debtors' side of the prison, and this was contrived at the exercise hour. When the political prisoners were being marched in, to give place to the debtors—there being but one exercise yard for the two classes—Duvergier and Laverderie escaped the warder's eye, and hid in the garden, until the debtors came out for their constitutional. Nowadays, the warder would have counted his flock, both on coming out and on going in ; but the colonel and the captain seem to have had no difficulty, either in attaching themselves to the debtors or in taking refuge, after the exercise hour, in the cell of a debtor who was a party to the scheme.

So far, however, the fugitives had succeeded only in changing their quarters in the prison ; and the next step was to procure for them two visitors' passes. These passes, deposited with the gate-warder when visitors entered, were returned to them as they left the prison. How to place in the warder's hands passes bearing the names of two " visitors" who had not entered the prison ? The adroit Eugène thought it not too difficult.

He had a friendly warder at the gate who was much interested in some sketches which Eugène was making in the prison, and went down to him one day with his portfolio in his hand. " A few fresh sketches you might like to look at." While the Argus of the gate was amusing himself with Eugène's drawings, Eugène himself feigned astonishment at the number of visitors to the prison, as evidenced by the quantity of passes lying loose on the table. He expressed no less surprise that the warder should have so little care of them ; why not keep the passes in a handy case, such, for example, as Eugène used for his drawings ?

The warder thought he would ask the governor for one. " You need n't trouble the governor," said

Eugène; "take mine. Look, what could be better!" and in filling the portfolio with the visitors' passes, he slipped in two others.

At that psychological instant, Duvergier and Laverderie presented themselves at the gate.

"Your names, messieurs?" and they gave the names which were entered on Eugène's passes.

The passes were turned up, the warder handed them over, and—still thanking Eugène for his present—bowed the fugitives out of the prison.

CHAPTER VIII.

THE ABBAYE.

IT was the monks, as tradition wills it, who hollowed out the cruel cells of the Abbaye de Saint-Germain-des-Près. The architect Gomard, insisting that cells were not included in the bond, withdrew when he had put his last touches to the cloisters. But in 1630, or thereabouts, no monastery was complete without its *oubliettes*, and the prior commanded his brethren to finish the work of the too-scrupulous Gomard. Thus was the Abbaye equipped as an abbaye should be.

What power indeed, spiritual or temporal, had not the privilege in those days of setting up its pillory, its gallows, its pile of faggots built around a stake! In Paris alone at this date some twenty separate jurisdictions possessed the right to fatten victims for the scaffold, and it might almost be said that the municipal divisions of the capital had gibbets for their boundaries.

In 1674, however, the situation changed somewhat. The authority of the Châtelet was enlarged by royal edict, which gathered to it the rights and privileges of all the lesser corporations, and confiscated the hal-

ters and the faggots of private justice. This was a
general blow, which none took more to heart than
the prior of the Abbaye of Saint-Germain-of-the-
Meadows. He had enjoyed the rights of "high,"
"middle," and "low" justice; he had imprisoned,
tortured, and despatched at his holy pleasure. Forthwith, he composed and addressed to Louis XIV. *un
mémoire éloquent*, which touched that pious heart.
The Royal will consented to restore to the prior a considerable portion of his ancient jurisdiction. Within
the extensive bounds of the monastery and its appan-
ages, the holy father might still consider himself
gaoler, tormentor, and executioner.

But his prison was now large beyond his pious
needs, and little by little the Abbaye took a more
secular character. The cells which the restricted
powers of the prior could no longer charge to the
full, were set apart for young noblemen and others
whose parents or guardians had an interest in nar-
rowing their borders. It was an age when parents
and guardians had an almost unlimited authority over
sons, daughters, and wards; and when fathers and
uncles seldom thought twice about applying for a
lettre de cachet. Sometimes young rakes were put
into temporary seclusion for quite satisfactory reasons; but very often the legal powers of parents and
guardians were used with abominable cruelty; and
young men were imprisoned for years, suffering the
treatment of criminals, merely to gratify the rancour
of a near relative; or were even, where there was a
fortune in question, confined expressly with the design that they should be secretly got rid of. A father

could or did authorise a gaoler to treat his innocent
son with a rigour that goes almost beyond belief; to
forbid him to petition anyone for release; to keep
him in solitary confinement; to feed him on the most
meagre rations. The nephew of a General Wurmser,
who had designs upon the young man's fortune, had
him imprisoned in the Abbaye on some vague charge
of dissipation. The young man was only twenty
years of age, but he entered the Abbaye with the
fixed conviction that his uncle did not intend ever to
release him, and this conviction was confirmed by the
hint conveyed to him by a turnkey, that he was to be
sent to the fortress of Pierre-Encise, or Ham. Within
a week, he had committed suicide in his cell.

Occasionally, young bloods of the period did penance in the Abbaye for practical jokes of a rather
questionable morality. A certain D——, a spend-
thrift of the first rank (who, however, rose afterwards
to great honour in the army), was at the last pinch
to settle his gaming debts. An uncle from whom he
expected a goodly legacy lay sick unto death in his
hôtel, and D—— gave out that the patient desired
the attendance of a notary. The notary arrived, and
the uncle dictated a will entirely in his nephew's favour. This being published, loans were forthcoming.
But the sequel was less satisfactory; for D—— presently found himself a prisoner in the Abbaye, and his
friend, the Chevalier de C——, in a cell of the Bastille; the former for having personated a moribund
uncle, and the latter for having aided and abetted
him in the swindle.

When Howard was making his memorable progress

through the " Lazzarettos of Europe," the Abbaye
was amongst the prisons which he visited.   He notes
that there were " five little cells in which as many as
fifty men were sometimes massed together."   The
Abbaye had undergone yet another transformation,
and was now the principal military prison of Paris.
It was reserved chiefly for the soldiers, both officers
and privates, of the *Gardes Françaises;* but delinquents of other regiments were sent there also ; and
a turbulent place the Abbaye seems to have been in
the days before the Revolution.   For, up to '89, the
French army recruited itself as best it could, and
principally from amongst the masses of the unem-
ployed and the vagabond classes.   They were bought
by recruiting sergeants, or swept into the ranks by
the press-gangs, and it may be supposed that the
stuff out of which the rank-and-file was manufactured
was sometimes of the rottenest.   Moreover, there
was little spirit amongst the officers to induce them
to train up into good fighting-men and self-respecting
citizens the peasants, beggars, and outcasts of whom
they found themselves in command.   The swagger-
ing, aristocrat captain, lording it over the colonel,
who was perhaps a mere soldier of fortune, scorned
the men beneath him.   His military rank, added to
the colossal difference in social rank between the
nobility and the people, gave him a double sense of
superiority ; there was no *esprit de corps*, no feeling
of comradeship in arms ; but, on the one side, a perpetual and galling assertion of authority, and, on the
other, a continuous struggle to secure some amount
of recognition and freedom.

Insubordinate soldiers were continually being thrust into the Abbaye, and there were strange scenes within those walls.

In the year 1784, say the authors of *Les Prisons de l'Europe*, two military prisoners were finishing their scanty meal.

"Our last day together, Desforges," said one. "You go to Château Trompette, I to Valenciennes. We're in for twenty years of it!"

"Yes, and for what, Dessaignes?" said the other. "For a quarrel with a clod of an officer risen from the ranks. Twenty years!"

"My dear Desforges," said the young aristocrat. "It is not a cheerful prospect.—Warm here, is n't it? Trees in leaf, and flowers smelling sweet—out there. Out there, where liberty lies, Desforges. Come, shall we be free?"

"Free! There are four bolts to the door, and another door at the end of the corridor."

"Who talks of forcing bolts?" said Dessaignes. "At what hour do they exercise us?"

"At six, as usual, I suppose."

"Yes; and once in the court-yard there is but one door to open."

"True; but the means of opening it?"

Dessaignes whipped up his mattrass, and displayed a pair of cavalry pistols (*pistolets d'arçon*) and a long dagger.

"Where—" began his friend.

"The barrister who came to see me yesterday conveyed the arsenal under his robe. Now, are these the keys to open a cage like ours?"

"None better! But I make one condition," said Desforges,—"that we are not to kill anyone."

"There will be no necessity. We shall go down armed to the court-yard; one of us will entice the concierge near the door, and the other will cover him with a pistol. A little determination is all we shall need."

Six o'clock struck, and the gaoler came to conduct the prisoners to the court-yard. They descended with their weapons in their pockets, and once in the yard Dessaignes was for losing not a moment. Their guard was the only attendant within sight, and as Desforges held him in talk, Dessaignes suddenly stepped behind and seized him by his coat-collar. The startled gaoler prepared to summon help, but before he could get out a word Dessaignes clapped a pistol to his forehead.

"Speak but one syllable," said he in a whisper, "and you will never utter another. Come, your keys!"

"Never!" replied the gaoler.

"Your soul to God, then, for your hour has come!"

The gaoler felt the muzzle at his forehead, and saw the glitter in the eyes of his captor. He hesitated.

"A second more, and I fire. Reflect!" said Dessaignes, quietly.

The gaoler's hand was already moving towards his keys when, all at once, his collar burst in the grip of Dessaignes, and he fell backwards. At the same instant, and by accident, Dessaignes' pistol exploded. The crack brought a dozen warders on the scene.

" Quick !" cried Dessaignes to his fellow-prisoner ; " up-stairs again !"

They gained their cell, Dessaignes shut and bolted the door, and together they barricaded it with all the furniture they could lay hands on.

" How much powder have we?" asked Desforges, under his breath.

"About four charges, but we shall not need it," replied Dessaignes. "Wait; I'll give them their answer."

The warders hammered vainly at the door.

"Gentlemen," called Dessaignes, "we may be induced to capitulate, but we shall not yield to force. You had better desist. We have powder enough here to blow the Abbaye to the gate of heaven."

A murmur of alarm arose on the other side of the door, and silence followed.

"You see!" observed Dessaignes, "these pious chaps will not mount unprepared into the presence of their Maker!"

The posse of warders was, in fact, withdrawn.

"But what shall we do next?" asked Desforges.

"For the present," said Dessaignes, "we shall wait. They will be wanting to make terms with us."

But the night passed, and no offer of capitulation was received. Two other things lacking were, supper in the evening and breakfast in the morning. The enemy had apparently changed their tactics; the blockade of the prisoners was complete, and so was the famine. The day wore on, and night came again; but not the paltriest offer of terms, nor a bowl of thin soup. The next day broke with a prospect as barren.

11

Towards noon a deputation was heard approaching.

"If you don't give us something to eat," cried Dessaignes, "sooner than die of hunger we will blow up the prison."

"To the gate of heaven. You have already said so," replied the voice of the governor.

"Then you mean to sacrifice all the innocent persons in the place?"

"Not at all! We have made our dispositions. The other prisoners have been removed. You two can ascend heavenwards as soon as you please."

Dessaignes glanced at his friend, and the expressions on both faces must have been interesting.

"To be candid," said Desforges, "my stomach sounds a parley."

"My own offers the same advice," said Dessaignes.

"Let us follow it," said Desforges.

"Gentlemen," called Dessaignes through the keyhole, "the war is over. Some bread, if you please, a bottle of wine, and a plate of meat. Those are our simple conditions of capitulation."

Agreed to; and the door was opened. A legal gentleman came from the King to hold an enquiry; but as Dessaignes' pistol had done no harm to anyone, and as the two prisoners had conducted their little campaign in a modest and inoffensive manner, no addition was made to their sentence,—which indeed was the equivalent of a "life" sentence at the present day. They were transferred to the Conciergerie, where their bonds were not too tight; their families kept them in money, and they received and dined their friends.

Desforges, the younger of the pair, seemed willing to accept his fate; but Dessaignes, whose blood was always tingling, ached for liberty. He watched his visitors out of the prison with hungry eyes. After all, the least cruel of prisons is a cage, and the wings will beat against the bars. Who knows what freedom means but the man who hears his lock turned nightly by some other man's hand?

One night, the two young prisoners had been allowed (an affair of a bribe) to give a dinner to some friends. The looseness of the rules permitted the presence also of the principal warders, whom the hosts took care to fill with wine. The table was surrounded by men in the sleep of liquor, and Dessaignes and Desforges slipped out, and presented themselves at the inner door of the prison. It was past midnight, and the turnkey was asleep in his chair. Dessaignes took a key from his belt at a venture, and tried the lock. It creaked, and the turnkey awoke. Dessaignes turned and stabbed him, and he slept in death. The first door was passed.

At the second door the turnkey was awake. So much the worse for him. Dessaignes' dagger was out and in again, and the turnkey dropped. Another key, another lock; the second door was passed.

At the third and outer door, the warder stood beyond the grille, safe, and shouted the alarm. The prisoners turned to retreat, but the third warder's cry had summoned another, who, quick to see the situation, slammed the first door to; and between the first door and the third Dessaignes and Desforges were trapped.

One warder murdered outright, a second on the point of death,—the fate of the assassin and his comrade could not be long in doubt. A prisoner gave evidence that he had been bribed to drug the first gate-warder; and both Dessaignes and Desforges were sentenced to be " broken alive." The decree was passed on the 1st of October, 1784, signed by Louis XVI., at the express request of two of his ministers, and carried out publicly in every terrible detail.

But darker scenes than this are preparing at the Abbaye. It was here that the Revolution may be said to have begun, and here that some of its worst crimes were perpetrated.

In June of 1789, there lay in the Abbaye certain soldiers of the *Gardes Françaises*, charged with refusing to obey their orders, out of sympathy with the National Assembly. Their situation in the prison became known, and a clamour arose for their release. "À l'Abbaye! à l'Abbaye!" was the cry; two hundred men set out from the Palais-Royal, and four thousand arrived at the prison gates. Every door of defence was staved in, and in less than an hour from the commencement of the attack, the democratic *Gardes* were released, and borne in triumph through Paris. This was one of the first demonstrations of the popular will. How quickly that will felt and appreciated its strength, and in what abandonment of cruel passion it was to find expression, most readers have learned. There is nothing in the annals of the world to be compared with the series of events in the Paris prisons in '92, to which history has given the

A STREET SCENE DURING THE MASSACRES.

CALIFORNIA

name of the September Massacres. In that deliberate slaughter, over one thousand men and women
perished, hewn in pieces in the prisons or at the
prison doors. The revolutionary committees had
packed the gaols with "suspected" persons, mostly
innocent of anything that could be laid to their
charge; and there they awaited such death as might
be decreed for them: salvation was all but hopeless.
There was talk at first of burning them *en masse* in
the prisons; then of thrusting all the prisoners into
the subterranean cells, and drowning them slowly by
pouring or pumping water on them. Assassination
pure and simple seems to have been resolved upon
"as a measure of indulgence." A mock form of trial
was held at all the prisons, that the butcheries might
be given an appearance of legality.

On Sunday, the 2d of September, '92, the barriers of
the city were closed, and early in the afternoon the
tocsin clanging from every steeple in Paris called up the
butchers to their work. Some thirty priests were far-
ing in five hackney carriages to the Abbaye prison,
and with them the slaughter was begun. One coach
reached the prison with a load of corpses; the occupants of the other four—Abbé Sicard excepted—
were killed as they alighted. Prisoners in the Abbaye
watched the carnage from behind their bars, and
said: "It will be our turn next."

To one of these prisoners, Journiac Saint-Méard,
one time captain in the King's light infantry, we shall
for the present attach ourselves. His *Agony of
Thirty-eight Hours* (*Mon agonie de trente-huit heures*),
much read at the beginning of the century, is amongst

the best of the contemporary records, and from that I
shall translate at some length.

This slow deliberate killing of the priests was done,
he says, amid a silence inexpressibly horrible; and as
each fell, a savage murmur went up, and a single
shout of *Vive la nation!* Women were there encouraging the men, and fetching jugs of wine for them.
Someone in the crowd pointed to the windows of the
prison and said: "There are plenty of conspirators
behind there; and not a single one must escape!"

Towards seven in the evening, two men with sabres,
their hands steeped in blood, entered the prison, and
began to carry out the prisoners for slaughter.

"The unfortunate Reding lay sick on his bed, and begged to
be killed there. One of the men hesitated, but his companion
said, '*Allons donc!*' and he slung him across his shoulder to
carry him out, and he was killed in the street.

"We looked at one another in silence, but presently the cries
of fresh victims renewed our agitation, and we recalled the words
of M. Chantereine as he plunged a knife into his heart : 'We are
all destined to be massacred.'

"At midnight, ten men armed with sabres, and preceded by
two turnkeys with torches, came into our dungeon, and ordered
us to range ourselves along the foot of our beds. They counted
us, and told us that we were responsible for one another, swearing that if one of us escaped, the rest should be massacred, without being heard by the President. The last words gave us a
little hope, for until then we had had no idea that we might be
heard before being killed.

"At two o'clock on Monday morning, we heard them breaking
in one of the prison doors, and thought at first that we were
about to be slaughtered in our beds, but were a little reassured
when we heard someone outside say that it was the door of
a cell which some prisoners had tried to barricade. We learned
afterwards that all who were found there had their throats cut.

" At ten, Abbé Lenfant, confessor of the King, and the Abbé de Chapt-Rastignac appeared in the pulpit of the chapel which served for our prison, and informing us that our last hour was approaching, invited us all to receive their blessing. An indefinable electric movement sent us all to our knees, and, with clasped hands, we received it. Those two white-haired old men with hands outstretched in prayer, death hovering above us, and on every side environing us : what a situation, what a moment, never to be forgotten ! "

Saint-Méard goes on to say how, during that morning, they discussed among themselves what was the easiest way in which to receive death. The slaughter in the streets never stopped, and some of them went from time to time to the window to observe and make reports.

" They reported that those certainly suffered the most and were the longest in dying who tried in any way to protect their heads, inasmuch as by so doing they warded off the sabre-cuts for a time, and sometimes lost both hands and arms before their heads were struck. Those who stood up with their hands behind their backs seemed to suffer least, and certainly died soonest. . . . On such horrible details did we deliberate."

Towards afternoon, overwhelmed by fatigue and anxiety, Saint-Méard threw himself on his bed and slept. He awoke after a comforting dream, which he felt certain was an omen of good fortune. But he and the others were now consumed by thirst ; it was twenty-six hours since they had had anything to drink. A goaler fetched them a jug of water, but could tell them nothing as to their fate.

The long agony of waiting drew to an end.

" At eleven at night, several persons armed with swords and pistols ordered us to place ourselves in single file, and led

us out to the second wicket, next to the place where the
trials were being held. I got as near as I could to one of
our guards, and managed little by little to engage him in conversation."

This man was an old soldier and a Provençal, and
when he found that Saint-Méard could talk the rude
patois of that district—scarcely intelligible in Paris—
he grew quite friendly, fetched him a tumbler of wine
to hearten him, and counselled him as to what he
should tell the judges. The Provençal let him stand
where he had a glimpse of the court, and he saw two
prisoners thrust to the bar and condemned almost
unheard; a moment later, their death-cries reached
his ears.

Two hours passed thus; it was one o'clock in the
morning, but still the judges heard, condemned, and
sent their victims out to die by sword and hatchet in
the street, where in places the blood was ankle deep,
and the dead lay in piles.

All at once Saint-Méard heard his name called.
"After having suffered an agony of thirty-seven
hours, an agony as of death itself, the door opened
and I was called. Three men laid hold of me, and
haled me in."

By the glare of torches,

"I saw that dreadful judgment bar, where liberty or death lay
for me. The President, in grey coat, sword at his side, stood
leaning against a table, on which were papers, an ink-stand,
pipes, and bottles. Around the table were ten persons, sitting or
standing, two of whom were in sleeveless jackets and aprons;
others were asleep, stretched on benches. Two men in shirts all
smeared with blood kept the door; an old turnkey had his hand
on the bolt . . .

" Here then stood I at this swift and bloody bar, where the best help was to be without all help, and where no resources of the mind were of avail that had not truth to rest upon.

" ' Your name, your calling ? ' said the President, and one of the judges added : ' The smallest lie undoes you.'

" ' My name,' I answered, ' is Journiac Saint-Méard ; I served twenty-five years as an officer in the army. I stand before you with the confidence of a man who has nothing to reproach himself with, and who is therefore not likely to utter falsehoods.'

" ' It will be for us to judge of that,' responded the man in grey."

The trial proceeded. Saint-Méard was accused of having edited the anti-revolutionary journal, *De la cour et de la ville*, but showed satisfactorily that he had not done so. Accused next of recruiting for the emigrants, at which there was an ominous murmur, " Gentlemen, gentlemen," pleaded the prisoner, " the word is with me at present, and I beg the President to maintain it for me,—I never needed it so sorely !" " That 's true enough !" laughed the judges, and the court began to shew itself more sympathetic. Saint-Méard, though, was not yet off the gridiron. " You tell us continually," said one impatient judge, " that you are not this and you are not that ! Be good enough then to tell us what you are."—" I was once frankly a Royalist." Another and louder murmur ; but the President put in : " We are not here to sit in judgment on opinions, but on their results " ; words of precious augury for the prisoner, who went on to say that he was well aware the old régime was done with, that there was no longer a Royalist cause, and that never had he been concerned in plots or Royalist conspiracies, for he had never in his life been con-

cerned in public affairs of any kind. He was a
Frenchman who loved his country above all things.

The questioning and cross-questioning came to an
end, and the President removed his hat.   " I can find
nothing to suspect in Monsieur.   What do you say ;
shall I release him ? " and the voice of the judges
was for liberty.   Thus finished, at two o'clock in the
morning, the " thirty-eight hours' agony " of Journiac
Saint-Méard.   He survived it some twenty years.

Alas for the hundreds upon hundreds whose agony
of yet longer duration finished under the arch of
pikes !

The escapes were not many.   Abbé Sicard, the
benevolent founder of the Deaf-and-Dumb Institute,
was set free on the earnest petition in writing of one
of his pupils. Beaumarchais, author of the *Mariage
de Figaro*, evaded the clutches of the judges after a
terrible period of suspense in the Abbaye.   The old
Marquis de Sombreuil was saved by his daughter.
She clung to his neck, imploring the cut-throats to
spare him to her.   " Say, then," said one of them,
dipping a cup into the blood at his feet : " Wilt thou
drink *this ?* " The brave girl gulped it down ; the mob
threw up their weapons with a roar of applause, and
opened out a way for both through their dripping
ranks.

But few fared as these did.   President Maillard, of
the grey coat, who was so well satisfied with Saint-
Méard, did not release, perhaps, one in fifty amongst
the accused at the Abbaye.   He is accused of " carrying about heads, and cutting up dead bodies."   Bil-
laud-Varennes went about from group to group of the

assassins who were massed in parties, encouraged
them in the name of the tribunal, and promised that
each man should be paid a louis for his " labour."

A contemporary sketch depicts him delivering a
speech on " a table of corpses " against the door of
the Abbaye : " Citizens, you are slaughtering the enemies of France. You are doing your duty." Indis-
criminate killing had been the legal order of the day.
There was no question of the guillotine during the
September massacres. Every citizen who could arm
himself was a Samson by privilege of the prison
judges ; and popular justice, called " severe justice
of the people," made the butcheries of September a
people's fête. It was not so much an act of patriotism
to assist in them as a dereliction of duty to hold aloof.
The " Septemberers " have been condemned as cannibals ; but they were common ratepayers of Paris to
whom the government of the day offered money to
kill as many " enemies of the republic " as should be
delivered to them. Most of these " enemies of the
republic " were persons to whom the republic was
scarcely known by name, and who asked only to be
ignored by it. They were killed in batches during
the September of '92, merely because they happened
to be thrust out at one particular door of their prison.
You came out at this door, and were received with
cheers ; you came out at the next door, and were
hacked in pieces. Which door it was, depended upon
the vote of the judges ; and this, as a rule, was the
determination of a moment. Saint-Méard's trial of
an hour was one of the longest.

The mere business of killing went forward until

numbers had lost their significance, and the lists of
the dead were but approximately reckoned. They
are all set down in black and white, and may still be
read—so many killed " in the heap (*en masse*), so many
" after judgment " (*après jugement*)—but the figures
have never been proved ; and one seeks in vain to
reckon the total, after the " three hundred families
belonging to the Faubourg St. Germain," who were
" thrown into the Abbaye in a night " ; and the " cart-
load of young girls, of whom the oldest was not
eighteen," and who, " dressed all in white in the
tumbril, looked like a basket of lilies." After this
batch, were guillotined all the nuns of the convent
of Montmartre.

Then there were the Swiss Guards, " remnants of
the 10th of August," to whom Maillard said : " Gentlemen, you may find mercy outside, but I am afraid
we cannot grant it to you here." The youngest of
them, " in a blue frock-coat," elected to go first. " Since
we must die," he said, " let me show the way " ; then,
dashing on his hat, he presented himself at the door
where the butchers stood ready to receive him ; a
double row of them,—sabre, bayonet, hatchet, or
pike in hand. For a moment he looked at them,
quite coolly ; then, seeing that all was prepared, he
threw himself between their ranks, and " fell beneath
a thousand blows."

When the killers began to flag, brandy mixed with
gunpowder was served to them. A woman passes,
carrying a basket of hot rolls ; they beg them of her,
and the bread, before being eaten, is " soaked in the
wounds of the still breathing victims." * The bri-

* Nougaret.

THE GALLANT SWISS.

gands of the Abbaye were not more than from thirty
to forty in number. Amongst them, says Nougaret,
" one youth, mounted on a post, distinguished himself
by his ferocity in killing. He said that he had lost
his two brothers on the 10th of August, and meant to
avenge them. He boasted of having cut down fifty
to his own weapon. Another brigand prided himself
on a total of two hundred ! "

Women looked on, adds the same authority, " sitting in carts on piles of dead bodies, like washerwo-
men on dirty linen. Others flung themselves upon
the corpses, and tore them with their teeth, danced
round them, and kicked them. Some of these Furies
cut off the ears of the dead, and pinned them on their
bosoms."

Some ten months after this carnage, tranquil amid
the din of the Terror, lies beautiful Charlotte Corday,
in her cell within the Abbaye walls. Her hour has
not yet come ; she bides it in perfect peace. By-and-
bye she will go to the Conciergerie, and thence the
next morning to the guillotine. Samson will lift the
fair head when he has struck it off, and smite the cheek
with his crimson paw, amid universal plaudits. " I
have found the sweetest rest here these two days,"
she writes from prison ; " I could not be better off,
and my gaolers are the best people in the world." A
memory of her lives as she " tripped smiling up the
steps of the scaffold, her hair cropped under a little
close-fitting cap, and wearing, by order of her judges,
a hideous red shirt, which descended to her feet. " She
blushed and frowned on the executioner when he
plucked the tippet from her bosom. Two moments
after, the knife fell on her."

After the Revolution, the Abbaye was again a military prison, and its subterranean dungeons were in existence in 1814. " The principal of these," wrote one who had inspected it, " is as horrible as any in Bicêtre ; sunk thirty feet below the level of the ground, and so fashioned that a man of average height could not stand up in it. One could scarcely remain here, says the doctor himself, more than four-and-twenty hours without being in danger of one's life."

The Abbaye was demolished in 1854.

CHAPTER IX.

THE LUXEMBOURG IN '93.

THIS was, above all others, the aristocratic prison of the Revolution. It was fitly chosen for the reception of that brilliant contingent of nobles, just ready to fly the country, whom the famous Law of the Suspects had routed from their hôtels in Paris. To confine them in the Luxembourg, converting that ancient and renowned palace into a dungeon of aristocrats, was in itself an apt stroke of vengeance on the part of the people. Few indeed of the historic dwellings of Paris could have put them more forcibly in mind of the tyrannies of kings and regents, of the splendid and licentious fêtes and orgies of princes and princesses of the blood, the cost of which was wrung from the lean pockets of those who were told to eat cake when there was no bread in the cupboard! Had not Marie de Médicis passed here, and Gaston de France, and Duchesse de Montpensier, and Elizabeth d'Orléans, who gave it to Louis XIV., and Louis XVI., who gave it, in 1779, to Monsieur his brother, who after the days of storm and terror was to reign, not too satisfactorily, as Louis XVIII.? Was it not here that Duchesse de Berri, in the early years of the eighteenth century, held those surprising revels the

details of which may be read only in secret and un-
published memoirs? Sedate historians merely hint
at them.* And, palace though it was, the revolutionary judges might have found ready to their hands
at the Luxembourg, bars, bolts, fetters and dungeons
enow. For that "symbolic hierarchy" of palace,
cloister, and prison, proper to all princely and noble
dwellings of the old régime, had existed at the Luxembourg; and during long years the penal justice of
priest and monk had passed that way.

This was the place to which the noble and courtly
suspects were conveyed by hundreds in August, 1793.
One can imagine, though but very faintly, with what
feelings they resigned themselves into the hands of
concierge Benoît. Their King had been decapitated;
their Queen, a prisoner elsewhere, was expecting her
husband's fate. They knew how little their sovereign's life had weighed in the people's balance; was
it likely that theirs would be of greater weight?
Judgment and death disquieted them.

"A diverting spectacle in its way," wrote one sar-
castic prisoner, "to see arriving in a miserable hack-
ney-coach two marquises, a duchess, a marchioness,
and a count; all ready to faint on alighting, and all
seized with the megrims on entering." Dames of
great rank came with their brisk femmes de chambre,
old noblemen with their valets, youths separated from
their governors and tutors,—children even; whole

---

* "Dans son Palais-Royal, au Palais de Luxembourg où demeurait la duchesse de B——, se célébraient le plus ordinairement ces parties de débauche.
L'on y voyait les acteurs figurer quelquefois avec un costume qui consistait à
n'en point avoir; et les princes, les princesses, se livrer sans pudeur aux désor-
dres les plus dégoûtans."—Dulaure, vol. viii., p. 187.

battalions of the most distinguished suspects, the
very flower of the aristocracy of France. The dungeons were not requisitioned, but hasty preparations
had been made for them. Under concierge Benoît's
polite and sympathetic conduct, they mounted the
splendid staircase—up which had flitted in a costume
of no weight at all the unblushing guests of De Berri
—to the splendid chambers, picture-gallery, ball-room,
salon, dining-room, and the whole sumptuous suite,
which rude partitions of naked lath and timber had
converted into some semblance of prison lodgings.
The wide windows had been armed with iron bars,
and guards were posted at every story.

The gallant company of French suspects found
some of the chambers in the occupation of a party of
English suspects, who had been placed under arrest
some weeks earlier, "as a response to the insults
offered by the English government to the Republic"
(*pour répondre aux insultes dirigées par le gouverne-
ment anglais contre la république*). Amongst them
were Miss Maria Williams, who had gone to France,
pen in hand, to see what liberty, equality, and fraternity were like in practice (and who returned to write
one of the dullest books on record); and Thomas
Paine, who was studying "The Rights of Man" under
alarming aspects.

This was the first Battue; the royalist suspects of
Republican France were the second.

The salons of the palace, made into prison chambers, were named afresh. Miss Williams and her
sister occupied the chamber of *Cincinnatus;* hard by
were the chambers of *Brutus, Socrates,* and *Solon;*

12

and the derisive name of *Liberty* was given to the
room in which nobles under special guard were confined in the strictest privacy.   High personages,
whose titles but a little while before might have
made their gaolers tremble, were lodged in every
quarter of the palace.   In this cabinet were Marshal
de Mouchy and his wife, "rigorous observers of
courtly etiquette"; a little way off, in chambers no
bigger than prison cells, the Comte de Mirepoix, the
Marquis de Fleury, President Nicolai, M. de Noailles,
and the Duc de Lévi.

Parlous in a high degree as the situation was for
all of them, they did not at this date suffer any
special discomfort, the deprivation of liberty excepted.   Their captors were satisfied at having them
under lock and key, and did not insult their captivity.   A gossiping history, which may be history or
fable, describes a visit of Latude to one of the political prisoners, a certain M. Roger.   The great pris-
on-breaker laughed the Luxembourg to scorn: "A
prison? You call this a prison, *mon cher?*   I call it
a *bonbonnière*, a *boudoir!*"

Indeed, to be precise, the Luxembourg was not exactly a Bastille.   There were sad and evil days in
store for these suspects, but they were days as yet
distant.   For the present, heart-questionings apart, it
was not too dismal a confinement ; and rumour went
so far as to hint that there were relaxations of an
evening which would not have discredited the character of the Luxembourg of history.

The palace-prison might be compared to an unsea-
worthy vessel in which one shipped for a compulsory

voyage, in dangerous waters, with a doubtful chart. One might reach port, or founder in mid-ocean. Meanwhile, there was no choice but to sail ; and the rotten ship had good berths and was well-provisioned.

The Luxembourg was not as yet governed as a prison, the suspects of the Revolution were under no extraordinary restraint, there was no surveillance, and the sentries allowed the prisoners to come and go as they pleased within the wide walls of the palace and its gardens. Their friends called upon them, and they wrote and received letters. One of them had a dog in his chamber which used to fetch and carry messages and packets between the " prison " and free Paris. A confectioner outside was allowed to furnish whatever was ordered for the tables, and the rich paid ungrudgingly for the poor. Plain *sans-culottes* came in as suspects with the nobles, and were regularly fed by them.

" How many are you feeding ? " asked one marquis of another.

" Twelve ; and pretty hungry ones."

" Well, what do you give them ? "

" Meat at dinner always, and dessert."

" That 's not so bad. My fellows want meat twice a day, and coffee once a week."

A strained position made matters easier. The nobles kept apart from the plebs, and took their share of snubs from the " common patriots " whom their purses kept in food ; but a sense of general danger minimised the hostilities of class. Succour, whenever needed, was never lacking. The regulation mattress for the beds is described as " of about the thickness of an omelette " and the bolster " of

the leanest " ; but bolsters and mattresses ran short in
a month or two, and the men stripped themselves of
coats and waistcoats to make beds for the women. It
was a camp or caravanserai, with the style of a court.

The aristocrats assembled of an evening in a common room which was always called the salon, pow-
dered and dressed in the fashion, saluted one another
by the titles which they had ceased to own, and
disputed precedence as at Versailles. Visits were
paid and returned, and never was a fool's paradise so
scrupulously ordered. It was admirable in its way ;
the old order would die by rule.

The prisoners were fortunate in their concierge,
Benoît. A veteran of seventy, gentle and genial, with
a heart as fine as the manners of his royalist prisoners,
he smoothed all paths, and ushered in a new-comer to
a lodging of four bare walls and a naked floor with
an apology that transformed it into a royal boudoir.
He seemed to know all his guests as they arrived,
and placed them where he thought they would find
the easiest entertainent and the most congenial
company. He played the part of master of cere-
monies, and put each guest into his proper niche.
In Benoît's hands, the marquis who had arrived without his valet found himself handling the broom, fetching water, and taking his turn at the spit, as if the
custom of a lifetime had used him to those offices.
It was Benoît who learned at once what money a
prisoner had brought in with him, and who saved the
needy suspect the humiliation of begging his meals,
by a whisper in the ear of a good-natured noble.

By-and-bye, the suspects had the gratification of

knowing that their perils, present and to come, were shared by the enemy himself. There arrived as a prisoner one evening a president of the revolutionary tribunal. It was one Kalmer, a German Jew, and reputed millionaire (he had an income of about £8000), who had been active in filling the chamber-cells of the Luxembourg. He presented himself in sabots and a costume of the shabbiest simplicity, and his reception was of the coolest. He displayed from the first a voracious appetite, and every day an ass laden with provisions was brought for him to the palace door. The ex-president seemed well disposed to end his days eating and drinking in the Luxembourg, and was not a little shocked on receiving the news that he had been sentenced to death, " for conspiring secretly with the enemy abroad." He went to the guillotine without a benediction.

Came next the much more notable Chaumette, ex-sailor, ex-priest, and recently Procureur of the Commune, in which capacity he had been foremost in demanding and promoting the Law of the Suspects. He was as chapfallen as a wolf in a snare, but he did not escape the mordant jests of the company. It was Chaumette who had declared in the Chamber that " you might almost recognise a suspect by the look of him." He himself was recognised on the instant.

" Sublime Procureur !" exclaimed one, " thanks to that famous requisition of yours, I am suspect, thou art suspect, he is suspect ; we are suspect, you are suspect, they are all suspect "—which indeed was the case, for at that date, as Carlyle says, " if suspect of

nothing else, you may grow," as came to be a saying,
" Suspect of being Suspect."

One night, the wildest rumour circulated in the
prison.   It was said that Danton, Camille Desmoulins, Hérault de Séchelle, Lacroix, Philippeaux, and
others, the head and front of the party of the Moderates, had been arrested by Robespierre's order, and
were to be sent forthwith to the Luxembourg.   It was
even so ; and the next night the news sped through
every corridor of the palace that Danton and his fellows had arrived, and were with the concierge.   The
prisoners swarmed to the reception room, and gratified their eyes with that unlooked-for spectacle.   The
brilliant Camille, whose young wife was a prisoner
with him, was denouncing the tribunal in a storm of
passion ; Danton bade him be calm : " When men act
with folly," he said, " one should know how to laugh
at them."   Then, recognising Thomas Paine, he said :
" What you have done for the liberty of your country,
I have tried to do for mine.   I have been less fortunate than you !   They will send me to the scaffold ;
well, I shall go there cheerfully enough !"   Camille
Desmoulins had brought with him some rather melan-
cholly reading—Hervey's *Meditations* and Young's
Night Thoughts.   The merry Réal, who had arrived
a day or two earlier, exclaimed against these works :
" Do you want to die before your time ?   Here, take
my book, *La Pucelle d'Orléans ;* that will keep your
spirits up !"

General Dillon, who was of the earliest batch of
suspects, was amongst the first to visit the imprisoned
Moderates in the chamber which had been set apart

for them.*   Camille was still fuming, and Danton playing the part of moderator.   Lacroix was debating with himself whether he should cut his hair, or wait till Samson dressed it for him.   Another of the party, Fabre d'Eglantine, lay sick in bed, tenderly nursed by his comrades.   He was saved for the scaffold, for the turn of the Moderates was not long delayed.   At the brief trial of the party, Danton and Camille showed a characteristic front to their judges.   " You ask my name !" thundered the Titan of the Revolution.   " You should know it !   It is Danton, a name tolerably familiar in the Revolution.   As for my abode, it will soon be the Unknown, but I shall live in the Pantheon of history !"   " My age," answered Camille, " is the age of the good *sans-culotte* Jesus Christ ; an age fatal to Revolutionists !"   Returning to the Luxembourg after condemnation, he said to Benoît : " I am condemned for having shed a tear or two over the fate of other unfortunates.   My only regret is that I was not able to be of better service to them."   Camille wrote with one of the wittiest pens of his day, and busied himself in the Luxembourg with a comedy called *The Orange*, the model of which was Sheridan's *School for Scandal*.   He had evoked in a greater degree than any other of the Moderates the sympathies of the suspects in the Luxembourg, and up to the last there was a general belief in the prison that both he and Danton would be saved by the intervention of Robespierre.   But Robespierre could not, if he would.   Executioner Samson received in due

---

* This general," says Nougaret, in his dry way, "drank a great deal.   In his sober moments, he played at trictrac."—Vol. ii., p. 61.

course his order to proceed with them—a document drawn up in the style and almost in the terms of a commercial invoice—and made his own note in pencil at the foot : " One cart will be enough."   Even at the steps of the guillotine, Camille turned to denounce the crowd.   " Leave that canaille !" said Danton, quietly ; " we are done with it."   To the headsman Danton said, as he stood on the scaffold : " You must show my head to the people.   It is a head worth looking at."

This hetacomb of the Moderates sent a thrill of fear through the Luxembourg.   Whose turn next ?

Up to this date, the principal political prisoners had enjoyed unrestrained communication with their friends outside, and General Dillon had private news twice a day from the tribunal.   Two days after the bloody despatch of the Moderates, the prisoners of the Lux-embourg were confined to their chambers.   Evening receptions and parties of trictrac (in one's sober inter-vals) were suppressed ; communication of every kind was forbidden ; and the journals of the day, which had been freely circulated in the prison, were no longer admitted.   The prisoners awaited " in silence and fear " the explanation of this rigorous *consigne*.

It was the outcome of the first of those rumours of a " plot in the prison."   A certain Lafflotte, a suspect of low origin, denounced General Dillon and one Simon (nicknamed in the prison Simon-Limon) as the author of a secret conspiracy.   The revolutionary journals were full of the affair, but it was never very clearly explained, nor, for that matter, was any pre-cise· explanation ever offered of other prison plots so-called. There were pretended discoveries and expositions of plots in the Luxembourg, Saint-Lazare, Bicêtre, and the Carmes. That the prisoners of the Revolution in all these goals were eager to recover their liberty, is a statement which may pass without dispute; and it is no less natural to suppose that they would have seized upon any means that offered a reasonable hope of escape. But the truth seems to have been, and it is rather curious in the circumstances (though the presence of so many women and children would have multiplied the difficulties) that no concerted efforts to break prison were ever made by the suspects. Statements or rumours to the effect that they were planning a forcible release for themselves, and that, once out of prison, they intended to put Paris to the sword, should have been regarded as quite too silly for credence. Surely those poor aristocrats had given proof enough of their weakness! Of all the enemies of the Republic, they were the least capable of harming it.

Dillon and Simon, nevertheless, were delivered over to Samson. The terror had begun for the prisoners of the Luxembourg.

An unexpected calamity succeeded. Benoît, most humane and benevolent of concierges, was arrested. It was as if the father had been snatched from his family, and the suspects were inconsolable; they had lost their best friend within the prison. The tribunal acquitted him, but he did not return to his post. Benoît had two successors at the Luxembourg within a space of weeks, the second of whom was a man who would have been regarded with terror in any

French prison at that epoch. This was Guiard, who had been fetched expressly from Lyons, where he had acquired a hideous celebrity as gaoler of the " Cellar of the Dead," the name bestowed upon the dungeon or black-hole in which the victims of the *commission populaire* passed their last hours between condemnation and execution.

A few days after the removal of Benoît, the prisoners awoke one morning to find that sentinels had been posted at every door. A stolid police officer named Wilcheritz, a Pole by birth, who had been nominated to a principal post in the prison, came round with the order that there was to be no communication between the suspects. They, believing that they were on the eve of another September massacre, prepared to bid each other farewell. On this occasion, however, it was merely a question of stripping them of their belongings. Money, paper notes, rings, studs, pins, shoebuckles, penknives, razors, scissors, keys, were gathered in cell after cell, and deposited in a heap in one of the larger rooms; no notes or inventory being taken. Wilcheritz and his inquisitors were the objects of some pleasantries which, it is said, "annoyed them greatly." One prisoner, after handing over his writing-case was asked for his ring. "What!" said he, "isn't the stationery enough? Are you setting up in the jewellery line too?" Another, when it was pointed out to him that he had retained the gold buckles of his garters, replied : " I think, citizens, you had better undress me at once." They entered the cell of the playwright Parisau. " Citizens," said the author, " I am really distressed; you have come too late. I had three hundred livres here, but another citizen has just relieved me of them. I hope that you will have better luck elsewhere. They tell me, however, that you are leaving us fifty livres apiece, and as I have only just five-and-twenty, no doubt you will make up the sum to me." "Oh no, citizen," returned the stolid Pole.—"Ah! I see. You are merely 'on the make,' citizen. It is unfortunate in that case that there are gentry in the prison more active than you. However, if you follow the other citizen, I dare say you will catch him up, and then you can settle accounts with him. You are the ocean, citizen, and all the little tributaries will join themselves to you."

In another apartment it was proposed to carry off his silver coffee-pot from a prisoner, who, to preserve it, explained that it was "not exactly silver," but "some sort of English metal." That was possible, observed Wilcheritz, for he had one just like it himself. "Ah!" returned the prisoner, "now that you mention it, I remember there was another like mine in the prison!"

Suspects belonging to the working-classes,—tailors shoemakers, engravers, and the like—were allowed to retain the tools of their crafts; and the barbers received their razors in the morning, returning them to the gaolers at night.

To all requests addressed to him by the prisoners, imploring information as to their fate, the phlegmatic Pole made answer: "Patience! Justice is just. This durance will not endure for ever. Patience!"

Patriots and nobles were now massed in hundreds

within the same walls, shared the same chambers, and
were fed from the same kitchen ; and all alike were
now in the same state of siege. What news penetrated within the palace-prison was not the most
inspiriting ; the tumbrils were moving steadily to the
guillotine, and in the copies of the *Courrier Republi-
cain* which were smuggled into the Luxembourg, the
principal intelligence was the " Judgment of the
Revolutionary Tribunal, which has condemned to
death " thirty, forty, fifty, or sixty " conspirators."

Word was passed that the *commissions populaires*
were to take in hand the cases of the suspects, which
was more comforting to the patriots than to the
nobles ; but the days crept on, and nothing happened.

The prisoners amused themselves by teasing
Wilcheritz, a fair butt for raillery, who carried out his
orders imperturbably, but was never a bully. The
day came of the " Feast of the Supreme Being," and
citizen Wilcheritz honoured it with a radiant suit.
His big feet were cramped in a pair of new shoes
with the finest of silver buckles. One of the
despoiled suspects fancied or pretended that he
recognised the buckles, and a whisper went round.
The prisoner whose coffee-pot had been appropriated
came to the rescue. " Citizens," he said, " those
buckles don't look to me like silver. They are *a sort
of English metal.*" " They have been in my family
for three generations, citizens, I assure you. I had
them long before the visitation," stammered Wilcheritz. " The visitation " had grown to be the polite
mode of reference to the act of spoliation. " Citizen,"
said the defender of Wilcheritz, " your answer is

complete.   You told us the other day that no good
Republican should stoop to wear jewellery, but no
citizen here would have the heart to claim your shoebuckles."

The coming of Guiard as concierge (*cet homme
féroce* is Nougaret's dismissal of him) quenched all
pleasantries, and made the palace-prison a prison
complete.   Two suspects hopeless of being brought
to the bar, had committed suicide by throwing themselves from their windows; Guiard ordered that no
prisoner should approach within a yard of his window.
The sentries had orders to enter every cell and
chamber, with drawn sabres, at midnight, rouse the
occupants from their beds, and count them.   At
intervals, all through the night, they were to hail one
another loudly in every corridor : *Sentinelles, prenez-
garde à vous !* " so that there should be no sleep for the
prisoners.   No letters were allowed to pass out from
or into the prison ; and no visitors were admitted.

Meals could no longer be sent in from the confectioner's, and a common table was established.   At
noon precisely, the bell was struck for dinner, and
the nine hundred prisoners were ranged in the
corridors, each with his *couvert* under his arm, a
wooden fork, knife, and spoon.   They descended by
batches to the dining-room, marching two and two,
and this singular procession was half an hour on its
journey.   Arriving at the dining-room, three hundred
took their places at the table, three hundred waited
with their backs to the wall, and three hundred cooled
their heels in the passage.

At this time, all money and paper notes, having

been taken from them, the suspects were receiving an allowance of about two shillings a day, though it is not quite clear what they were to spend it on.

At the distribution one morning, Guiard said significantly: "There won't be quite so many to receive it to-morrow!" That same night, a long row of tumbrils stopped under the walls of the Luxembourg, and one hundred and sixty-nine prisoners were dragged from bed to fill them.

It was the first seizure on the grand scale, and in a few minutes the whole prison was in confusion and panic terror. The warders were heard going from door to door, and calling the names of the victims; one from one chamber, two, three, or four from another. Here were sobbings and loud wails, and clinging embraces; husbands and fathers trying to animate the weeping women whom they were leaving; priests called for in the dark to bless together for the last time two who were to be separated. No one dared descend to the great gallery, but elsewhere there were frightened rushings to and fro; meetings and partings in darkened doorways and half-illumined corridors; friend seeking friend, and women and girls imploring with streaming eyes for leave to say good-bye again to the lost ones who were already seated in the tumbrils. Happy were the friends and whole families who were despatched together. In one moving instance, weeping was turned into joy. A family of father, mother, and two daughters were divided; the younger daughter was left behind, almost distracted; her name was not upon the list. Presently came another warder with another list.

The girl started from the empty bed on which she had thrown herself, snatched the list from the gaoler, and read her own name there. Carrying the sheet, and with a face beaming as if a free pardon had been handed to her, she ran down the corridor, crying: "Mamma, I have found my name! See, it is here! Now we shall die together!" So by minutes, of which each minute was an æon, that night of horror was exhausted, and at day-break the long file of tumbrils dragged scaffold-wards.

Not less wretched was the situation of the hundreds who remained. Racking fears were their portion day and night; death was in their hearts. Every evening a new list came in. The "ferocious" Guiard had a very suitable assistant in a turnkey called Verney, whose duty is was to read out the roll of the proscribed, and who did it with a terrible art, dallying with the syllables of a name, and pausing to watch the strained faces around him. Sometimes instead of reading the list, he would pass it round, when the struggle to reach it prolonged the agony. An eyewitness of the scene has left a description:

"In the evening, those prisoners who were allowed to do so as-sembled in one of the large rooms and played, or made a pretence at playing, vingt-et-un, chess, and other games. While these were in progress, the terrible Verney, head turnkey, appeared, bringing what was called the lottery list. This little paper contained the names of those who were to go the same night to the Conciergerie, and the next morning to the guillotine. The fatal list went round amid the most pitiful silence. Those who found their names on it rose pale and trembling from the table, embraced and bade farewell to their friends, and left us. Verney would then pro-duce the evening paper, where we read the list of the day's dead,—the dead who had been at the table with us the night before ! I was playing chess one evening with General Appremont, General Flers looking on. I had just put him in check when the summons came for him, and Verney carried him off. Flers took the vacant seat, with a pretence of finishing the game, when he too was called. This officer had proved his courage in battle a score of times, but I have never seen terror so horribly painted on any human countenance. His whole visage seemed undone, and when he struggled to his feet, he could scarcely support himself. He gave me his hand, speechless, and staggered from the room." *

In the Luxembourg as in the other prisons at this epoch there were miserable creatures, also under lock and key, who made a kind of trade of denouncing their fellows. The Luxembourg had seven of these spies, who assisted in preparing the lists, " embellishing " them, as they said, with details which they had scraped together or invented in the prison. These wretches enjoyed and boasted of the terror which they inspired ; and the chief of them, Boyaval (a tailor by trade, who had served in and deserted from the Austrian army), used to say that anyone who looked askance at him in the Luxembourg might count on spending the next night in the Conciergerie ! Scarcely a suspect whom Boyaval denounced escaped the guillotine, and one night he scandalised the prison by offering love to a young widow of a day, whose husband he had sacrificed. The husband was an artist, who had painted portraits in the Luxembourg of nobles who had reason to suppose that they would leave their families no other legacy. He was accused of assembling the nobles in his room, and

* Les Prisons de l' Europe.

plotting with them against the Republic. As lightly as this, during the Terror, were lives devoted to Samson, in every prison in Paris. The "plots" were not credible, and it is impossible at this date to suppose that they were ever credited; but Paris was still obedient to the word of the Danton whom it had guillotined, that "one must strike terror into the aristocrats"; and these "prison plots" served to fill the tumbrils to the last.

An epidemic of sickness came to crown the sufferings of the dwindling population of the Luxembourg. They were reduced almost to the last extremity of despair. They had no news from without, except the nightly list of the proscribed, and the nightly journal, with its monotonous tale of executions. Between morning and evening, there was no other event, except the swift good-bye at night to the friends or relatives whose names were mumbled out by Verney. A silence almost unbroken had settled on the prison; parties of ghosts assembled at dinner, and whispered together in the common-room until bedtime. Their misery culminated in the epidemic of sickness. The rations had been cut down to one meal a day, and Guiard was the caterer. The wasted prisoners sent back their rotten meat to the kitchen, and lived on bread and thin soup. Half the prison fell ill; poisoned or underfed. Doctor's aid could be had only on a warrant from the police, and applications remained a week or a fortnight at the bureau. Samson had a rival in diseased or exhausted nature; and Guiard's requiem for the dead was an unvarying formula: " Peste! there 's another lost to the guillotine!"

13

This agony of a season was dissolved in an hour. The "walking corpses" *(les cadavres ambulans)* of the Luxembourg were recalled to life by the revolution of the 9th of Thermidor. It came with the din of the tocsin, and the beat to arms which, until that day had gathered the rabble to follow the tumbrils to the guillotine. The tocsin continued, and the rattle of the drums increased, and the trampling of feet towards the Luxembourg grew louder. The remnant of the suspects gathered in the gallery : the last massacre was to come. No! The doors were burst open ; a shout went up. Robespierre had fallen. The Reign of Terror was finished.

CHAPTER X.

THE BASTILLE.

" . . . if once it were left in the power of any, the highest, magistrate to imprison arbitrarily whomever he or his officers thought proper (as in France is daily practised by the Crown), there would soon be an end of all other rights and immunities."—BLACKSTONE.

AFTER enduring for centuries an oppression as rigorous and as cruel as any nation had ever been subjected to, this idea dawned, almost in an hour, upon the mind of France. It did not matter that the King who occupied the throne at this time was, if not at all a wise one, at least one of the most humane, and distinctly the best intentioned, and the only French sovereign who had ever really cared to soften the lot of his prisoners. He did not soften their lot in the least, because he was weak and indolent, and in the hands of the least honest of his ministers ; but his predecessors, almost without exception, had lent their efforts or their sanction to the support of that old malignant policy, descended from the feudal times, that prison was properly a place of torment. The quick aspiration of liberty, born at last of a wretchedness that was past enduring, inflamed the heart of the whole nation. It took Paris, as it were, by the throat. What thing in Paris opposed itself most visibly to the "natural rights" and liberty of man? Paris said: The Bastille! Up then, and let the Bastille go down. They went there, a very ordinary crowd of rioters, and overturned it. The Bastille, which the superstitious fears of ages had thought impregnable, fell like an old ruined house (which it was) in a midsummer gust. But the fall of it shook Europe to its foundations, and before the dust had vanished, it was seen that the Bastille had carried with it the throne of France, and every shred and vestige of the system which that throne represented.

This then must have been the most terrible prison in Europe? Not at all. It was the most renowned; and, as a prison, no other name is ever likely to be greater than, or as great as, the Bastille; but at the time of its destruction it was no more than the shadow of its ancient self, and at no period of its existence was it a worse place than any other of the old State prisons of France. Vincennes was quite as cruel a hold as the Bastille had ever been; there were, I think, uglier dens in the Châtelet and in Bicêtre; and the torture-chamber of the Conciergerie had perhaps witnessed more inhuman spectacles than any other prison in Paris.

But when, in July, 1789, a prison was to be destroyed, as the chief symbol of the tyranny of kings, it was upon the Bastille that Paris marched, as by instinct. Why was this prison abhorred above all the rest? Mainly because what had once been a fact had survived as a tradition,—that the master of the Bastille was the master of France; and the master of the

THE BASTILLE.

Bastille was, of course, the King. In its beginnings, the Bastille was merely a gate of Paris, as Newgate was originally nothing more than the New Gate of London. It came next to be a very common little fort, for the defence of the Seine against the English and other pirates. But it grew by-and-bye to be a stout castle and prison, over against the royal residence of Vincennes; and when, on the approach of an insurgent force, the King could signal from his window at Vincennes to his commandant in the Bastille, just opposite, and the guns of both places could be primed in time, the plain between them was secure. The Bastille came thus to hold a place quite distinct from that of any other prison in Paris, and one which threatened in a much higher degree the liberties of the citizens. It was considered impossible of capture; and while the King's standard shook over the great towers of the Bastille, Paris and France were secure to him; and, in the popular imagination, his principal stronghold was also his principal prison. In this point of view, and it was the popular point of view, the Bastille was a double menace to Paris. It was the King's best means of keeping importunate subjects at arm's length, and it was also the most redoubtable of the prisons he could shut them in. Both ideas were to some extent erroneous. The Bastille, considered as a fort, was never as formidable as its name; and, as a prison, the Kings of France seldom favoured it above the Dungeon of Vincennes.

But let us seek now to put the Bastille in its proper and exact place amongst the historic gaols of France. In recent years, one or two French writers of distinction, and others of no distinction whatever, have come forward as the apologists of this too famous keep, who would persuade us that it was not only a very tolerable sort of prison, but even, in cases, a rather desirable place of retirement, for meditation, and philosophical pursuits. M. Viollet-le-Duc has assured us, quite gravely, that the famed *oubliettes* (the bottoms of which were shaped like sugar loaves, so that prisoners might have no resting-place for their feet) were merely ice-houses! It is not denied that these cells existed, and those who care to believe that a mediæval architect built them under the towers of the Bastille as store-chambers for ice to cool the governor's or the prisoners' wine, are entirely welcome to do so.   These were amongst the places of torment in which Louis XI. kept the Armagnac princes, who were taken out twice a week to be scourged in the presence of Governor l'Huillier, and "every three months to have a tooth pulled out."   The author of *The Bastille Unveiled* has attempted to explain away the iron cage in which the same King confined Cardinal Balue for eleven years, and which, I believe, is still in existence.   An English apologist (whose work extends to two bulky volumes) says that "prisoners were less harshly treated in the Bastille than in other French and English prisons"; that "the accusations of prisoners having been tortured in the Bastille have no serious foundation"; that the majority of the chambers "were comfortable enough"; that one of the courtyards "resembled a college playground, in which prisoners received their friends, and indulged in all kinds of games."   We hear of tables which

were so sumptuously furnished (three bottles of wine
a day, amongst other comforts) that the prisoners
complained to the governor that he was feeding them
too well. We are presented with printed rules to
show how carefully the sick were to be attended to,
and what were to be their ghostly ministrations
in their final hours. We are told, without a smile, that
it was really not so easy for people to get into the Bastille as the world in general has supposed ; and that,
once there, their situation was not too helpless, inasmuch as the governor must present to the minister
every day a written report upon the conditions of the
prison. Under the pen of this or the other indulgent
writer, the horrors of the Bastille have vanished as by
process of magic. Unfortunately, the horrors are,
with quite unimportant exceptions, facts of history.

The government of the Bastille was precisely similar to the government of the other State prisons of
France. Edicts notwithstanding, these prisons were
practically the *property* of their successive governors.
To this unwritten rule the Bastille was not an exception. The governor in possession at this or that epoch
might or might not be the creature of the minister
through whose interest he had bought his office at a
sometimes exorbitant price ; it was, at all events, understood that, whatever limits were set to his authority,
he was fully entitled to get back his purchase money ;
and this, as had been shown, he could seldom do except by villainously ill-using his prisoners. There
were governors who did not do this, and then indeed came a blessed period for the prisoners. Then
food was good and plentiful, the faggots were not

stinted in the fire-place, the beds were not rotten and
lousy, the foul linen went to the wash, and the threadbare clothes were replaced, the cells were made proof
against wind and rain, the governor was prompt in
looking into grievances, and all went as well for the
prisoner as it was possible that it should go in a gaol
of old Paris. But when a new Pharaoh arose, who
was avaricious, and a tyrant, and a bully, and who had
bought his prison as a speculative investment, then
the clouds gathered again, and the wind blew again
from the east, and the old tribulations began afresh.
Now, as the records of all the French prisons of history leave no doubt as to the fact the bad governors
were many, and the good governors were few, and
that within his prison walls the governor was only less
than omnipotent, readers of these pages will not expect often to find prisoners of the Bastille regaling
themselves with three bottles of wine a day, or asking
to have their tables ordered more plainly, or receiving
the free visits of their friends, or playing at " all kinds
of games " in courtyards resembling college play-
grounds. Sprigs of the nobility and young men of
family, shut up for a time for making too free with
their money, or for running away with a ballet-dancer,
had perhaps not too much to complain of in the Bastille ; there were certain prisoners of rank, too, who
came off lightly ; and now and again there were other
prisoners who enjoyed what were called the " liberties
of the Bastille," and who were allowed a restricted in-
tercourse. But the general rules for the keeping and
conduct of prisoners in the Bastille were of the severest
description, and they were carried out for the most

part with inflexible rigour.   Privations and humilia-
tions of all kinds were inflicted on them ; and redress
for injuries, or for insults, or for mean and illegal annoyances, the outcome of the governor's spleen, was
not more easy to obtain in the Bastille than in the
Dungeon of Vincennes.

The statement that "it was not so easy to enter
into the Bastille" is from Ravaisson, the compiler of
the *Archives de la Bastille*.   He gives his reasons,
which are sufficiently curious.   Incarcerations, says
Ravaisson, were accomplished with the utmost care,
and the Government insisted upon the most stringent precautions, inasmuch as, "acting with absolute
authority, it felt the danger of an uncontrolled responsibility."   Sore indeed would be the task of
proving by example that the absolute monarchy had
many compunctions on this score, when tampering
with the liberties of its subjects.   "Extreme care
was taken to avoid errors and abuses" in effecting
incarcerations in the Bastille ; and the great safeguard
was that "each *lettre de cachet* was signed by the King
himself, and countersigned by one of his ministers !"
One need go no further than this.   M. Ravaisson
spent from fifteen to twenty years in studying and
arranging the archives of the Bastille, and his knowledge of his subject must have been immense.   Was
this the writer from whom one would have expected
the suggestion that the King and his minister, in
signing a *lettre de cachet*, took care to assure themselves that no injustice was being done, and made
themselves immediately and personally responsible
for the guilt of the victim whom it was to consign to

captivity in the Bastille? Leave aside the cases in
which the document was used to imprison a person
in order that charges or suspicions might afterwards
be inquired into,—though there are countless instances
to show, (1) that no proper investigation was held,
and (2), that the clearest proofs of innocence were
not always sufficient to procure the prisoner's liberation. But what shall be said of the cases, infinitely
more numerous than these, in which no charge was
ever formulated, and in which none could have been
formulated, save some fictitious one inspired by private greed, hatred, or vengeance? Where in these
cases was that "greatest care" which "was taken to
prevent errors and abuses"? Kings and their ministers sent to the Bastille and other prisons many thousands of prisoners who had no justice, and who never
expected justice. But these same "closed letters,"
duly signed and sealed, were the instruments of imprisoning hundreds of thousands of other persons—
to whom life was sweet and liberty was dear—in
whose affairs neither King nor minister had the most
shadowy interest, and whose very names most probably they had never heard of. During the reign of
one King, Louis XV., one hundred and fifty thousand *lettres de cachet* were issued. For how many of
those was Louis himself responsible? They carried
his signature, but is it necessary at this day to say
that the King wrote his name upon the blank forms,
which the minister distributed amongst his friends?
The lieutenant-general of police also had his blank
forms at hand, in which it was necessary only to insert
the names of the victims. Wives obtained these

forms against their husbands, husbands against their wives, fathers against their children, men-about-town against their rivals in love, debtors against their creditors, opera-dancers against the lovers who had slighted them. If one but had the ear of the King, or the King's mistress, or the King's minister, or the King's chief of police, or of a friend or a friend's friend of any of these potentates, there was no grudge, jealousy, or enmity which one might not satisfy by means of a *lettre de cachet*,—that instrument which was so sure a safeguard against the " errors and abuses " of imprisonment, because it carried the signature of the King and his minister ! And the cases in which these scraps of paper were used merely for the ruin, the torment, or the temporary defeat of a private enemy, often had the cruellest results. The enemy and the enmity were forgotten, but the *lettre de cachet* had not been cancelled, and the prisoner still bided his day. Persons who had never been convicted of crimes, and other persons who had never been guilty of crimes, lay for years in the Bastille, forgotten and uncared for. " There are prisoners who remain in the Bastille," said Linguet (who spent two years there), " not because anybody is particularly anxious that they should remain, but because they happen to be there and have been forgotten, and there is nobody to ask for their release." Captain Bingham, the English apologist of the Bastille, discussing the cases of certain criminals who were arbitrarily dealt with by *lettres de cachet*, says that in England at the present day they " would be prosecuted according to law, and most probably committed to prison." Very good !

But is there no difference between the situation of
the criminal who, after conviction in open court, is
sent to prison for a fixed term of weeks, months, or
years, and that of the "criminal" who goes to prison
uncondemned and untried, and who cannot gauge the
length of his imprisonment? Far enough from being
"not so easy" to get into the Bastille, the passage
across those two drawbridges and through those five
massy gates was only too dreadfully simple for all
who were furnished against their wills with the "open
sesame" of the *lettre de cachet*.

The interior of the Bastille had nothing worse to
show than has been discovered in the chapters on
Vincennes, the Châtelet, and Bicêtre. There were,
perhaps, uglier corners in the two last-named prisons
than in either of the two more famous ones. The
Bastille, however, has stood as the type, and the almost
plutonic fame which it owes to romance seems likely
to endure. Romance has not been guilty of much
exaggeration, but this saving clause may be put in,
that what has been written of the Bastille might have
been written with equal truth of most other contemporary prisons. Its eight dark towers, its walls of
a hundred feet, its drawbridges, its outer and its four
great inner gates, its ditches, its high wooden gallery
for the watch, and its ramparts bristling with cannon,
—these external features have been of infinite service to romance, and romantic history. But within
the walls of the Bastille there was nothing extraordinary. Lodging was provided for about fifty prisoners, and it was possible to accommodate twice that
number.

The fifth and last gate opened into the Great Court.

some hundred feet in length and seventy in breadth, with three towers on either side. The Well Court, about eighty feet by five-and-forty, lay beyond, with a tower in the right and a tower in the left angle. Each tower had its name : those in the Great Court were *de la Comté, du Trésor, de la Chapelle, de la Bazanière, de la Bertaudière,* and *de la Liberté;* those in the Well Court were the *du Coin* and the *du Puits.* The comely garden on the suburban side of the château was closed to all prisoners by order of De Launay, the last governor of the Bastille, who also forbade them the use of the fine airy platforms on the summit of the towers. The main court was then the only exercise ground, a dreary enclosure which Linguet describes as insufferably cold in winter (" the north-east wind rushes through it ") and a veritable oven in summer.

The *oubliettes* have been mentioned. Besides these there were the dungeons, below the level of the soil ; dens in which there was no protection from wind or rain, and where rats and toads abounded. The ordinary chambers of the prisoners were situated in the towers. The upper stories were the *calottes* (skullcaps), residence in which seems to have been regarded as only better than that below ground. " One can only walk upright in the middle." The windows, barred within and without, gave little light ; there was a wretched stove in one corner (which had six pieces of wood for its daily allowance during the winter months), and one has no reason to doubt the statements of prisoners, that only an iron constitution could support the extremities of heat and cold in the *calottes.* In contrast to these, there were rooms which had fair

views of Paris and the open country. The lower
chambers looked only on the ditches; all the chambers (and the stairs) were shut in by double doors
with double bolts; and all, with the exceptions of
those which a few privileged persons were allowed
to upholster at their own cost, were furnished in the
most beggarly style.　But in all of these respects,
nothing was worse in the Bastille than elsewhere.

In principle, the dietary system here was the same
as in other State prisons.　The King paid a liberal
sum for the board of every prisoner, but the governor
contracted for the supplies, and might put into his
pocket half or three-fourths of the amount which he
drew from the royal treasury.　In the Bastille, as in
other prisons, there were periods when the prisoners
were fed extremely well; and in all these prisons
there were persons who, by favour of the Government or the governor, kept a much more luxurious
table than was allowed to the rest.　But one must
take the scale of diet which was customary.　Two
meals a day were the rule.　On flesh days, the dinner
consisted of soup and the meat of which it had been
made; and for supper there were "a slice of roast
meat, a ragout, and a salad."　Sunday's dinner was
"some bad soup, a slice of a cow which they call
beef, and four little pâtés"; supper, "a slice of roast
veal or mutton, or a little plate of haricot, in which
bones and turnips are most conspicuous, and a salad
with rancid oil."　On three holidays in the year,
"every prisoner had an addition made to his rations
of half a roast chicken, or a pigeon."　Holy Monday
was celebrated by "a tart extraordinary."　There was

always or usually dessert at dinner, which "consists of an apple, a biscuit, a few almonds and raisins, cherries, gooseberries, or plums." Each prisoner received a pound of bread a day, and a bottle of wine. De Launay's method of supplying his prisoners with wine was no doubt the usual one. He had the right of taking into his cellars about a hundred hogsheads, free of duty. "Well," says Linguet, "what does he do? He sells his privilege to one Joli, a Paris publican, who pays him £250 for it; and from Joli he receives in exchange, for the prisoners' use, the commonest wine that is sold,—mere vinegar, in fact."* A prisoner of the same period sums up the matter thus: "There is no eating-house in all France where they would not give you for a shilling a better dinner than is served in the Bastille."

Apart from all exceptional hardships and privations, the oppression of the first months of captivity in the Bastille must have been very terrible. The prisoner who was not certain of his fate, and who did not know to whom he owed his imprisonment, lay under a suspense which words are inadequate to describe. Mystery and doubt environed him; his day-long silence and utter isolation were relieved only by the regular visits of his gaoler. He was not allowed to see anyone from without, and could not get leave to write or receive a letter. Nothing could be done for him, he was told, until his examination had been concluded; and this was sometimes delayed for weeks or months. If he were a person of some consequence in the State, powerful enough to have enemies at Court, his

* *Mémoires sur la Bastille.*

examination in the council-chamber of the Bastille was conducted in a manner quite similar to (and probably borrowed from) that adopted by the Inquisition. He was asked his connection with plots or intrigues which he had never heard of ; he was coaxed or menaced to denounce or betray persons with whom perhaps he had never associated ; papers were held up before him which he was assured contained clear proofs of his guilt ; and he might be told that the King had unfortunately been inflamed against him, and would not hear his name. If, mystified by threats, hints, and arguments which had no meaning for him, he asked to be confronted by an accuser or witnesses, his requst was not allowed. These were the exact methods of the Inquisition. The lieutenant of police, or the commissioner from the Châtelet, who presided over the interrogation, would not hesitate to tell the accused that his life was at stake, and that if his answers were not complete and satisfactory he would be handed over forthwith to a *commission extraordinaire*. Every device was resorted to (says the author of the *Remarques politiques sur le Château de la Bastille*) in order to draw from the prisoner some sort of admission or avowal which might compromise either himself or some other person or persons in whom the Government had a hostile interest. The examiner might say that he was authorised to promise the prisoner his freedom, but if he allowed himself to be taken by this ruse it was generally the worse for him ; for, on the strength of the confession thus obtained, he was told that it would be impossible to release him at present, but every effort would be made, etc. If the ministry had reason to suspect that the prisoner was really a dangerous character, and involved in political intrigue, there was little hesitation in resorting to torture.

Ravaisson says that only two kinds of torture were applied in the Bastille: the " boot," and the torture by water. Well, these were sufficient; but it is to be remembered that the archives of the Bastille date only from about the middle of the seventeenth century, and it is improbable that the *Salle de la Question* of this prison was less horribly equipped than that of any other. The ordeal of the "boot" needs no description; for the torture by water, the victim was bound on a trestle, and water was poured down his throat by the gallon, until his sufferings became unendurable. Torture was practised in the Bastille as long as it was practised in any other French prison; a man named Alexis Danouilh underwent the Question there ("ordinary" and "extraordinary") in 1783 —after the date at which Louis XVI. had forbidden and abolished it by royal edict. To so small an extent had the absolute sovereigns of France control over the administration of their own prisons of State!

At no point in the existence of an ordinary captive of the Bastille is there any occasion to exaggerate his pains. Such as they were, they were very real; and scant reason is there to wonder at the bitterness, the vehemence, and even the violence of tone which characterises the memoirs or narratives of those who had endured them. The apologists of the Bastille will beg us to believe that the histories of Linguet and certain others are mendacious, have been refuted, and

14

so forth.   The gifted, caustic Linguet, who is one of their particular bugbears, was not the most upright man, nor the most scrupulous writer, in the France of his day; but the essential parts of his narrative are confirmed by the statements of a host of others.   It is not because Linguet has said that the Bastille walls, which were from seven to twelve feet thick, were from thirty to forty feet thick (which he might quite possibly have supposed) that we are to discredit his account, highly wrought as it is, of the general conditions of life within the prison.   It is not more highly wrought than the accounts of other prisoners of the Bastille, the accuracy of which has not been questioned.   These other histories are plentiful, and we are under no necessity of resting upon the better-known narratives which, for their qualities of style or their greater picturesqueness, have been so often reproduced.   Far on into the eighteenth century— indeed until within a few years of our own—there lay in the Bastille victims of public or private injustice, whose complainings, stifled in its vaulted ceilings, have sent us down a faint but faithful echo.   What of Bertin de Frateaux, who was walled in there from 1752 until his death in 1782 ? What of Tavernier, who, imprisoned in 1759 (after a previous ten years' sojourn in another gaol), was liberated only by the wreckers of the Bastille, on the 14th of July, 1789 ?   Here, too, in 1784, lies the Genoese, Pellissery, imprisoned, in 1777, for publishing a pamphlet on the finances of Necker.   Dishonourable terms of release are offered him which he will not accept, although " rheumatic in every joint, scorbutic, and spitting blood for fifteen months, owing to the atrocious treatment I have had here during seven years." Here, two years later, is Brun de la Condamine, the inventor of an explosive bomb, which he has importuned the ministry to make test of. After a captivity of four years and a half, enraged at the indignities he receives, he makes a wild attempt to escape. Here, at the same period, is Guillaume Debure, the oldest and most respected bookseller in France, lodged in the Bastille for refusing to stamp the pirated copies of works issued by his brethren in the trade; treated apparently like a common malefactor, and released only on the indignant representations of the whole bookselling fraternity of Paris. Thus lightly was the liberty of the subject held, even while the Revolution was fermenting.

The prisoner who was released never knew until then the full bitterness of the treatment he had endured. It was perhaps the acutest part of his sufferings, that the letters he had written to family and friends, the entreaties he had addressed to ministers, magistrates, and chiefs of police, brought him never a word in answer. It was thus that was produced in so many cases that sense of utter desolation and abandonment by the whole world which resulted in the madness of very many prisoners. Those who were restored to liberty with their reason unimpaired learned that their letters and petitions had never been received. They had never, in fact, passed out of the Bastille. It was well to have the truth of this at any time; but we are to remember the prisoners who died in the belief that their dearest ones had denied them one kind or sympathetic word. When the Bastille was sacked, piles of letters were found which had never passed beyond the governor's hands. Amongst them was one which (considering the circumstances of the writer, and the fact that no line was ever vouchsafed him in response) may be regarded as perhaps the very saddest ever penned: " If for my consolation," wrote the prisoner to the lieutenant of police, " Monseigneur would have the goodness, in the name of the God above us both, to give me but one word of my dear wife, her name only on a card, that I might know she still lives, I would pray for Monseigneur to the last day of my life." This letter was signed " Queret Démery," a name known to nobody, but which will be remembered while the Bastille is remembered. One does not choose to ask, were there even a chance of an answer, how many other letters not less piteous than this were read and drily docketed by governors of the Bastille.

This inveterate and almost inviolable secrecy in which the government of the Bastille enwrapped the majority of its prisoners seems on the whole to have been the most cruel feature of its policy. After reading some fifty volumes of cells with rats in them, and dungeons frozen or fiery, and torture-rooms, and filthy beds, and food not enough to keep life on, one is shocked to find that the due and natural poignancy of sympathy with human suffering begins insensibly to weaken. But this refinement of pain, inflicted as a part of the routine, upon the common prisoners of the Bastille, revives the sense of pity. It was the habit to pretend that prisoners who were dungeoned there were not in there at all. Asked as to the fate of this prisoner or the other, ministers would respond with a blank look, assure the questioner that they had never heard the prisoner's name, and that, wherever he might be, he was certainly not in the Bastille. The governor and chief officers of the prison, who saw the prisoner every day, would say that he was not in their keeping, and that no such person was known to them. The common practice of imprisoning men in the Bastille under names other than their own made these denials easy. At other times, when it was desired to prejudice his friends or society against a prisoner, the answer would be, that the less said about him the better. The nominal cause of his imprisonment, his friends were told, was not the real one; the Government had their information, and if it could possibly be published the prisoner would be known in his true character. The prisoner himself was often told that his friends had ceased to believe in his innocence, or that they thought him dead, or that they had given up all hope of procuring his release. The Bastille and the Inquisition were singularly alike in their methods.

Dreary beyond expression must have been the daily round for all but the privileged few. "Every hour was struck on a bell which was heard all through the Faubourg St. Antoine." The sentries on the rampart challenged one another ceaselessly throughout the night. There were prisoners in solitary confinement to whom no other sounds than these ever penetrated, except the grating of the key in the lock which announced the daily visits of the gaoler. This was the life of such prisoners as the Iron Mask, and of Tavernier, who told his liberators that, during the thirty years of his captivity, he had passed nineteen consecutive ones without crossing the threshold of his cell. Exercise in the yard, for those who enjoyed this favour, was limited to an hour a day, and this period might be reduced to a few minutes if there were many prisoners to be exercised in turn,—for, in general, the utmost care was taken to prevent them from meeting one another. If a stranger were shewn into the yard, the prisoner who was taking his mouthful of air had to retreat to a cabinet in the wall. These walks were solitary, except for the presence of a dumb sentinel ; and, unless the prisoner were now and then permitted or compelled to share his chamber with a fellow-captive, not less solitary was his whole existence. The most stringent rules were in force respecting the admission of friends or relatives. " Strangers cannot enter the Bastille," ran the official injunction, " without very precise orders from the governor"; and such rare interviews as were permitted took place in the council-chamber, in the presence of this officer or his deputy. The length of the interview was always fixed in the letter which the visitor bore from the lieutenant of police, and nothing might be said relative to the cause of the prisoner's detention.

A certain Mme. de Montazau, visiting her husband in the Bastille, took with her a little dog, and, while pretending to caress it in her own Portuguese tongue, was trying to tell Montazau what efforts she was making for his release. " Madame," interrupted De Launay, his gaoler's instinct aroused, " if your dog does not understand French you cannot bring him here." Even such poor barren visits as these were of the rarest possible occurrence.

But, M. Ravaisson will tell us, prisoners were frequently visited by the lieutenant of the King or some other high personage. It would be more to the point to say that such visits were occasionally inflicted, for the comfort that prisoners derived from them was slender. Abbé Duvernet receives the visit of the minister Amelot, who tells him that he can have nothing to complain of, since he has had access to the prison library. The Bastille library, by the way, seems to have been founded not by the Government, but by a prisoner who was confined there early in the eighteenth century. Abbé Duvernet had made a catalogue of the collection. "I have catalogued your library," he replied to the minister, "and there are not ten volumes in it which a man of ordinary education would trouble himself to read. Library, indeed! Listen, monsieur: when a man has had the hardihood to expose one of the blunders of you ministers, you will spend any quantity of money to be avenged on him. You will hunt him to Holland, England, or the heart of Germany, if it costs the State two thousand pounds. But to afford a little solace to the poor devils in your Bastille, by buying a few books for them to read—no! I dare be sworn that Government has not spent ten pounds on books for this place since the Bastille was built!"

"Well, monsieur l'abbé," said Amelot, "may I ask why you are here?"

"Why am I here! Because you yourself gave

some one a *lettre de cachet*, which had your own name
and the King's attached to it.   I am very sure that
his Majesty knows nothing of my detention, or the
motive of it; but *you* can scarcely pretend to the
same ignorance.   Or, will you have me believe that
you set your signature to these *lettres* without knowing what it is that you are signing?"   Then, turning
to Lénoir, the Lieutenant of Police, the Abbé asked :
" Do *you*, sir, demand *lettres de cachet* of M. Amelot
without giving him a reason? Come, as you are
both here together, perhaps one of you will be good
enough to tell me what is the excuse for my imprisonment."   I have condensed this interview from *Les
Prisons de Paris*.   It is not likely that ministers and
chiefs of police were often faced in this style by prisoners of the Bastille, but it is probable enough that
most interviews of the kind ended with the same
fruitless inquiry on the part of the prisoner.

It may be inferred from this how much protection
was afforded to prisoners by the daily reports of the
governor or the major to the minister, who was nom-
inally responsible for the Bastille.   These reports, in
fact, seem to have been merely a part of the system
of espionage which was regularly practised there.
The governor writes :

" I have the honour to inform you that the sieur Billard was
engaged with the sieur Perrin yesterday, from six to nine in the
evening.

" This morning M. de la Monnoye saw and spoke with Abbé
Grisel a good half-hour.

" M. Moncarré had an interview with his wife in the afternoon,
in accordance with your instructions.

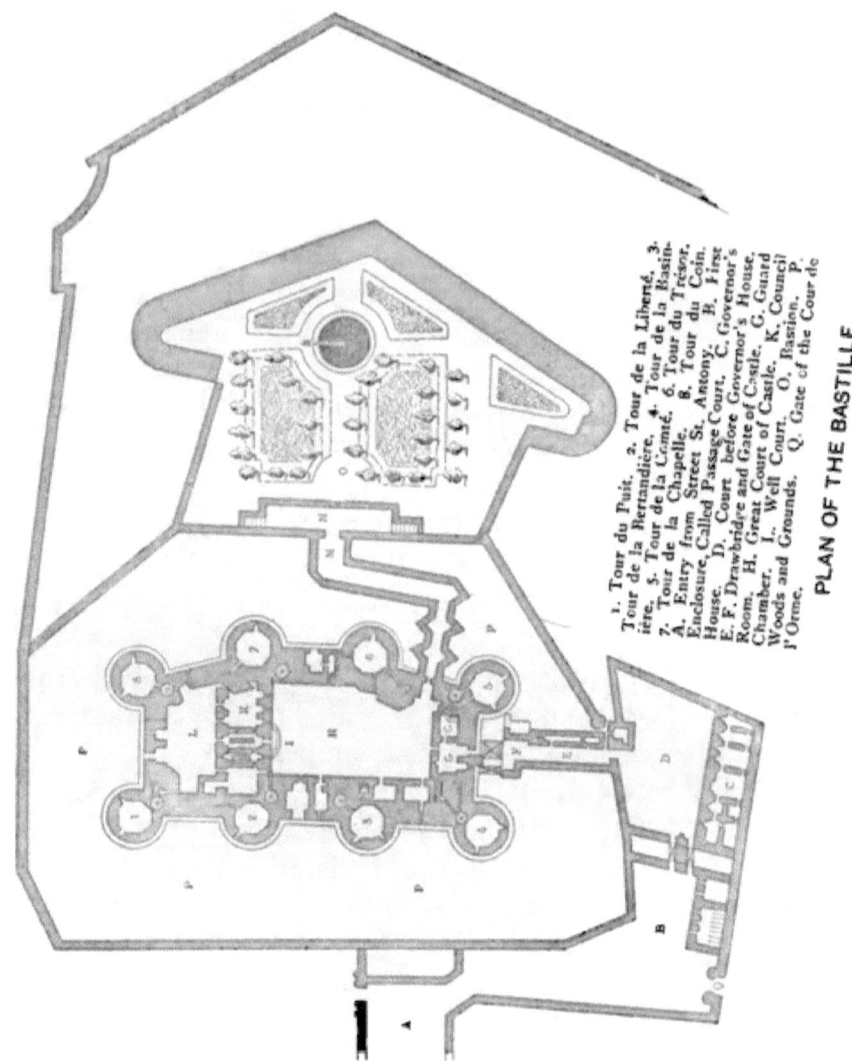

1. Tour du Puis. 2. Tour de la Liberté,
Tour de la Bertaudière. 4. Tour de la Basin-
ière. 5. Tour de la Comté. 6. Tour du Tresor,
7. Tour de la Chapelle. 8. Tour du Coin,
A. Entry from Street St. Antony. B. First
Enclosure, Called Passage Court. C. Governor's
House. D. Court before Governor's House,
E. F. Drawbridge and Gate of Castle. G. Guard
Room. H. Great Court of Castle. K. Council
Chamber. I. Well Court. O. Bastion. P.
Woods and Grounds. Q. Gate of the Cour de
l'Orme.

PLAN OF THE BASTILLE.

" In obedience to your instructions of the 28th of this month, I have handed letters to Abbé Grisel and M. Ponce de Léon.—I am, etc."

The library which Abbé Duvernet dismissed with contempt was not at the disposal of every prisoner. Both books and writing materials were in the nature of indulgences, and doled out sparingly. The rule was terribly precise on the subject of relaxations of any kind. It stated, in so many words, that : " As regards a prisoner, the governor and the officers of the château cannot be too severe and firm in preventing the least relaxation in the discipline of the Bastille ; they cannot pay too much attention to this, nor punish too severely any act of insubordination." How often was that rule interpreted in favour of a sojourn in the dungeon or the " ice-chamber " ?

Not only the governor and his immediate subordinates, but every turnkey, sentinel, guard of the watch, and invalid soldier on the staff was a gaoler and spy in himself. The inferior attendants of the Bastille were encouraged and sometimes directly charged to feign sympathy with a political prisoner, in order to lure him into some indiscreet avowal ; but in the discharge of their ordinary duties they were enjoined to be watchful and mute. Amongst their orders were the following :

" The sentinels will arrest immediately anyone of whom they have the slightest suspicion, and will send for a staff-officer to settle the matter.

" The sentinel will not let out of his sight, on any pretext, prisoners who are exercising in the court. He will watch carefully to see whether a prisoner drops any paper, note, or packet.

He will be careful to prevent prisoners from writing on the walls, and will report upon everything he may have remarked whilst on duty.

"When the corporal of the guard or any inferior officer is ordered to accompany a prisoner who may have leave to walk in the garden or on the towers, it is expressly forbidden him to hold any conversation with the prisoner. The officer is there solely to guard the prisoner, and to prevent him from signalling to anyone outside the walls."

Prisoners of a devout character must have been shocked by the studiously cynical mode of worship in the Bastille. The chapel was a dingy den on the ground floor of the prison, which Howard describes as containing

"five niches or closets ; three are hollowed out of the wall, the others are only in the wainscot. In these, prisoners are put one by one to hear mass. They can neither see nor be seen. The doors of these niches are secured on the outside by a lock and two bolts ; within, they are iron-grated, and have glass windows towards the chapel, with curtains, which are drawn at the *Sanctus*, and closed again at the concluding prayer."

As not more than five prisoners were present at each mass, only ten could hear it each day. " If there is a greater number in the castle, either they do not go to mass at all (which is generally the case with the ecclesiastics, prisoners for life, and those who do not desire to go) or they attend alternately : because there are almost always some who have permission to go constantly."

If a prisoner, sick and at the point of death, asked that masses might be said for his soul, he was told that it was not customary for masses to be said in the

Bastille, either for the living or for the dead. " No prayers are offered up in the Castle," ran the word, " except for the King and the Royal Family." If it were promised him that he should be prayed for in a church outside the prison, he was sent out of captivity with a lie in his ear ; for information of his death was withheld from his family. He was buried by night and in secrecy in the graveyard of St. Paul's, and the record of his name and rank in the parish register " were fictitious, that all trace of him might be oblite-rated." The register of the Bastille, in which his real name and station were recorded, was a volume closed to the world. That false book of the dead, which a turnkey edits by his lantern's glimmer in the sacristy of St. Paul's, adds a mountain's weight to the sins of the keepers of the Bastille. There is no reason why its memory should not increase in detestation.

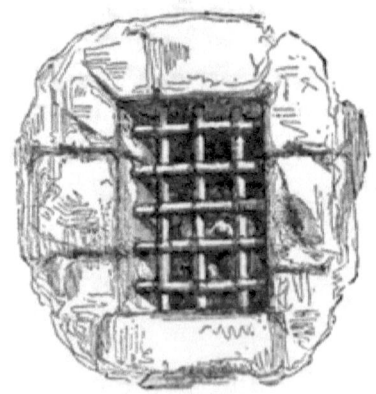

CHAPTER XI.

THE PRISONS OF ASPASIA.

I T is not easy, in telling the story of the prisons of old Paris, to avoid mention of the subject with which this chapter is concerned. That subject is not, however, an attractive one, and readers whom it repels are invited to let the chapter go.

According to the authors of *Les Prisons de l'Europe*, Charlemagne was the first monarch of France who "formally punished" the calling of the *femme publique*. His edict swept the field, so to speak; the *femme publique* (known then, however, as the *femme du monde*) and all who gave asylum to her were absolutely banned. The prison, the whip, and the pillory were their portion; the keepers of houses of ill-fame had to carry the pillory on their backs to the market-place, and the women whom they lodged had to stand in it. This edict, completely prohibitive, was in force during four centuries, and its principal result seems to have been to augment the custom of Aspasia. She and her industry increased a thousand-fold.

The state of France in this respect struck Saint Louis with horror on his return from the Holy Land. His *ordonnance* of 1254 bade the women of the town

renounce their calling, on pain of being deprived of
house and clothing, "even of the clothes in which
they stood up." If, after being warned, these women
continued as before, they were to be banished the
country. But, wiser and more humane than Charlemagne, Saint Louis set apart for repentant Magdalens a shelter in the convent of the Filles-Dieu, and
drew from his private purse the moneys to lodge and
maintain two hundred of them.

The new law, enforced with as much rigour as the
old one, proved every whit as impotent. Aspasia
went her ways in secret, and devised many arts. She
borrowed the manners and the costume of her more
respectable sisters *(Les prostituées singèrent les ma-
nières et le costume des femmes honnêtes)*, glided into
the churches, and went with sidelong glances through
the most frequented places of the town. This clandestine pursuit of the calling, and the hypocrisy
which of necessity it bred on every side, were beyond
measure distressing to Saint Louis. A good king,
and a pious one, he considered the matter deeply,
and then, in the interests, as he believed, of public
and private morals, he resolved upon a novel and
hazardous measure. It was, to allow the *femmes publiques* a degree of liberty, and the exercise of their
calling, under certain strict conditions. Amongst
other regulations, they were to live in houses specially
appointed to them, and these houses were to be
closed at six o'clock in the evening, no person being
allowed to enter them after that hour.

Thus, strangely enough in one point of view, the
King who won the name of "Saint," and whose

memory has been justly cherished, was the first to give legality in France to the calling of Aspasia. Yet this was also the King who, above all others on that throne, had sought to keep in check the moral disorders of his kingdom. It was only when he had seen that measures of repression were of worse than no avail, inasmuch as the immorality of the town appeared always to increase in proportion to the stringency of laws, whilst the secrecy of the traffic confounded the *femme du monde* with the "respectable" woman, that he resolved upon giving to the former a domain and status of her own. In this manner, the unrecognised *femme du monde* was transformed into the *femme publique*, a woman with a standing of her own, and with the King's authority to prosecute her mournful industry.

She entered under the special jurisdiction of the Provosts of Paris, who from time to time made various enactments on her account. Thus, in 1360, the chief magistrate forbade the *femmes publiques* to wear certain specified apparel in the streets; and, in 1367, a police order confined them to particular streets in Paris, "a measure rendered necessary by their unseemly behaviour in all places, to the great scandal of everyone."* During the next two hundred years they were occasionally transferred from one quarter of Paris to another, and Parliament more than once took upon itself to "regulate their costume."

In 1560, an edict given at Orleans formulated afresh the stern prohibitions of Charlemagne. Once more, the calling of Aspasia was forbidden through-

* *Les Prisons de l'Europe.*

out the whole of France. The difficulties of enforcing this new-old *ordonnance* were great everywhere,
but nowhere so great as in the capital; and the
Provost, it is said, was five years in concerting his
measures. The statement is easily credited. Paris
herself was little in sympathy at that date with laws
to restrict the liberty of Aspasia; and it cannot be
said that the average citizen had received much
encouragement to virtue from the examples of the
Court, the nobility, the clergy, or the magistracy itself.
Dulaure asserts in his *Histoire de Paris* that "*La
prostitution était considerée à l'égal des autres professions
de la société.*" The *femmes publiques*, he adds, formed
a corporation by themselves, received their patents,
as it were, from the the hands of Royalty, "*et même
étaient protégées par les rois. Charles VI. et Charles
VII. ont laissé des témoignages authentiques de cette protection.*" The commerce to which was extended the
august protection of the throne "*était encore favorisé
par le grand nombre de célibataires, prêtres et moines,
par le libertinage des magistrats, des gens de guerre, etc.,
Les femmes publiques, richement vêtues, se répandaient
dans tous les quartiers de cette ville, et se trouvaient
confondues avec les bourgeoises, qui, elles-mêmes,
menaient une vie fort dissolue.*" Provosts of Paris
sometimes refused to put in force laws which themselves had framed against the "daughters of joy";
and in so refusing they seem usually to have had
with them the sympathies of the town.

This being in general the attitude of society in
Paris, it might be thought that the attempt to revive
the code of Charlemagne would be received with

small popular favour. It appears to have been received with no favour whatever. Seven years, from 1560 to 1567, did the Provost prepare his way, and then the edict was launched. It was read aloud at either end of every street in which Aspasia had her dwelling, and in several of these streets a violent resistance was offered, by the women as well as by their friends and protectors, to the not too-willing agents of the law. By main force at length the women were taken as by press-gang, their streets were closed, the temple of Venus was demolished, and there were once more no *femmes publiques* in Paris.

So, at least, did the Law assure itself; what then had become of them? As may be supposed, the great majority were still in Paris. Not a few were in prison (but for short periods only); the rest were scattered throughout the town, or in the villages surrounding Paris. As in the days of Charlemagne, and before the second decree of Saint Louis, Aspasia had merely disguised herself. No Magdalen repented on the order of the State. She sought a retreat until the passing of the storm, and in a little while the history of the affair repeated itself : *la prostitution clandestine inonda Paris.*

Matters continued apparently without the slightest improvement until 1619, when the authorities could devise no better plan than a renewal of the prohibitions of 1565. The *femmes publiques* were commanded by proclamation to betake themselves to some domestic or other occupation, or to quit the town and suburbs within four and twenty hours. The utter infeasibility of the injunction is not more striking than its stupendous absurdity. Imagine the whole corporation of Aspasias, *richement vêtues*, converting themselves at a day's notice into seamstresses, cooks, or chambermaids. It would have been so easy for them to find employers! Saint Louis had shewn himself more generous, more thoughtful, and more sensible in opening his private purse to lodge and maintain the would-be penitents of the order amongst the recluses of the Filles-Dieu. Needless to say, the foolish and impossible decree was quite barren of result. During the next sixty-five years, that is to say until 1684, no definite legal action was taken with respect to the position of the *femme publique*. Unlicenced and unacknowledged, she fared well or ill according to the laxity or the vigilance of the bench and police, who sometimes harried and sometimes tacitly or openly abetted her. The secret or semi-open practice of her calling was often as profitable as the pursuit of it by sanction of the Crown, but it was attended by the risks of an illegal industry, and in seasons when provosts or lieutenants of police shewed an unwonted activity, Aspasia went to prison. Thus she fared, now sparkling in the finest company, now pinched for a meal, and now doing penance on the prison flags, or perhaps sick (eight to a bed) in Bicêtre hospital, until 1684. At that date, another move was resolved upon, and for the second time Aspasia had the gracious permission of the State to style herself *femme publique*, and to sell her liberty to the police, to buy *une licence de débauche*,—for this was what it came to.

At the period arrived at, it was no longer merely a

15

question of irregularities to be repressed, but of the public health to be preserved; and in the new regulations the hospital was named along with the prison. From this time forward, a brief interval under the Consulate excepted, it does not seem to have been questioned in France that women who chose to do so, or who might be driven to do so, were entitled under specified conditions to enter on the calling of *femme publique*. What steps must be taken to secure the dubious privileges of the order, and what dissuasions were employed by the magistrate who dispensed them, will presently be shewn.

Up to the reign of Louis XIV., the monarch responsible for the provisions of 1684, there was no special prison for the women of this class, who, when under lock and key, were herded with female offenders of all degrees. The first special prison for the *femmes publiques* was the Salpêtrière, built by Louis XIV., under the designation of "Hospital General." At this era, the women arrested were not put upon their trial, nor was any formal judgment pronounced against them. They were under the sole jurisdiction of the newly appointed lieutenant of of police, who dispatched them to prison on the King's warrant, which took the form of a *lettre de cachet*. Curious, that the *fille de joie* should be placed in this respect on a footing of equality with the prince of the blood, the nobleman, and the prelate!

At about the end of the eighteenth century (say, towards 1770), the police authorities distinguished two classes of women of the town, the *femmes pub-*

liques, or authorised women, and a numerous and unlicenced class, of more dissolute habits, officially stigmatised as *débauchées*. To strengthen the line of demarcation between the two classes, the *femmes publiques*, or the majority of them, were inscribed on the police registers (paying a fee of twenty sous), and being to a certain extent *protégées* of the State, the treatment accorded to them was generally of a more lenient character. The terms of their imprisonment (for soliciting in the streets or public places, for brawling and rioting, for signalling from their windows, etc.,) were entirely at the discretion of the lieutenant of police; but it would appear that they were frequently released, at the request or on the bond of a parent, sister, or other relative, after a brief confinement. The houses in which the members of the unlicenced class lived together were continually raided by the police, who descended upon them after dark, "*parce que les femmes en étaient arrivées à ce degré de scandale, qu' on ne pouvait plus les arrêter pendant le jour, à cause du désordre qu'elles causaient, et des collisions qu'excitaient leurs amants et autres adhérents.*"

Eighteenth-century documents concerning these houses are still to be read, and some of them have a curiously modern flavour. There are complaints of householders, and the reports of the police agents whom these complaints set in motion. A certain, M. Ledure, writing under date of the 23d of July, 1785, asks the attention of the police to an unlicensed house of ill-fame adjoining his own, and details his annoyances with a freedom of expression which debars translation. The burden of his protest is, that being a gentleman with a family of daughters, and the holder of a position which obliges him to entertain "des personnes de distinction," his existence is rendered intolerable by the worse than light behaviour of the "females over the way." He can scarcely even get into his own house of an evening.

"To satisfy M. Ledure," runs the police report, "we began by visiting, in Beaubourg Street, the house in which the women complained of were lodging. We arrested there, Marguerite Lefèbvre, the other women having taken themselves off. . . . In response to the complaints of the residents in Rohan Street, against the women living at No. 63, we forced an entry there, and arrested the woman Rochelet, and the two *filles d'amour* kept by her. We fetched them out, to take them to Saint-Martin "—a house of detention, from which the women were transfered to the Salpêtrière,—" but, although our guard was composed of five men with fixed bayonets, we were so set upon by the man Rochelet, a hairdresser, and twenty blackguards with him, that we had to let the women go."

The origin of the prison of Saint-Martin, abolished by Louis XVI., is quite unknown. It was a small confined place with a villainous reputation. Regarded by the authorities as a temporary lodging for both classes of public women, a sort of fore-chamber of the Salpêtrière, no attempt was ever made to render it decently habitable. The dark and dirty cells were absolutely destitute of furniture; a truss of straw, thrown from time to time on the stone floor, was both bed and bedding. The food was strictly in keeping; all that the prison gave was a loaf of black bread a day, and whilst prisoners who could afford it were allowed to do a little catering for themselves, the rest soaked their black bread in the soup provided by charitable societies.

Every petition to improve Saint-Martin was answered by the formula that no one stayed there above a few days, which was a callous misstatement of the facts. It is true that the women arrested " by order of the King" were not detained after their *lettres de cachet* had been obtained; but the women of the other class, who were arrested by simple act of police, and tried at the bar as ordinary offenders, lay for weeks or months at Saint-Martin, awaiting the pleasure of a judge of the Châtelet. When the cases to be disposed of were numerous, a part only were heard, and the women whose fate was still to be pronounced were remanded for a further period of weeks or months to Saint-Martin. It was thus not less a prison in the ordinary meaning of the word than what the French call a *dépôt*; and when its inconveniences were no longer to be endured, Louis XVI. abolished and demolished it, and constituted by letters patent the Hôtel de Brienne as a *prison des femmes publiques*, under the name of *La Petite Force.* This continued to be the temporary prison until the revolutionary era, and here at least the women had air to breathe and beds to lie on.

The first rules for the conduct of the Salpêtrière were issued from Versailles in April, 1684, over the signatures of Louis XIV. and his minister Colbert,

The women were to hear mass on Sundays and Saints' days; to pray together a quarter of an hour morning and evening, and to submit to readings from "the catechism and pious books" whilst they were at work.

They were to be soberly attired in dark stuff gowns, and shod with sabots; bread and water with soup were to be their portion; and they were to sleep on mattresses with sufficient bed-gear.

The nature of their tasks was left to the discretion of the directors, but the labour was to be "both long and severe." After a period of probation, prisoners of approved behaviour might be employed at lighter occupations, and receive a small percentage of the profits, which they were to be at liberty to spend on the purchase of meat, fruit, *"et autres rafratchissements."*

Swearing, idleness, and quarrelling with one another were to be punished by a diminution of rations, the pillory, the dark cell, or such other pains as the directors might think proper to inflict.

These continued to be the rules for the prisons of the *femmes publiques;* their spirit is modern, but we shall see later on to what extent they were enforced.

In no long time, indeed, after the decrees of 1684, the conditions of life in the Salpêtrière seem to have been little if at all better than those in Saint-Martin. Six women shared a cell by night; the one bed which was supposed to hold them all accommodated four; two of whom slept at the head and two at the foot, while the two latest comers made shift on the bare floor. When one of the bed-fellows got her dis-

charge, or went sick to Bicêtre, the elder of the floor-
companions took the vacant place in the bed, resign-
ing her share of the boards to a new *fille d'amour*.
Complaints evoked the cut-and-dried response that
the bed was intended to hold six. The cells were
always damp, and "*il y regnait absolument, et surtout
le matin, une odeur infecte, capable de faire reculer.*"
Despite the lack of sanitation, and the fact that the
food was always of an inferior quality, the death-rate
was not abnormal in the Salpêtrière.

Such was the first regular prison of the *femmes
publiques*, and its régime. The sensible intentions of
Louis XIV. were never realised, nor does the
character of the monarch himself permit it to be
inferred that he was very seriously concerned on the
subject. The Salpêtrière continued to receive, if not
to chasten, the "daughters of joy" until two days
before the September massacres, when, as the beds
for six were wanted for political prisoners, they were
restored to liberty.

The year '91 saw the overthrow of everything, and
the women of pleasure, so-called, entered upon
halcyon days. Aspasia, left to her own devices, was
"regarded as exercising an ordinary trade." Scan-
dals and disorders followed, and when the public
health was again in danger, there being neither control nor supervision of this traffic, a new census of
the women was ordered. This was in 1796, but the
work was so badly done that the opening days of the
Directory found the situation more deplorable, if
possible, than ever. Strange to say, the dissolute
Directory (which admitted to its salons "gallant

dames" who lacked nothing of the status of *filles d'amour* save inscription on the police registers) turned a severe eye upon the morals of the public. The police were bidden to be active in the haunts of Aspasia, but Aspasia had not forgotten the Republican doctrine of liberty, and when haled before the bench she gathered her lovers and friends about her in such numbers, that the cloud of witnesses in her favour quite overawed the magistrates, who were fain to let her go free.

The Consulate renewed the attack. It was at this era that the Central Bureau, which displaced the old office of Lieutenant of Police, was created, with a special sub-department called the *Bureau des Mœurs*. This department gave its attention principally to the sanitary aspects of the matter. Then was established the *Préfecture de Police ;* and the new prefect, M. Dubois, ordered a fresh numbering of the women, which was made in 1801. The police, however, continued to ask for larger powers, which, to be brief, were conferred on them by article 484 of the *Code Pénal.* There were here revived at a stroke the *ordonnances* of 1713, 1778, and 1780, which gave to the heads of police, " *une autorité absolue sur les femmes publiques.*"

During the period which has been thus hastily reviewed and which commenced soon after the close of the Reign of Terror, three prisons in succession served for the women of the town : La Force, Les Madelonnettes, and Saint-Lazare.

For many years—indeed, until the year after the battle of Waterloo—they were taken to prison in

the keeping of soldiers, who led them through the
streets in broad day; a crowd following, the women
in tears or swearing, the crowd jeering or applauding.
If a woman were well known in the town, there was
an attempt to rescue her, and she was often snatched
from the soldiers before the prison was reached.
This public scandal, and bitter humiliation to all
women above the most degraded class, was allowed
until the year 1816, when the *femmes publiques* were
conveyed to prison in a closed car.

They went to the Force, which has not left a kinder
memory than the Salpêtrière. Prison rule was an
art as yet in its infancy, and there was scarcely an
idea of cleanliness, moral control, or discipline. The
Force, it is said, was "as inconvenient a place as
could be found for its purpose." The infirmary,
always an important department of prisons of this
class, was "unwholesome and wretchedly ventilated."
The women were altogether undisciplined, and as
workrooms had not been opened they passed their
days in idleness and gaming. In the summer months
they swarmed in the yard; in winter, they slept,
played cards, quarrelled, and fought in dusky and
ill-smelling common-rooms. They had no keepers
but men, before whom they displayed the most cynical effrontery. It is asserted that, on the days on
which clean linen was distributed, the women were
accustomed to present themselves before the warders
in the precise state in which Phryne astonished her
judges.* These things were noised, and the prefect

---

* Un ancien gardien de la Force nous a dit que le samedi, jour où on leur
donnait des chemises, pendant l'été, elles se mettaient entièrement nues dans
le préau pour les recevoir des mains des gardiens.—*Les Prisons de l'Europe.*

of police had to devise afresh.   In 1828, the *filles d'*
amour were transferred from the Force to the
Madelonnettes.   The record of the Madelonnettes
in this connection is not important, except that here
it was attempted to employ the women at some
strictly penal tasks.   This project was more fully devel-
oped at Saint-Lazare, to which prison all classes of
women of the town were relegated in 1831.   At this
date, the number of registered public women in Paris
was 3517.

Before penetrating within the prison of Saint-Lazare, the reader will be curious to know by what
means a woman desirous of doing so enrolled herself
in this singular militia.   She must seek the countenance and aid of a magistrate of Paris, whose task
was in equal measure a delicate and a painful one.
Without doubt, it was a strange spectacle ; a woman
presents herself before a magistrate and says that, re-
nouncing her woman's modesty, her hope or desire of
an honourable future, she wishes to be cut off from the
world, that she may cast herself *dans la prostitution
publique*.   At first sight, she seems to make the
magistrate her accomplice, but that this was not the
case the sequel will shew.

The applicant underwent a most minute interrogation.   She was asked if she were a married woman,
a widow, or a spinster ; if her parents were living and
whether she lived with them, or why she had separated from them.   She was asked how long she had
inhabited Paris, and whether she had no friends there
whose interest the magistrate might evoke for her.
She was asked whether she had ever been arrested,

how often, and for what causes. She was asked whether she had ever followed the calling of *femme publique* in any other place, and finally, what were the true motives of her application. Procès-verbal of the examination was drawn up, and the applicant had then to be seen by a medical man attached to the police service. Next, her certificate of birth was asked for, and if she could not produce it, and had been born out of Paris, she must give the name of the mayor of her department. The magistrate wrote forthwith to the mayor, and after setting forth the facts which the applicant had submitted in her examination, requested him to report upon them, asking particularly whether the relatives of the woman could not be moved to induce her to return to them. All this was done in the case where the girl or woman went alone to solicit her enrollment, but it has to be said that not infrequently one or both of the parents of the applicant attended with her at the bureau, to support her request !

When every effort of the magistrate had proved unavailing, a final procès-verbal was prepared, to the effect that such-and-such a female had requested to be inscribed " *comme fille publique*," and had been enrolled on the decision of the examining magistrate, " after undertaking to submit to the sanitary and other regulations established by the Prefecture for women of that class." Thus, and in all cases by her own act, was she launched upon those turbid waters.

Of the 3517 women on the Paris police registers in 1831, 931 were from Paris and the department of the Seine, 2170 from the provincial departments, 134 from foreign countries, and the remaining 282 had been unable or unwilling to satisfy the authorities as to their place of birth. There were amongst them seamstresses, modistes, dressmakers, florists, lacemakers, embroiderers, glove-makers, domestic servants, hawkers, milliners, hairdressers, laundresses, silk-workers, jewellers, actresses or figurantes, acrobats, and representatives of many other trades and callings, together with six teachers of music, and one "landscape painter." As regards the education of this army of outcasts, rather more than one-half were unable to sign their names on the cards or badges which they received from the bureau ; a somewhat smaller number appended " an almost illegible signature" *(fort mal, et d'une manière à peine lisible)* ; whilst a hundred, or thereabouts, wrote " a neat and correct hand."

As for the causes which induced them to cast in their lot with their sister pariahs, they were traceable for the most part to the weaknesses or defects of the social organisation. Thus, a majority of the women pleaded "excess of misery," and the class next in point of numbers were "*simples concubines ayant perdu leurs amants, et ne sachant plus que faire.*" A large proportion had lost both parents, or had been driven from home ; many had left the provinces to seek work in Paris ; some were widows who could find no other means of supporting their children ; and others were daughters looking for bread for aged parents, or for younger sisters and brothers.

And now, standing on the threshold of their prison, we may ask what were the commoner causes which sent these unfortunates to Saint-Lazare. It has been made sufficiently clear that by the act of procuring their licences they sold their liberty to the police. This indeed was the sole condition on which enrolment could be obtained. The *femme publique*, in becoming such, bought herself an army of masters; the whole force of police were in authority over her, and almost equally so were their agents and spies, and the medical men in their employ. She had subscribed obedience to all the regulations invented by the Préfecture, and she was under perpetual surveillance. The great power of the police over her rested on her submission in writing to the prefect's "*règlements sanitaires*" and his "*mesures exceptionelles de surveillance*," and infringement of the most arbitrary enactment brought her within the danger of prison. Failing to render her prescribed visit to the police doctor, she was almost certain to find herself a day or two later in Saint-Lazare. Special rules and regulations apart, the irregularities of life and infractions of common law which at times were almost inevitable in the calling she had entered on, were amongst the causes contributive to her troubles with the powers at whose mercy she had placed herself. On the whole, one gathers that the *fille de joie* paid at siege rates for that none too felicitous title.

She seems to have found herself often on the less desirable side of the prison door; and as the class of *filles publiques* in Paris has always included some of the handsomest and some of the most ill-favoured, some of the most elegant and some of the least refined, some of the brightest and some of the most

villainous women in the town, it may be supposed
that the floating population of Saint-Lazare (which
amounted sometimes to fourteen hundred) offered a
marvellous variety of types.

It was the place of waiting for women and girls
whose applications to be registered had not been disposed of, and for the women who were to be tried on
police charges; and it was also the place of punishment for those who had received sentence.

The position of the untried was in many respects
worse than that of the convicted prisoners. The
former had the privilege, to be sure, of hiring what
was called a private room, but if they went in penniless they were in a bad case indeed. They had no
right to the full prison rations, and were fed strictly
on bread and water. The convicted prisoners were
warmly clad in winter, but the untried were not allowed to add to the clothing they took in with them
a wrap or comforter from the prison wardrobe. In
hard weather the public women of the poorer class
seem to have suffered keenly both from hunger and
from cold. Untried, and presumably innocent (and
many honest women were sent to Saint-Lazare on the
vaguest accusations or suspicions of the police), they
were compelled to receive the visits of the doctors,
which were not always of the most delicate character.
Women awaiting trial sometimes offered money to
escape this humiliation, and the case is recorded of a
girl who preferred suicide to submission.

It was better, in respect of physical comfort, on the
penal side of the prison. There the women were clad
to the season, fed not meanly, and lodged with a cer-

tain decency. The untaught and feckless had opportunity to learn a trade, for the workrooms were now conducted on a much more practical principle, and the small bonuses bestowed on the industrious were to some extent a corrective of the *femme publique's* inveterate indolence. There was, for the first time in the history of French penal discipline, a clean, more or less wholesome, and well ordered infirmary for the treatment of maladies peculiar to that class.

In the material point of view, in a word, the prison of Saint-Lazare was, for convicted prisoners, an infinitely better place than any of its predecessors. But the régime from the standpoint of morals left more than a little to desire.

Certainly, it offered none of the grosser features of the old system. The male attendants had disappeared. The principle of work had been established, and discipline was pretty well maintained in the wards, cells, and refectories. When the women had lived together in all but absolute idleness, their prison was always in a state of disorder, and often in a state of uproar. Quarrels were of daily occurrence, and a quarrel usually issued in a fight. Two women, armed with combs or holding copper coins between their fingers, stood up to do battle for an absent lover, whom each claimed for her own ; and the other prisoners made a ring around them, not so much in the interests of fair play, as to see that each combatant got her due share of " punishment." If the warders attempted to interfere, they probably retired with broken heads.

There was almost no restraint upon the women,

and the lack of discipline, which permitted sanguinary fights at any hour of the day, pervaded the entire system. The *femme publique* could receive what visitors she pleased, and her lovers and friends crowded the "parlour," and laughed, sang, and swore at their ease. They brought her money, food, clothing, and whatever else she desired. As long as her purse was filled, she was never without luxuries, and she selected from amongst her fellow-prisoners some table companion, called a *mangeuse*, with whom she shared her meals. This companionship was usually a *liaison*, the character of which permits no more than a reference; the cult of Sappho was universal in the women's prisons.

At a pinch for money, or for food more dainty than the prison kitchen furnished, the women had recourse to the prison usurers. These were old crones, very familiar with prison, who committed some petty offence which would entail about a month's confinement; a strictly commercial speculation on their part. They took in with them a certain sum of money, with which they bought clothes from, and made loans to, necessitous prisoners. To procure money a woman would sell the clothes on her back, until "*elle restait presque nue, et dans un état indécent.*" Others borrowed from the old women at a fixed rate of interest, which was never less than fifty per cent. These were regarded as debts of honour, and the payments were punctually made.

Letters might be written and received without the scrutiny of the director; and the *écrivains publics*, or scriveners of the prison, were continuously employed in composing for their illiterate bond-sisters (always, of course, at a price) epistles to lovers outside, which are described as *brûlantes d'amour*. All unknown to the authorities, betrothals of a very curious kind were made through the prison post.

Five male prisoners at La Roquette, let us suppose, were on the point of completing their sentences ; but the prospect of liberty without a companion of the other sex held no attractions. Where were the fiancées to be found ? At Saint-Lazare, where five engaging hearts might be expecting their release at about the same date.

In the men's prison there was always an artist whose services could be hired for an affair of this kind, and to him the five gallants would present themselves, with a request for " a bouquet."

" Of how many flowers ? " asked the artist.

" Five."

The artist then traced on paper five separate flowers, to each of which a number was attached ; and the five prisoners made their choice of a blossom. From La Roquette the " bouquet " was magically wafted to Saint-Lazare, and once there it seldom failed to reach the hands it was destined for. The recipient summoned to her four other single hearts, and each of the five chose her flower. The same mysterious agency which had introduced the bouquet to Saint-Lazare conveyed a fitting answer to La Roquette, and the affair was arranged.

But the new brooms of the Préfecture swept out of the system all these injurious relaxations. At Saint-Lazare, the director took note of every letter that

16

passed into or out of the prison, and the *écrivains publics* had need to chasten their epistolary style. At Saint-Lazare, Aspasia had no clothes to sell for pocket-money, for the black gown striped with blue, which was her daily wear, was the property of the State. At Saint-Lazare, she could hold no receptions of her lovers ; and the presents of money and jewels with which they sought to solace her through the post could not be converted into spiced meats ; for all Aspasia's moneys and other valuables were taken care of by the director, who rewarded her good behaviour with a few sous at a time. At Saint-Lazare, she could seldom use her comb as a weapon of offence, and the hours which had been devoted to the duel were absorbed by some industrial or penal task.

All this implied a moral reform of no inconsiderable kind ; but, as has been stated, the morals of the new régime were not perfection. The great shortcoming in this respect was that no attempt was made to classify the prisoners.

This, however, in such a prison as Saint-Lazare should have been regarded by the authorities as a paramount duty and necessity. It has been suggested, though not yet expressly stated, how great a variety of types this population embraced. Not all of these were *femmes publiques*, and of those who belonged to that class by no means all were of a really abandoned or degraded character. There were prisoners scarcely out of their teens, who had not yet quite crossed the Rubicon, and who were importuned day and night by the old and vicious hags to be rid once for all of their virtue, and betake themselves to the "life of pleasure."

The crones who had traded as clothes-dealers and money-lenders in the older prisons were not less active in Saint-Lazare, albeit in another and baser capacity. They acted here as the agents and procuresses of the women who kept houses of ill-fame in Paris and the provincial towns. A large proportion of the population of Saint-Lazare were essentially women of the people, girls fresh from the restraints and hard monotony of shop and warehouse. They were in prison perhaps for the first time, paying the penalty of some not very serious offence against the law. But they would leave the gaol with its taint upon them, and whither should they go? The young and pretty ones amongst them were flattered by the addresses and importunities of the harridans who were there to recruit for the *maisons de tolérance*, and who promised them silk gowns, fine company, and gold pieces. There were here also wives of the middle class, whose first false step in life had changed its whole aspect for them, and who knew that home was closed to them forever. There were young *filles d'amour* who had sickened of their calling almost before the ink had dried on the page of the register which they had signed, and who longed for a means of escape.

This was good soil to work in, and it would be unjust to say that it was quite neglected. The prison was visited by sisters of mercy and other charitable women, and there were even at that date homes and refuges for the penitent, whose agents sought in the prison and at the prison door to rescue the young offenders, and those whose feet were still half-willing to lead them back to virtue. But for inexperience which lacked strength of character, and for indecision which had no moral or religious sign-post, the influence of the prison was omnipotent. Without separation of the classes there was no hope for the weak, and the classes were not separated. At the moment of her release, at the door of the prison itself, the woman who had made no plan for her future found three to pick from. Philanthropy was ready to receive her into one of the houses of refuge. But she was hungry and ill-clad, and a toothless procuress came forward with an offer of clothes, a dinner, and a soft bed. If she still wavered, there was a skulking limb of the law on the watch—probably the creature by whom she had been arrested—whose " protection " was hers if she would accept it ; and in this case, at least, refusal was indeed dangerous. For the police spy knew the " history of the case " and would dog the steps of his victim.

It resulted that, up to close upon the middle of the century, the prison of Saint-Lazare, its intelligent aims notwithstanding, was largely a recruiting ground for the *maisons de tolérance* of Paris and the departments, and a place in which uncertain virtue had every opportunity to decline into finished vice. The *maisons de tolérance* have been mentioned once or twice in this connection, and a word in explanation will dispose of them. The *femme publique* had her own house or lodging, or she lived with others of her calling, under a common roof, a *maison de tolérance.* Licences for these houses were obtained from the *Bureau des Mœurs* by a process similar to, though less tedious than, that which has been described.

The applicant was almost always a retired *femme publique*, and her request to the prefect was usually composed for her by an *écrivain public*, who kept an office for the purpose, under the discreet sign, "*Au tombeau des secrets.*" He had two styles of composition, the plain and the ornate. Adopting the first, he would write :

"Monsieur le Préfet : M——, a native of Paris, and inscribed on your registers during the past eighteen years, has the honour to request your permission to open a licenced house. Her excellent conduct during the lengthened period of her connection with a class which is not remarkable for sober living, will, I trust, be a sufficient guarantee for you that she will not abuse her new position, etc."

For a sample of his finer style, the following petition will serve :

"To his Excellency, the Prefect of Police, whose signally successful administration has changed the face of Paris.

"You will be gracious enough, Monsieur le Préfet, to pardon the importunity of my client, Mme. D——, who solicits your authority to open forthwith a *maison de tolérance*. She knows and appreciates the responsibility which this undertaking involves, but the austerity and circumspection of her conduct, her calm and peaceful life in the past, proclaim her fitness ; and the inquiries which you may deign to make on my client's account can only result to her advantage."

This was the tenor, and these the terms, of the official requests to the prefect ; and if the applicant could show that she was in a position to support an establishment, she generally received her licence. Amongst the women whom she lodged, and the frequenters of her house, she was styled at different periods *maman, abbesse, supérieure, dame de maison,*

and *maîtresse de maison*.   During the Consulate and
the Empire, she might be sent to prison as a *femme
publique;* but after the Restoration it became the
custom to punish her—on any conviction involving
the conduct of her house—by suppression of her
licence.

If, however, no attempt at classification was made
by the prison director, certain distinctions of rank
existed which were generally acknowledged by the
prisoners themselves.   The authors of *Les Prisons de
Paris* mention a class of elegant adventuresses who
were always apart in Saint-Lazare, and who stood as
the shining examples of the aristocracy of vice.   The
passage is interesting and worth translation :

"Amongst the class of swindlers, so numerous in Saint-Lazare,
who boast their skill in exploiting the ambitious fools of Paris,
you might recognise beneath the prison cap, so coquettishly
worn, dames whom you had met perchance in the most elegant
houses in town, and whose protection you might have sought.
This one was a countess, that one a baroness, and, rightly or
wrongly, the badge of nobility was painted on the panels of their
carriages.   Did you need the friendly word of a minister or the
countenance of a capitalist, it was enough that you were known to
have one of these angels for your friend.   There were four of them
in the sewing-room of Saint-Lazare,—rogues and swindlers of
the first water !   For years these corsairs have laid violent hands
on all fortunes they could come at, but they continue to hold a
position in society which is in itself a more scathing satire on the
morals of the age than any which I am able to imagine.   At
intervals, these dames are lodged for a time at the country's
cost in one or other of the houses of detention, without, however,
losing one jot or tittle of their prestige in the world of fashion !
When they reappear, society receives them open-armed, as poor
banished exiles who have returned to the fatherland, or prodigal
children whose wanderings are ended."

Nothing delighted plebeian Saint-Lazare so much as to hear the countesses and baronesses discussing the merits, as a gallant, of this or the other minister, nobleman, poet, or banker of renown; and the interest culminated when the question arose as to which of the two could produce the greater number of letters signed by names with which all Paris was familiar.

Roving like satellites around these gaudy planets were a small class of habitual criminals who, out of prison, served the noble adventuresses in several offices, as spies, go-betweens, receivers, etc. These also enjoyed a certain celebrity in the prison. One of them used to open chestnuts with a knife with which, in a passion of jealousy, she had all but murdered her lover, and which had become an object of the devoutest worship since the lover had gone to hide his scars under the red jacket of the galley-slave. Another woman arrived at the prison in a flutter of pride, eager to display a novel charm which decorated her ears. She also had lost her latest lover, but *Monsieur de Paris* had been kind enough to extract for her two teeth from the head which he had just severed. The disconsolate mistress had had them set in gold as earrings! Nearly all these women carried on the neck, arms, and upper portion of the body specimens of the work of the professional tattooer; they preserved in this way the names of their successive lovers, and the figured emblems sometimes included the most ignoble devices.

Of the licenced women whore stricted themselves mainly if not entirely to the calling of *femme publique,* Saint-Lazare recognised two separate orders. They were the *Panades* and the *Pierreuses.* The *Panades* carried a high chin in the society of their humbler associates; they were generally members of some *maison de tolérance,* where, so long as the mistress found it profitable to maintain them, they lived in luxurious indolence; fed, and pampered, and extravagantly dressed; captives, but in gilded fetters. In prison they separated themselves, as far as it was possible, from the rest, to whom they never addressed a word. They would be known only by some delicate or romantic name: Irma, Zélie, Amanda, Nathalie, Arthemise, Balsamine, Léocadie, Isménie, Malvina, Lodoïska, Aspasie, Delphine, Reine, and Fleur de Marie.

The *Pierreuses* regarded them with the bitterest jealousy, and spited and abused them at every opportunity. Memories of a gayer past intensified the feelings of the *Pierreuses;* they too had been *Panades* until the *abbesse* had cast them out, faded and worn, to join the foot-sore legion of street-walkers. They used to whisper mockingly: "You may sneer, you *Panades;* but we were like you once, and you'll be like us;" and as for the prophetic part of the reproof, it was more than likely to be realised. Like the *Panades,* the *Pierreuses* had a peculiar set of names: Boulotte, Rousselette, Parfaite, la Ruelle, la Roche, le Bœuf, Bouquet, Louchon, la Bancale, la Coutille, Colette, Peleton, Crucifix, etc. To the *Panade,* prison was a place of horror and disgrace; to the *Pierreuse* it was often the kindest home she had; and as years advanced on her, and the gains of her trade grew ever miserably smaller, the poor creature felt never so happy as in the hands of the police, on the once dreaded journey to Saint-Lazare.

There was a strangely sympathetic side to this saddest of the prisons of Paris. The sick and worn-out were always tenderly regarded by their fellow-prisoners, and a woman who brought in with her a child in arms was an object of intense and almost affectionate interest. If a woman died in the prison, it was not unusual for the rest to club together to provide a substantial and costly funeral, and masses for the repose of her soul. Sometimes the affections of the whole prison, directed upon one weak girl, had the result of saving her from ruin and insanity.

In the early years of the Restoration, Marie M——, a pretty peasant girl, was sent to Saint-Lazare for stealing roses. She had a passion for the flower, and a thousand mystical notions had woven themselves about it in her mind. She said that rose-trees would detach themselves from their roots, glide after her wherever she went, and tempt her to pluck their blossoms. One in a garden, taller than the rest, had compelled her to climb the wall, and gather as many as she could,—and there the *gendarmes* found her. She was terrified in prison, believing that when she went out the roses would lure her amongst them again, and that she would be sent back to Saint-Lazare.

This poor girl excited the vividest interest amongst the *femmes publiques* in that sordid place. They plotted to restore her to her reason, christened her Rose, which delighted her, and set themselves to make

artificial roses for her of silk and paper. Those
fingers, so rebellious at allotted tasks, created roses
without number, till the cell of Marie M—— was
transformed into a bower. An intelligent director of
prison labour seconded these efforts, and opened in
Saint-Lazare a workroom for the manufacture of
artificial flowers, to which Marie M—— was introduced as an apprentice. Here, making roses from
morning till night, and her dread of the future dis-
pelled, the malady of her mind reached its term with
the term of her sentence, and she left the prison
cured and happy, The authors of *Les Prisons de
Paris*, from whose pages her story is borrowed, declare
that Marie M—— became one of the most successful
florists in Paris.

CHAPTER XII.

LA ROQUETTE.

THERE is to be a flitting of the guillotine. For nearly fifty years executions in Paris, which are not private as with us, have taken place immediately outside the prison of La Roquette, known officially as the *Dépôt des Condamnés*.

Four slabs of stone sunk in the soil, a few yards beyond the gaol door, mark the spot where, on the fatal morning, at five in summer, and about half-past seven in winter, the red " timbers of justice " are set up by the headsman's assistants.

But La Roquette is to be demolished, and the dismal honour of furnishing a last lodging to the condemned will be conferred on La Santé. This change effected, the guillotine will flit to the Place Saint-Jacques. Criminals of a modest habit will not approve the change, but the murderer with a touch of vanity (and vanity is notoriously a weakness of murderers) will doubtless welcome it ; for the progress from the prison to the scaffold will be somewhat longer.

When the doors of La Roquette are thrown open, the victim, bareheaded and manacled, has but a few paces to shuffle to the spot where old M. Deibler awaits him, with his finger on the button of the knife.

Between La Santé and the Place Saint-Jacques there is rather more than the length of a thoroughfare to be traversed, and, as in the old days, some form of tumbril will probably be called for.

It is a pity, of course, for it has been proved abundantly that this kind of spectacle is anything but good for the public health. Humane and enlightened opinion on the subject has ceased to be that which Dr. Johnson gave utterance to. "Sir," said the Doctor to Boswell, "executions are intended to draw spectators. If they do not draw spectators, they do not answer their purpose. The old method [Tyburn had been abolished] was most satisfactory to all parties : the public was gratified by a procession, the criminal is supported by it ; why is all this to be swept away ?"

The sheriffs of the year 1784 gave the answer in a pamphlet which exposed all the horrors and indecencies of the public progress to the gallows. As for the " support " accorded to the criminal, he might, if he were unpopular, be nearly stoned to death before the hangman could despatch him.

Public executions in Paris are not, and have never been, the scandalous exhibitions that they were in London during the whole of the last century, but the scene in the neighbourhood of La Roquette for four or five hours before a guillotining is something less than edifying.

In leaving its present site for the Place Saint-Jacques the guillotine will only be returning home. The Place Saint-Jacques was the scene of punishment for nineteen years and a half ; it was dispossessed in favour of La Roquette in 1851. The first person to suffer death at the Place Saint-Jacques (the Place de Grève having been abandoned) was an old man named Désandrieux, sixty-eight years of age, condemned for the murder of a man whose age was eighty-four. Owing to the disgraceful neglect of the authorities, Désandrieux lay in prison one hundred and twenty-eight days before he was led to execution. After him came the parricide, Benoît, the atrocious Lecenaire, David, the regicides Fieschi, Morey, and Pepin, and other murderers of greater or less notoriety. The Place Saint-Jacques saw the guillotine erected thirty-five times, and beheld the fall of thirty-nine heads.

At this date the *Dépôt des Condamnés* was remote Bicêtre, which, as we have seen, was also the gaol from which the criminals convicted in Paris were despatched on their journey to the *bagne*.

A vivid picture of the condemned cell, or *cachot du condamné*, very painful in its blending of the imaginative with the realistic, is given in Victor Hugo's *Le Dernier Jour d'un Condamné*. It was a day when that veil of decent mystery which our age casts over the last torturing hours of the condemned had not been woven ; and callous curiosity could, for a trifling bribe to the turnkey, uncover the grating behind which the criminal in his strait-waistcoat was couched on mouldy straw.

It was a veritable journey from Bicêtre to the Place Saint-Jacques, by way of the Avenue d'Italie and the outer boulevards ; midway along the Boulevard d'Italie the guillotine came in sight, and for five and twenty minutes before he reached it, the miserable victim had the death-machine for his horizon, the huge blade gripped between the blood-red arms gleaming deadlier moment by moment.

The progress was even longer and more wretched when La Grande Roquette was substituted for Bicêtre as the prison of the *condamné à mort*. On a day in mid-December, 1838, a certain Perrin was carried to death from La Roquette to the barrière Saint-Jacques. An icy rain was falling, and the streets beyond the Seine were so choked with mud that at certain points the vehicle became almost embedded in it, and had to be hauled along by the crowd. Think of riding to one's death in that fashion! The Abbé Montès, riding beside the young assassin, saw him shivering, and insisted on covering him with his own hat. At the scaffold, Perrin was lifted from the cart almost dead from cold and exhaustion.

From that date there began to be a talk of changing the place of execution, but the proposals had no result, and during the next thirteen years five and twenty murderers traversed the whole length of Paris in their passage to the guillotine. Amongst them may be named the regicide Darmés, the terrible and dreaded Poulmann, Fourier, chief of the famous band of the *Escarpes*, the *garde général* Lecompte, who fired on Louis-Philippe at Fontainebleau, and Daix and Lahr, the assassins of General Bréar. At length, in 1851, the Place Saint-Jacques ceded its dubious honours to the Place de la Roquette,—which is now about to restore them.

As La Roquette (or properly La Grande Roquette,

to distinguish it from La Petite Roquette, the prison for juvenile offenders, which stands opposite) is to be abolished, it will be interesting to make a brief survey of the place in which some of the most celebrated French criminals of modern times have awaited the visit of M. Deibler, with his scissors and pinioning straps.

Here the "toilet of the guillotine" has been performed on Orsini, Piéri, Verger, La Pommerais, Troppmann, Moreau, Billoir, Prévost, Barré and Lebiez, Campi, Pranzini, and so many others, down to Vaillant and Emile Henry.

It would be impossible even to summarise all that has been said and written in France in favour of abolishing the guillotine. It was vigorously advocated during the Revolution itself, while the scaffold was flowing with blood.

Under the Convention, Taillefer rose one day with the demand : " Let our guillotines be broken and burned !" At the sitting of the of " 9th Vendémiaire, year iv," Languinais exclaimed : "Should we not be happy if, having begun our session by establishing the Republic, we were able to end it by pronouncing once for all against capital punishment !"

At the last siting of the Convention, Chénier in energetic terms denounced the guillotine. A voice called out : "What o'clock is it ?" A voice responded : " The hour of justice." A moment later this vote was proclaimed : " Dating from the publication of the general peace, the punishment of death shall be abolished throughout the French Republic."

That vote has not yet become effective !

After a long sleep the question re-awoke on the lips of M. de Tracy, son of the orator who had been amongst the first to entreat that the code of France might be cleansed of blood.   In the same historic mention we must gather in the names of the Duc de Broglie, the Marquis de Lally-Tallendal, the Marquis de Pastoret ("A man attacks me ; I can defend myself only by killing him : I kill him.   For society to do the same thing, it must find itself in precisely the same situation.") de Bérenger, Lafayette, Glais-Bizoin, Taschereau, Appert, Léon Fancher, and Guizot the historian.

" If," added the authors of *Les Prisons de Paris*, " all these enlightened publicists and statesmen, with M. Guizot amongst them, did not succeed in pulling down the scaffold, at an epoch when, to quote M. de Bérenger, the very executioners were weary, it must be concluded, we suppose, that it is necessary to proceed with prudent hesitation, and, by a gradual abolition, to convince the most timid and incredulous that society has nothing to dread from this reform."

This was written fifty years ago, and as "prudent hesitation" has not yet attained its goal it is still possible to penetrate within the condemned hold of La Roquette.

The prison is chiefly interesting in this day as the fore-scene of the scaffold.   It is built with a wealth of precautions ; and escape, if not imposssible by ordinary means, is exceptionally difficult to compass.   No successful flight from La Roquette has been recorded in modern times.

Three iron *grilles* and four doors of massive oak

conduct to the great court-yard. The foundations of the prison are in layers of freestone; the two walls which enclose the buildings are of a thickness proportionate to their elevation, and the builder took care to efface the angles by rounded stonework. Buildings surround the court-yard on the north, east, and west, and the prison chapel occupies the south.

For the ordinary prisoner (convicts awaiting shipment to the penal colonies, or undergoing short sentences of hard labour), the day at La Roquette begins early. The warders are at their posts soon after light, and the second bell summons the prisoners half an hour later. Thirty minutes are allowed for dressing, bed-making, and cell-cleaning, and at the third bell there is a general descent to the yard, each prisoner receiving his first allowance of bread as he goes down. After half an hour's exercise the regular labour of the day begins, and at nine o'clock there is a distribution of soup. Between nine-thirty and ten the prisoners take another turn in the yard, and the second period of work lasts till three in the afternoon. At three is served another allowance of bread, with vegetables or meat according to the day; and from half-past three to four the court-yard echoes again the monotonous tramp of hundreds of pairs of sabots. The last sortie—there are four in all—varies with the seasons; and after supper the prisoners are locked in for the night.

Fifty years ago, there was here and there in the *bagnes*, and the general prisons of France, a priest of exalted ideals, and such unwearied patience as the task demands, toiling to reclaim the *condamnés* who

17

were his spiritual charge.   One such was the Abbé
Touzé, chaplain of La Roquette at about the middle
period of our century.   The Abbé set himself to inquire what causes sent men to prison at that day,
what might be done or attempted to prevent them
from returning there; and knowing that the part
which thinks may be reached through the part which
feels, it was in the sanctuary of the heart that he
began his experiments on a population whose emotions are none too easily turned to moral or religious
profit.   To a Touzé in France, a Horsley in England, prison is not all the barren vineyard which a
lazy chaplain finds it ; and the *aumônier* of La
Roquette did not labour in vain.   He has been mentioned here as a herald of the philanthropic scientist
of later days, who has occasionally done for the
prison world what genius alone—with religious fer-
vour for its basis—can accomplish there.

When the secret history of the condemned cell
comes to be written, the material will be furnished
for a new and important chapter in the history of
criminal psychology ; but it must not be a patchwork
of lurid gossip on a background of stale religious
sophisms, such as Newgate chaplains of the last century were not above compiling and selling for their
profit in the crowd on a hanging Monday ; nor a
mere spicy morsel for the sensation-hunter, such as,
for example, the copious gutter-stuff printed and circulated about Lacenaire, who drew the gaze of Paris
to the condemned cell of La Roquette some half-
century ago.

Thief, blackmailer, and assassin, this was a wretch

whose blood defiled the scaffold itself, yet his position
in the condemned cell was made little less than heroic.
A loathsome murderer, he was for weeks the fashion
in Paris. His portrait was hawked about the quays
and boulevards;

"from all sides exquisite meats and delicate wines reached his
cell; every day some man of letters visited him, carefully noting
his sarcasms, his phrases composed in drunkenness or studiously
calculated for effect; women, young, beautiful, and elegantly
attired, solicited the honour of being presented to him, and were
in despair at his refusal."

Criminals as indifferent as, but less notorious or
less popular than Lacenaire, idling the weeks while
their appeal was under consideration, were chiefly
anxious as to whether the charity of the curious
would keep them in tobacco until their fate was
decided.

If the tobacco ran out, and the supply seemed not
likely to be renewed, the prisoner sometimes met
that and all other unpleasantnesses, immediate and
prospective, by taking his own life—not because he
feared the guillotine, but because suicide (which, with
the limited means at his disposal, was probably far
the worse death of the two) offered the shortest cut
to nothingness.

Lesage, calculating that his *pourvoi* or appeal would
run just forty days, summed up without a tremor the
days that remained to him. "Thirty-two days I 've
been here; eight to follow. If I don 't get a sou or
two, *je manquerai de tabac*. Five sous a day to
smoke, and ten to drink,—that's not much for a poor
chap to ask, the last eight days of his life!" Seem-

ingly, this modest address to charitable Paris was coldly answered, for a day or two later Lesage was found dead in his bed. The companion of his guilt, Soufflard, in the adjoining cell, had already taken poison.

In all condemned cells there is a considerable proportion of criminals for whom the prospect of a violent and shameful death seems to hold no terrors whatever. The chief warder of Wandsworth prison, an experienced observer of death on the gallows, assured me that he remembered no instance in which the victim had needed support under the beam, and he cited the case of Kate Webster, who, with the halter about her neck, put up her pinioned hands to adjust it more comfortably. Dr. Corre * found that out of 88 criminals condemned to death, of whom 64 were men and 24 women, about two-fifths of the men "died in a cowardly manner," whilst only about one-fifth of the women showed a lack of self-possession.

Let us pass into the *cachot du condamné à mort*, the condemned cell of La Roquette.

Three types are found in the condemned cell : the indifferent, the penitent, and the impenitent. The indifferent is a lymphatic creature (there have been several female prisoners of this type), scarcely susceptible of any normal emotion, and—of whichever sex—as cold in repentance as in crime.

The second category includes offenders quite removed from the ordinary criminal classes. Several of these, impulsive murderers, reprieved from the

* *Les Criminels.*

gallows, were pointed out to me at Portland last summer, and one I remembered in particular—a handsome, well-set man, not yet middle-aged, trudging along under a warder's eye round and round the infirmary yard, who had been seventeen years in confinement. The impenitent of this order is such an egoistic maniac as Wainwright, who, the night before his death, paced the yard of Newgate with the governor, smoking a cigar, and recounting his successes with women; or he is a criminal of the great sort, strong in mind as in body, the fearless disciple of a dreadful philosophy of his own, which lets him face death as boldly as he inflicts it, and which, at the last, inspires him only with a hatred of the law that has vanquished him.

Poulmann was a criminal of this type; an ultra-sanguine temperament, an athletic form, a constitution physically and morally energetic, an Herculean force of body, and a pride which the *cachot du condamné* could not reduce. "It shall never be said that Poulmann changed!" was his first and last confession. A "monstrous atheist," he admitted that he had prayed for the woman who was condemned with him: "But there can be no God, since Louise also is to die." Abbé Touzé suggested that the last days of Louise might be embittered by his impenitence. This shook him for a moment, but he returned to himself: "No! Poulmann will never change."

But, alike for the weak-hearted, the indifferent, and the valiant, the way to the scaffold is rendered in these days as easy as may be. Victor Hugo's condemned man in the old, abhorred Bicêtre was turned

out by day among the *forçats* awaiting their despatch
to the *bagne;* they made sport of him, and ghastly
jokes about the "widow" or guillotine—time-hon-
oured amongst the criminal classes—were pointed
afresh for his benefit.

His treatment at the hands of the prison officers
was scarcely less callous; no one had a thought or
cared that this poor wight was biding the morning
when he should be rudely severed from all the living.

The position of convicts cast for death in the Newgate of the early years of this century was every jot
as cruel.

It was thus under the old order; it is more commendable to-day. The tenant of the condemned cell,
withdrawn from the stare of the world, is surrounded
by people who have no desire but to soften the few
days or weeks that remain to him. He is no longer
on view at a price. He has not, like Lacenaire, the
privilege of refusing the visits of duchesses, nor the
indignity to endure of being exposed at a few francs
per head to the indecent gaze of sensation-mongers.

In La Roquette nowadays no one can admire or
contemn him until he shuffles out to meet his fate
just beyond the prison door.

The condemned cell is, as in most modern prisons,
both in France and England, the most comfortable
quarters in the building. There are actually three
cachots des condamnés, as there are two in Newgate,
and those in the Paris gaol are better lighted and
rather more spacious.

The last scene of all, though it is a public execution, is no longer a feast for the ghouls. Justice is

done swiftly, and the crowd sees little more than the preparation in the grey morning hours. The preparations, however, are sufficiently enticing to draw to the Place de la Roquette the riff-raff of Paris, the frequenters of the night-houses, of the boulevards, the women of the town, and some foreign amateurs of the scaffold who, like George Selwyn, would "go anywhere to see an execution."

Selwyn, by the way, would find the spectacle in the Place de la Roquette tame enough after some that he had witnessed. He went to Paris on purpose to be present at the torture of the wretched Damiens, who, after suffering unheard of pains, was torn asunder by four horses. A French nobleman, observing the Englishman's interest in the savage scene, concluded that he must be a hangman taking a lesson abroad, and said : "*Eh bien, monsieur, êtes vous arrivé pour voir ce spectacle ?*"—"*Oui, monsieur.*"—"*Vous êtes bourreau ?*" "*Non, monsieur,*" replied Selwyn, "*je n' ai pas l' honneur ; je ne suis qu' un amateur.*"

It is after midnight that the rush begins to the spot where the scaffold is raised, and for hours the throng continues to increase in numbers and variety. All night there is feeding and drinking in the public-houses around, and, as it used to be in the Old Bailey, windows commanding a view of the scene are hired at any price.

A swarm of pressmen wait through the night just outside the prison gate. At this time the victim himself is probably unaware that his last hour is at hand.

When day has dawned, two carts come out from a

street adjoining the prison, bearing the disjointed
pieces of the guillotine.   The headsman's five brawny
assistants (one of whom is his son and probable suc-
cessor) set up the machine, and the knife falls three or
four times to test the spring.

Then the guard arrives ; and when the city police,
the *Gardes de la République*, and the mounted *gendarmes* are marshalled, the crowd behind can see only
the top of the guillotine.   A place within the cordon
is reserved for the press.

The genius-in-chief of the ceremony does not appear until the doors of the prison are thrown open.
He is within, preparing the victim, and coaxing him,
when the toilet is finished, to take a cigarette and a
little glass of rum.

Louis Stanislas Deibler, the *Monsieur de Paris*,
came to Paris in 1871, as assistant headsman to Roch.
He had been a provincial executioner, but, in 1871,
a new law ordered that all criminals condemned in
France should be despatched by *Monsieur de Paris*.

Deibler, who was born in Dijon in 1823, is a joiner
by trade.   His first head (as chief executioner) was
Laprade's, in 1879, and the case was one of his worst.
Laprade, who had murdered his father, mother, and
grandmother, felt a natural disinclination to join them
on the other side, and struggled so desperately on the
scaffold that Deibler had to thrust his head by main
force into the lunette.

M. Deibler is lame, and usually carries a very old
umbrella.   " Scenes " on the scaffold are rare.   The
victim may struggle for a moment, but it is only for a
moment that, in the practised hands of the assistants,

he can postpone the inevitable. In general, the whole affair lasts but a few seconds.

There is no such thing as a "last dying speech" from the guillotine. Even if the man were not too dazed to speak, time would not be allowed him. There is time only for the last ministrations of the Church, which are almost always rejected.

The instant the criminal is secured on the bascule, M. Deibler touches the spring, the knife shears through the uncovered neck, there is a spurt of blood in the air, and all is over.

The head and body are enclosed at once in a rough coffin, and trundled off with a guard of mounted *gendarmes* (officials and priest following in a cab) to the Champ des Navets, or Turnip Field, at Ivry Cemetery, where a burial service is read. The remains are then handed over to one of the medical schools for dissection, and what is left is interred.

THE END.

www.ingramcontent.com/pod-product-compliance
Lightning Source LLC
Chambersburg PA
CBHW020850020726
47497CB00005B/1344